the latest, **Kid Got**
Shot (David Fickling £10.99, 13+), can stand alone. It is a suspenseful, sharply written mystery in which super-intelligent Garvie ("like Sherlock — but lazier") picks up clues faster than the police after an autistic schoolboy is found dead in an empty storage facility. Peopled with credible characters including Garvie's ally, Sikh policeman DI Singh, and his loitering friends with their dubiously acquired skills, it is fresh, funny and compelling.

A notable anthology of stories for you...

Also by Simon Mason

KID GOT SHOT

SIMON MASON

David Fickling Books

31 Beaumont Street
Oxford OX1 2NP, UK

Kid Got Shot
is a
DAVID FICKLING BOOK

First published in Great Britain in 2016 by
David Fickling Books,
31 Beaumont Street,
Oxford, OX1 2NP

Hardback edition 978-1-910989-14-2
Trade paperback edition 978-1-910989-24-1

1 3 5 7 9 10 8 6 4 2

Papers used by David Fickling Books are from well-managed
forests and other responsible sources.

DAVID FICKLING BOOKS Reg. No. 8340307

A CIP catalogue record for this book
is available from the British Library.

Printed and bound in Great Britain by Clays Ltd, St Ives plc.

Only your actions shall go with you
— Guru Granth

1

The others were already there, waiting in the darkness, and Garvie Smith went through the park gate and across the slippery grass towards them. Haphazardly arranged on the tiny swings and miniature roundabout of the Old Ditch Road kiddies' playground, dim, low-slung and damp, Smudge, Felix, Dani and Tiger raised hands and touched knuckles with him, one by one, and he settled down among them, yawning.

Smudge looked at him. 'What you got for us, big shot?'

Garvie shook his head.

'What, not even the Rizlas?'

'Next time.'

'Next time! Might not be a next time, mate. The world's a strange and uncertain place. Who knows what's going to happen in the future?'

Garvie looked at him; yawned again. 'We all know, Smudge. Nothing, that's what. And, if we're not that lucky, maybe a bit less than nothing.'

He took out his Benson & Hedges and offered them round, and Smudge passed him the almost-empty half-bottle of Glen's cheapest and the sherbet lemons, and they sat there smoking, drinking, sucking sweets and grumbling.

Ten o'clock on a Friday evening in Five Mile. The wind getting up, drizzle, a few smokes and a bit of banter before the cop car came by to chuck them off.

Half an hour passed.

Smudge had another go. 'Come on, Garv, you haven't said hardly nothing since you got here. Anyone'd think you were fretting about your exams.'

No one who knew anything about him would think Garvie was fretting about his exams; he was not only the boredest but also the laziest boy in the history of Marsh Academy, perhaps of the whole city, or even the whole history of boys anywhere. Slacker Smith, all brain and no energy, the despair of his school. Black-haired, blue-eyed and sixteen years old, sloppy in slouch jeans, hooded sweatshirt and broken-down high tops, he sat on his stamped-metal circus horse with a cigarette dangling out of the corner of his beautiful mouth, rocking gently, breathing out smoke, gazing in quiet boredom across the black grass towards the city lights downtown. The truth was, exams didn't bother him. What bothered him was the people who talked about them. His mother, for instance. Uncle Len. Miss Perkins, Marsh Academy's principal enforcer. A few weeks earlier, as a result of some bother with the police, during which, through no fault of his own, he'd missed a good deal of school work, he'd been officially assured that his exams would be deferred – only for the school to decide a few days later that he'd be sitting them anyway. He would sit his exams as scheduled, Miss Perkins had told him, he would fulfil his potential as required, he would at long last show the world the abilities of a boy with a certified record IQ and famous photographic memory. Only he wouldn't. He didn't like Miss Perkins. He didn't like the world either and he wasn't going to do anything for it. What had it ever done for him?

'So what's your problem?' Smudge asked.

'Nothing,' Garvie said. 'Or a bit less.'

A disturbance came from down Old Ditch Road, a bass bumping noise shaking the ground. After a moment a car appeared alongside the hedge that divided the park from the street and came to a throbbing, brightly lit standstill by the park gate a few metres away, a tall black Cadillac Escalade Platinum with limo tint windows and Lexani wheels in electric egg-yolk yellow, hi-vision headlamps pulsing, coloured light panels racing like lasers along the roof. It fumed with music for twenty, thirty beats and suddenly fell silent. Transfixed, the boys stared at it as the nearside back window slid down with a thin whine and a face appeared, grinning and blinking. Smudge let out a small burp of fear.

The face looked at Garvie.

'Got a light for me, boy?' A hoarse, whispery voice.

Garvie looked back, puffing smoke, thinking about it. 'No,' he said at last.

3

Smudge stifled a moan.

The back door swung open and a short, skinny guy stepped out and stood there. He was wearing a black leather jacket over an outsized retro tracksuit in turquoise and a Dirty Rat swag hat, and his glasses flashed in the streetlight as his head bobbed, idiot eyes blinking big and slow. He was no longer grinning.

'You got a light,' he said, nodding towards Garvie's cigarette.

Garvie took a long drag on his Benson & Hedges, dropped it and ground it out with the heel of his shoe.

'No, I haven't,' he said.

Smudge groped hastily in his pocket for matches and made a few faltering squeaks, but fell silent as more car doors opened and two men in matching vests got out. They were big men, blank-faced behind shades, and they stood in the road as if waiting for instructions.

Blinkie grinned again. He was a fool. Everything about him was idiotic: his gangster outfit, monster bling, dental grille, those enormous, inhuman eyes. His teeth were too big for his mouth. He was the only white man in Five Mile with cornrows. But he was a fool no one laughed at. People were very careful around Blinkie. He was what was commonly known as 'a bit psycho'.

The street was quiet for a moment, no sound but a car on the other side of the park. Blinkie looked at his watch.

'Shouldn't you be in bed, boy?' he said to Garvie.

'Shouldn't you be in prison?' Garvie said.

Smudge flinched so hard he almost fell off the swings, and Blinkie stopped grinning. He took a step towards Garvie, and one of the men behind him leaned forward and muttered something, and he hesitated and glanced down the road.

He looked back at Garvie. 'Know what I like?' he whispered.

Garvie shrugged. 'I'm guessing it's not normal clothes. Or mirrors.'

'Fun,' Blinkie said. 'So I'll be seeing you.'

He slipped back into the car, the door closed with a satisfyingly shushy clunk, the music pumped out again and the rocking car slid away down Old Ditch Road like a fairground ride.

Garvie got to his feet and sauntered towards the gate after it, and Smudge and Felix called after him, anxious as baby birds.

'What you doing now? Are you insane? What if he comes back?'

'Relax. He's not coming back.'

'How do you know?'

Garvie reached the gate as the squad car drew up with its lights turned down low, and he went up to it and tapped on the window.

The window came down and a policeman in a bullet-proof turban looked out, and Garvie looked at him in surprise for a moment.

'You've just missed them,' he said. 'They went that way,' he added.

Detective Inspector Singh made no reaction. He said, 'What are you and your friends doing here?'

Garvie said, 'What are *you* doing here, on the night shift? It's usually Constable Jones here who comes along to move us on.'

Jones, the driver, scowled, but Singh simply asked again, 'What are you doing in the park?'

'Swings, mainly. Sometimes we go on the roundabout.'

Singh waited patiently.

'OK, you've got me,' Garvie said. 'Smoking, drinking, occasionally doing drugs.' He stretched his arms out wide. 'Do you want to search me?'

Constable Jones made a move to get out of the car, and Singh put a hand on his arm to stop him.

To Garvie he said, 'Go home, Garvie, and tell your friends to go home too.'

The window went up, and the squad car pulled away, and Garvie stood there a moment thoughtfully, before returning to the playground.

'That was lucky,' Smudge said. 'Plod turning up just in time to scare Blinkie off. Thought you'd successfully killed yourself, talking like that.'

'You need to check your watch, Smudge. Half ten. That's the time Plod usually turns up.'

'Not always, mate. Not always at this time neither.'

Garvie shook his head. 'Ignore the noise, Smudge. Find the signal.'

'What signal?'

'Plod shows up, what, four times a week? Weekdays it's half past, Saturdays eleven, Sundays he doesn't come. That's a two in three chance of him turning up exactly when he did.'

'Yeah, but . . .' Smudge fell silent.

'Also,' Garvie said, 'proves I'm not stoned.'

'Does it?'

'I know it's Friday. If all I knew was it wasn't Sunday, it'd be one in two, wouldn't it? If I was so out of it I didn't know what day of the week it was, it'd be three in seven. But I'm not stoned, so I get better odds.'

Smudge said warily, 'Well, if you put it like that . . .'

'Besides,' Garvie said, 'I saw the car on the other side of the park before it arrived.'

Nodding, he left them there and walked back to the gate, out into Bulwarks Lane and along Pilkington Driftway, homeward.

The wind had picked up. Clouds tore themselves to pieces and tossed the bits across the dark sky, wire fences chattered as he went past, litter scudding across the road. The flats at Eastwick Gardens were dim in the darkness. Garvie let himself into the lobby, retrieved the book he'd left under the stairwell, *Modern World History Student Book*, and went up the stairs to Flat 12, where his mother was preparing to go out for her shift at the hospital. She was an imposing lady from Barbados with a broad face, greying hair clipped into a halo and a Bajan accent thick as pork pepperpot, and she regarded Garvie mistrustfully.

'You were a long time fetching that book,' she said.

Garvie shrugged. 'Felix hadn't finished with it so I had to wait a bit.'

'Two hours? What was he doing, rewriting it?'

'And then we got caught up discussing the French Revolution and stuff.'

Her mistrustful look grew more mistrusting, but she looked at her watch and went to get her coat, hanging by the door.

'OK. At least you're back now. You can do a bit of revision and get to bed at a reasonable time for once.' She looked at him through narrowed eyes. 'You're not thinking of going out to the kiddies' playground, right?'

Garvie returned her stare. 'What would I want to go there for? There's nothing going on there.'

For a moment longer she regarded him with that flat look of disbelief. Then the door closed behind her. Sighing, Garvie drifted into his room, kicked his way through discarded clothing and lay down on his bed, staring up at the ceiling. The incident with Blinkie had been a momentary diversion. There was nothing to do at the kiddies' playground, nothing to do at home.

He sighed again, put his hands behind his head and focused on the ceiling.

2

After they left the park Singh and Jones continued their rounds, the squad car sliding quietly under the streetlights, up and down the hills of Brickfields and Limekilns, through the spacious suburbs of the affluent north, around the ring road, back towards town. The city grew quiet, the hours passed slowly, eleven o'clock, twelve, one o'clock, two, as they tracked the frail linkages of lights rippling across the estates, thinning out along the ring road, massing in grids around the tower blocks of the deserted business district, as at last they approached the police centre downtown and the end of their shift.

A city of light and dark, Detective Inspector Raminder Singh thought to himself, looking out of the window as he sat silent and unbending beside the slouching Jones, his posture and appearance as usual absolutely correct from the soles of his regulation boots to the tip of his police-issue turban, thirty-two years old, ambitious, uptight. A chequered city, a city of endless permutations, of luck and chance, where a man could make a life, or fail to. It was the end of a long shift. Jones was grunting and scratching irritably as they slowed to turn into the drive to the sallyport.

That was when the call came through.

Jones took it, listening to his headset with disgust. Frowned.

'*Where?*' he said bitterly into his microphone. 'For God's sake. Next shift can take it. We're back already. They'll be here any minute.'

Singh looked at Jones, who openly scowled back at him.

'Alarm going off,' Jones said to him. 'East Field industrial park. Be the wind, night like this.'

Singh said decisively, 'We'll take it. McKendrick can hand over when the others arrive.'

Jones pouted at him, but Singh stared him down and he swung the car round viciously in the road and they went at speed back down Cornwallis Way, heading west towards the ring road. Without speaking again they drove across the flyover onto the dual carriageway and turned east, the speeding car buffeted by shouldering gusts of wind. Northwards the humped darkness of Brickfields slid past, then the pale lots of empty retail parks, then the brighter glow of The Wicker, the city's fluorescent strip of clubs and casinos. Ahead were the tower blocks of Strawberry Hill streaked into life by the shadows of racing clouds, and the low, dense mass of Limekilns. Impassively Singh watched it all go by. Everywhere the wind-pressed city seemed to bend under wavering lights, as if the whole town swayed underwater.

With a show of petulance Jones put the siren on.

'It's going to be a false alarm,' he said. 'You know that, don't you?'

'Then we'll log it and be on our way.'

He switched on the radio channel, and the car prickled with background static.

At the sewage plant they turned south, away from the city into the darkness of farmland, accelerating along an unlit country lane towards the industrial estate. A robotic voice broke in over the radio.

'Hey, you guys. Report just in.'

Singh took up the handset. 'Try to remember Airwave Speak, McKendrick.'

'Loosen up, Tango-man. Do you want this information or what?'

Singh bit his lip. 'Go ahead, police centre.'

There was a snicker at the other end of the line. 'OK then. Some guy walking his dog just phoned in, says he thinks he heard gunshots.'

'Where?'

'East Field somewhere. Could even be the industrial park. But you know phone-ins. Nights get all the paranoids. Chance of it being true: slim to invisible. I'm just doing my job passing it on. OK, I'm off. The others are coming in now. Enjoy your field trip, children. Tango, Tango.'

They came to the end of the lane, pulled into the industrial estate through an open gate in a high wire fence and went slowly down the pitted, unlit road between decaying warehouses and low-rent lock-ups. Jones turned off the siren. From up ahead came

11

the squawk of a burglar alarm, the noise flapping in the wind like a far cry from out of a stormy sea.

'Told you,' Jones said.

The warehouse stood before them, dark and shut as if disused and undisturbed for centuries, the alarm echoing emptily from inside.

'Wait,' Singh said, peering through the window. 'There.' He pointed the other way along an access road towards a lock-up glinting in the darkness, light spilling out of flung-open main doors.

Jones pursed his lips, said nothing.

Singh put his hand on the door handle. 'You check the warehouse. I'll see what's happening down there.'

Jones hesitated. 'You heard what McKendrick said. You strapped?'

'I never carry a weapon.'

Jones shrugged, and they got out together and went in different directions.

Like much of the estate, the lock-up was a beaten piece of industrial architecture from the dawn of time, two storeys of mouldy brick and iron girders, once a factory, then a warehouse, now the cheapest sort of storage, its ground floor sub-divided into a dozen smaller units, the upper floor disused for years, unsafe and prone to water damage.

Singh glanced back at Jones disappearing casually into the shadow side of the warehouse up the road. There was no one to see Singh go into the police-manual crouch. Tense, alert and rigidly correct, he crept crab-wise to the main doors of the lock-up and peered through before swinging inside, cocking his head like an animal tracking a scent. The lobby was bare but for a reception desk used apparently as a bin. Three doors led off it. One was half open, light shining through it, and he slid silently to the side of the doorway and cocked his head again. For a moment he heard nothing; then, faintly, from just the other side of the door, vague noises. A scrape of feet? A hiss of talk? Hairs went up on the back of his neck. Peering through the crack between the door and jamb, he saw nothing. He leaned backwards, took a breath and pounced suddenly through the doorway into a square, brightly lit, whitewashed concrete room. It was empty except for a boy. Dressed very neatly in school uniform, he was lying on the floor staring impassively up at the ceiling. He still had his glasses on. Next to him was his school bag, and next to that an empty violin case, and next to that a handgun. The pool of blood he was lying in had reached the bag and the case but not the gun.

Singh rushed over, already talking into his radio.

The boy moved his lips, blinked once and stopped breathing.

'No,' Singh said, uselessly. He put his fingers on the chest of the boy's soaked shirt and felt the gun-shot wounds slippery under his touch, and looked around, still talking into his radio, issuing instruc-tions and giving directions. Beyond the room was a short corridor between padlocked units, at the end of it an open door. From above came the noise of something being knocked over, a clatter immediately stifled. Wind, Jones would have said.

With a thud of boots Jones ran in swearing.

'Occlude the wound,' Singh said.

Jones stared, white-faced and astonished. 'It's too late.'

'Do it anyway. Assist the paramedics when they get here.'

Leaving Jones crouching indecisively over the boy, Singh ran down the corridor and through the door at the far end to the bottom of an unlit metal staircase, and went up two steps at a time to the level above. There, the whole of the upper storey lay before him, dark and disorganized, its low ceiling supported on iron girders, empty spaces filled here and there with incomplete breeze-block partitions and piles of building materials. A prickling smell came off it of wet plaster and rust. Weak light shone through in torn patches from broken skylights.

Everything was silent; nothing moved as Singh swept his flashlight over cracked concrete and gleaming puddles.

He waited.

Nothing. No sound. No movement.

Quietly, he crept as per the police manual round the perimeter, cocking and uncocking his head, scanning the debris around him, and took up a strategic position in the corner of the building. From there he began to sweep across the warehouse with his flashlight once more, and someone hiding behind a rack of old ridge tiles leaped up and blundered into him, and he fell sideways, his torch skittering across the floor. Then he was on his feet running, dodging girders and rubble looming at him out of the darkness, chasing in and out of the shadows after a bulky figure hunched and hooded, their footsteps echoing in the emptiness. Doglegging around a girder, the other man skidded and fell and Singh tumbled over him, grabbing wildly at nothing. Up again, they ran the other way, the man gasping and groaning, Singh silent, elbows pumping. He caught him by a pile of used tarpaulins, got a blow in the face and after a brief struggle they came apart and stood facing each other in a dusty beam of moonlight, panting and swaying.

The man was taller than Singh by a head, and broader. In his hand something metal glinted. He swung it up and round, and Singh skipped backwards, keeping his distance. Some memory came to him then, not of the police manual but of *viraha yudhan* from martial-arts classes in Lucknow when he was a boy. It was a vision of sudden clarity: he could see the orange dust of the ground, the flawless blue of the sky. It loosened him, he felt his body relax, and as the man reared upwards and lunged forward, he spilled sideways light-footed and finger-punched twice him in the armpit. He yanked the man's head round by his hood and chopped down with his elbow on the side of his neck.

The man lay at his feet, still.

Singh closed his eyes briefly, saw again the orange ground, the blue sky, heard the silence of his teacher. He murmured the required phrase *Waheguru ji ki fateh* – Victory belongs to God – and turned anxiously towards the staircase as he heard the noise of the ambulance arriving outside, in time for the man at his feet but too late for the boy downstairs.

3

Next morning's media was dominated by news of the murder of a sixteen-year-old schoolboy shot dead on East Field industrial estate. For the present his identity was withheld for legal reasons. A man named as Martin Magee was in police custody, having been apprehended at the scene of the crime by serving patrolmen on the City Squad night shift. The city's chief constable, a quiet-faced man with a reputation for implacable efficiency, appeared on television in a hat overflowing with gold braid, to express disgust at the crime. In interviews, Detective Inspector Dowell, in charge of the investigation, praised the diligence of the two patrolmen who had made the arrest and assured the city's public that justice would swiftly follow. Although no formal charges had been brought yet, a gun had been retrieved from the scene of the crime, and there was a witness – Dowell said – who had seen the suspect dragging the boy into the lock-up moments before the police arrived. Dowell would not be drawn on the boy's reasons for being at the estate; nor would he comment on the rumours that he had been found wearing the uniform of the Marsh Academy at Five Mile and that he'd had with him his school bag and violin case. These rumours spread quickly, however, and a widespread sense of outrage grew, together with bewilderment as to what a boy, dressed for school and carrying his school things, could possibly be doing in a disused building on a semi-derelict industrial estate at two o'clock in the morning.

Given that it was the second killing of a juvenile in Five Mile in two months, in fact the second killing of a student from Marsh Academy, the media coverage was extensive and intense; many commentators took the opportunity to ask what had become of a place where this sort of thing could happen not once, but twice, where violence was so intimately part of daily life and where security forces seemed unable to prevent it breaking out.

All day such stories dominated the media, overshadowing other overnight news in the city: an armed robbery at a corner shop in Strawberry Hill; a small pile-up on the ring road; a break-in at Jamal's in Five Mile; and suspected arson at a house at Tick Hill.

Back at the police centre in Cornwallis Way, Singh sat outside Interview Room 3, waiting to be summoned by Inspector Dowell to be told his role in the forthcoming investigation. As usual, by personal preference, he was in uniform, crisp and correct, complete with Detective Inspector insignia – though, as a result of the recent disciplinary action against him, he was not currently performing a Detective Inspector's duties. Temporarily, he was a 'patrolman' again. As he thought of it, he stiffened his posture and concentrated on the dossier on his lap. Marked *Homicide: Classified*, it was open to an official school photograph of a Year Eleven boy in Marsh Academy uniform. The boy had wet-looking light-brown hair brushed flat across his scalp and black-framed glasses with thick lenses that magnified his pupils to the size of squash balls. His uniform was neat but shabby in places and looked too tight for comfort. His expression was self-contained, his mouth set, his eyes deadpan. His lack of smile was unnerving. He didn't look as if he had chosen not to smile – he looked as if smiling was something he knew nothing about.

Singh stared at the photograph. The boy's hands were visible at the bottom of the picture. They weren't relaxed but clenched, holding on tightly to the neck of a violin.

He closed the dossier and sat there, rigidly upright, thinking. The name of the boy in the photograph, currently protected, was Pyotor Gimpel. The school had provided the police with a copy of a statement of special educational needs issued in recognition of Pyotor's autism spectrum disorder. The rest of the school report was strikingly bare. Pyotor had been gifted at music and mathematics, average or poor in other academic subjects. His disciplinary record was impeccable. His social circle was described as 'nil'. There had been no connection between him and Martin Magee, nor any possibility of one.

Waiting for Dowell on his plastic seat in the over-lit corridor, Singh thought of these things. But what he thought of most of all was the photograph, and the impassive expression on Pyotor's face. He could not get it out of his mind. It was exactly the same expression he had seen himself in the lock-up the previous night as the boy lay dying at his feet.

4

Jamal's convenience store stood in a row of shops along Bulwarks Lane, a long, shabby, busy road running eastwards through Five Mile from the edge of the Marsh fields by the Academy almost as far as the ring road and the car plant. Like everything in Five Mile, it did its job and no more. At the shops there were three bus stops, a pelican crossing and a taxi rank. There was litter, cracked concrete, a savoury smell of petrol fumes and deep-fried food, and the shops themselves, sitting as if squashed under a line of first-floor flats with grimy windows: a mini-supermarket, newsagent's, launderette, hairdresser's, bakery, kebab and burger places, and, round the corner, O'Malley's bar. They did their jobs too, without any fuss.

At Jamal's, chipboard panelling covered one of the two front windows, a shiny metal plate the other. There was a new split in the door, pinned with metal brackets. Garvie glanced at them idly and moved on.

'Third break-in in a month, yeah?' Khalid said. 'Like a vendetta, know what I mean?' He looked at Garvie sourly. 'Abbu's still on crutches, got all these attacks going on; I ask myself, what's the point?'

Garvie said nothing. He watched Khalid getting

his Rizlas from a shelf above the counter. Since his father broke his leg, Khalid had run the shop, and the strain was showing. He was nineteen, thin-faced, bent-nosed, with bruise-like shadows under his eyes. He had developed a nervous tremor, Garvie noticed, in his left hand.

The shop was even untidier than before. The racks of sweets at the till – packs of gum, chocolate bars, penny chews in green-and-yellow wrappers – were mixed up and overflowing. Garvie whistled to himself. He glanced at the headlines in the Saturday evening newspapers. *Fear in Five Mile. Schoolkid Gunned Down. Murder Academy.*

'Bad news about the Gimp,' he said.

Khalid shrugged. 'Didn't know him.'

'Second murder in two months, man. That's tough.'

Khalid shrugged again, as if to say he had his own problems, and Garvie put down the Rizlas.

Khalid sneered. 'That it, yeah? No baccy to put in it or nothing?'

'Got all I need, thanks.'

'Not baccy you're smoking these days. I know.'

Garvie put the money on the counter and Khalid cracked down the change. His phone rang and he looked at it, scowling. He went down the shop to the far end, and disappeared through a door plastered with posters for ice cream and hairspray. 'Nah,' he was saying. 'I need them, like, really big. Like mega-locks. You got-mega locks? . . . Why? *Why?* 'Cause I got, like, mega-burglars kicking down my doors, that's why.'

Garvie turned to Sajid, Khalid's younger brother, thirteen years old, sitting in his basketball kit at the end of the counter with Jamal's laptop. White T-shirt, navy shorts: Marsh Academy colours. Sajid played point guard for school, and took his basketball seriously: a match every Saturday morning and fitness drills twice a week. A pity he wasn't taller. Alone at the counter, staring at the screen, he looked younger than he was, vulnerable. Rumour was, his brother gave him a hard time.

'Twenty pence,' Garvie said, holding up the pack of Rizlas.

'So?'

'Mark-up, say, twelve per cent.'

Sajid shrugged.

'Do the maths. Cost to your brother is 88% of retail price: 17.6 pence. Margin 2.4 pence a pack. On a box of two hundred and twenty packs, a profit of five pounds twenty eight. Takes, say, a month to sell a box. Seventeen pence a day. Yeah, your brother's right.'

'Right about what?'

'Crap money on Rizlas. What's the point? Why doesn't he pack it in and sing in a boy band instead?'

Sajid clicked his tongue. Concentrated.

They heard Khalid come back into the shop, still talking on his phone as he stacked shelves down one of the aisles. 'I don't know what you talking about, man,' they heard him say. Then: '*A grand!*'

Garvie went on, conversationally. 'I'll tell you why, Sajid. Look at the rest of the stuff here. High-price booze and cigs, high-turnover soft drinks, all the food and that. Factor in the long hours, the number of greedy punters like me. What do you reckon?'

Sajid ignored him.

Hidden in the background, Khalid hissed, '*What?* He's got to be having a laugh, innit?'

Garvie said, 'Open fifteen hours a day seven days a week fifty-two weeks of the year, sale made every five minutes, each sale three items at an average price of three quid. Same mark-up. You're clearing a profit of, what, seventy grand. Seventy thousand seven hundred and sixty-one pounds and sixty pence, if you want to be exact. That boy band'll have to wait.'

Still Sajid ignored him. As he leaned forward, peering at his screen, the neckband of his T-shirt slid down to reveal two long bruises round the side of his neck. After a moment he self-consciously pulled his T-shirt up, glanced round at Garvie, who was still watching him.

Garvie nodded at the laptop. 'Ring of Valor?'

Sajid nodded.

'Can't beat *WoW*, eh? Old games are the best.'

Sajid shrugged.

'You like playing the arenas?'

'Yeah.'

'Who do you play with?'

Sajid glanced nervously down the aisles. 'Not really playing with anyone,' he said as Khalid came towards them, still talking on the phone.

'Nah, man, it's got to be a mix-up. I'm telling you, I didn't get no message. Listen. *Listen!* I'm not being funny nor nothing, but you got to talk to him. It's just like not happening, all right?' He stamped up the aisle to the counter where Garvie stood. 'You still here? What you doing now, nicking stuff?'

Garvie put the Rizlas in his pocket. 'Just chilling.'

'Why do people think it's all right come in, hang out here, buy nothing, crowd up my shop?'

He snarled at Sajid in Urdu, and the boy slid away from the laptop at once and went into the back room, Khalid shouting after him. 'How many times I got to tell you, spending all your time on that games shit!'

'Three times in a month,' he said to Garvie. 'Yeah, well, don't worry about me. I got protection.'

'Have you?'

'Yeah. Getting it anyway. I'll introduce you when it arrives. Name of Genghis. Know what I mean? On a big chain and everything.'

'OK then.'

'Then we'll see.'

'OK. No need to get worked up, man.'

'No need to get . . . ? All these burglars, right? All these bandits, yeah?' He shouted after Garvie, who was already going out of the door. 'All these wasters coming in here, not buying nothing, just nicking stuff!'

The broken door swung. Khalid's phone rang again, and he hurried towards the back room, talking angrily. 'Nah, man!' he shouted. 'I told you! I want it in and out, three days tops.'

5

Garvie strolled along Bulwarks Lane across Pollard Way and turned into Old Ditch Road, heading for the kiddies' playground. Shredded blossoms torn off cherry trees by the recent winds lay like party-coloured fish-flakes in the gutters. It had rained before, would rain again, but now the sky was momentarily clear, last of the light fading in an ugly pink glow as Garvie went through the park gate and across the damp grass.

As usual, the others were already there.

'What you got for us tonight, big shot?'

Garvie put down the Rizlas, all twenty pence worth.

'That it?'

He produced a smallish package wrapped in foil and put that down too, and Smudge grinned.

'Knew you'd come through in the end.'

The sun went down, the sky flared up and turned dark, and they sat on the miniature roundabout and tiny swings, passing round the smokables, talking, inevitably, about the murder – specifically about Pyotor Gimpel, whose name, so scrupulously guarded by the police, was nevertheless already known to everyone in Five Mile.

'I don't get it,' Smudge said. 'First Chloe, now the Gimp. What's going on? Like suddenly Five Mile's the murder capital of the world. See the paddy wagons down by the taxi rank? All the cops in the country seem to have moved in.'

The police presence in the estate was unnervingly conspicuous, cruisers and Black Marias parked on every corner. Murders of school kids were rare. The murder of a school kid like Pyotor Gimpel was freakish. Five Mile was in a state of shock.

'The Gimp?' Smudge said. 'Give me a break. Why should anyone want to shoot the Gimp. Sherlock?'

'Why wouldn't someone want to shoot him?'

'What do you mean?'

'Well, what do you know about him?'

Smudge pondered. 'Don't know nothing about him. Except he was weird.'

Felix fixed him with one of his thin-faced, long-suffering looks. 'Statemented, Smudge. On the spectrum. He couldn't help it.'

'That's what I'm saying. Not weird like deliberately. Just a weirdo, you know, *officially*.' With effort he imposed on his potato face an expression of casual insight.

Felix shook his head sadly. 'There are all sorts of weirdos, Smudge, and some of them don't even know they're weird.'

'True enough,' Smudge said, his expression loosening until he looked almost normal. 'Take Garv, for example. All right, it's a fair point. Come on, what do we actually know about the Gimp? Speak up.'

Garvie, sitting smoking on a dwarf-sized rocking horse, ignored them. The others pooled information about the Gimp the same way they pooled cigarettes and vodka: bits and pieces picked up here and there. None of them knew him personally; he wasn't that sort of boy. Although he was one of theirs – part of the common scene – he was a loner. They were used to him, they'd seen him around every day, but they knew almost nothing about him.

'He played the violin,' Smudge said. 'That's pretty weird. I mean, who plays the violin nowadays except people in museums?'

It was one obvious aspect of the Gimp's oddity. Another was his unsettling neatness. By choice he wore full school uniform, his shirt always tucked in, his wet-looking hair always brushed down flat, always wearing a tie, though he didn't have to, looking like a boy from the past in an old photograph. He was small for his age, but his clothes always looked too tight, as if he had outgrown them. In the mornings when he arrived and at breaks he used to sit alone on a bench by Bottom Gate, always the same spot, with his violin case on his lap, impassive and uselessly alert, as if waiting for a bus. Tiger had seen him taking random pictures with his phone; so had Smudge. He spoke seldom, with a quiet, slurry Polish accent. Generally he was silent and immobile. Felix had several times seen him delicately eating an apple from a brown paper bag. No one had ever seen him with a friend. He was quiet, lonely, inoffensive, weird.

'Thing is,' Smudge said, 'he was in his own world all the time; he wasn't wised up like the rest of us. Natural victim, that's what he was. Someone could take advantage of a kid like that. What d'you reckon, Garv?'

Garvie said nothing. He smoked.

'Well, anyway,' Smudge went on, 'question is, what happened?'

The others went on discussing it while Garvie smoked quietly. There were various theories already flying around the internet, some of them not entirely stupid. It could have been a straightforward case of mistaken identity. Or a race attack. Perhaps the Gimp had seen something he shouldn't have and had to be silenced. He could easily have got involved in something he didn't understand. But why was he in the lock-up with Magee in the first place? He'd been kidnapped, perhaps. Or tricked. Lured there under false pretences, taken advantage of, like Smudge said. But it was hard to explain the bizarre fact that a schoolboy like the Gimp had been at that place with that man at that time, apparently dressed for school. At this point, really, there were only bizarre explanations. One was that he'd been killed in a shoot-out with Magee, to which he'd carried a gun in his violin case. Smudge, a reliable provider of bizarre ideas, thought it possible that the Gimp had sleepwalked to the lock-up. He'd heard of a man who sleepwalked to his car and sleep-drove fifty miles to a cheap hotel to meet a woman he'd never seen before in his life.

'That's what he told his wife. He was shocked to find himself there. Think how shocked the Gimp would have been when he woke up in that lock-up. Especially when Magee then shot him. What do you think, Garv?'

Garvie had said nothing now for twenty minutes. Sitting on his rocking horse, he continued to smoke, gazing across the field towards the city lights downtown. The others watched him curiously.

'Not bothered then?' Smudge said. 'Not interested?'

Garvie blew out smoke, dropped his cigarette, ground it out.

'I am interested, actually.'

Smudge grinned. ''Cause of the sleep-walking, I bet.'

Garvie ignored him. He took out another Benson & Hedges and tapped it thoughtfully on his knee. He tossed it suddenly into the corner of his mouth, lit up and blew out smoke in a long blue stream.

He said, 'Go back to what you said about him. The sort of kid he was.'

'Natural victim.'

'Control freak, you said. A loner, even at home with his Polish grandparents in that flat somewhere in Strawberry Hill. Good with lists, bad with people. A planner. Capable of violence.' He puffed out a little smoke. 'Doesn't sound like a natural victim to me.'

They looked at each other. 'We didn't say any of that.'

'Course you did. You said he always sat on that bench by Bottom Gate. Strawberry Hill way, where the Polish shops are. Where else do you think he lived? And who do you think dressed him up like that and gave him an apple in a brown paper bag every day? No one born in the last fifty years. What about that thick old Polish accent? He'd lived here nearly all his life. He can't have spoken much English at home. The other stuff's just obvious. Kept his hair neat, tucked in his shirt, brushed his hair down flat. Obsessive, a control freak. Always sat in the same spot. Had a plan and stuck to it. Took pictures of people but never talked to them. Bad with people. What would he do with all those pictures, with his orderly mind? Put them in order, catalogue them. Make a list. That's what you said. And that's the way he was.'

Smudge scratched. 'Well, all right. But . . . capable of violence? This is the Gimp, Garv. You said it – he hardly dared speak to anyone.'

'Did you ever see anyone sit in his place on that bench? Did you ever see someone try to take his violin off him?'

Smudge admitted he hadn't. It was universally accepted, if unexplained, that the Gimp was never parted from his violin: he even took it into the toilets with him. Smudge scratched. 'So . . . What're you saying?'

Garvie got off the rocking horse, put his cigarette pack in his jacket pocket. He drifted as far as the edge of the shadow and paused. 'I'm saying, don't wonder how he was lured out there. Don't wonder if he was taken advantage of.'

'What then?'

Garvie smiled. 'Wonder where he got his gun from.'

There was a bit of a silence after he said this. And by the time Smudge had opened his mouth again Garvie had gone, and they were watching him disappear across the grass towards the gate.

6

First thing Monday morning there was a special assembly at Marsh Academy. It began at nine thirty, to give staff and students time to clear the new security procedures and make their way through the groups of police stationed at the school gates and the entrances to the main blocks. There were even policemen on the stage alongside the teachers; they stood immobile and impassive in front of a screen showing a greatly enlarged school photograph of an unsmiling boy with wet-looking hair and a tight grip on his violin, as Mr Winthrop, the head teacher, addressed Year Eleven on the subject of Pyotor Gimpel, who had been, Mr Winthrop said, a diligent student, a dutiful son and grandson and a valued member of the Marsh Academy community.

'He trusted, as we all do, that life would at least treat him fairly. But that trust,' Mr Winthrop said emotionally, 'was betrayed.'

There was silence in the hall, from the teachers and policemen on stage, and from the students sitting in rows in the auditorium. And, coincidentally, there was silence between three boys not in the hall at that moment, not in school at all, but walking down a country lane past the sewage plant. Smudge,

Felix and Garvie Smith. They went through the gate in the tall wire fence into East Field industrial estate as far as the access road and came to a standstill, and stood there staring.

Not only the lock-up but also a radius of fifty metres of waste ground around it had been cordoned off behind scrub-clean plastic screens, three metres high, as if the whole area had been wrapped up ready to ship to a nearby laboratory or art gallery. Boiler-suited officials wearing face masks, boots and gloves went in and out, fetching and carrying and looking busy.

'You got to give them credit,' Smudge said. 'I mean, look how white it all is. You don't usually get that effect this side of Christmas.'

There was a group of press photographers drinking coffee on the broken-up verge, and uniformed constables with dogs going up and down the road sniffing things. Garvie gave them a wide berth. He wasn't keen on dogs, especially not police dogs, particularly not large ones.

'It's not their bite you've got to worry about,' Felix said, 'it's their bark. It can really put you off if you're in the middle of something.'

They walked past police vehicles parked haphazardly along the verge, some with their strobes still going.

Felix said, 'Will your uncle be here, Garv?'

Garvie shook his head. 'Been and gone by now. Forensics are the early birds. Yesterday morning he'd have been here. Just the lab grunts now. Maybe the inspectors.'

Felix said, 'Like that Singh guy who bust you up last time?'

Garvie sighed. 'I told you before, it was all a misunderstanding.'

Past the empty police vehicles they walked as far as two unmarked cars, one a top-of-the range Humvee, the other a nondescript Ford. In the Humvee were two policemen, who turned to look at them.

Felix said quickly, 'Let's go and play somewhere else.'

The car window came down and a face appeared.

'Hi,' Garvie said, strolling over. 'Did you find out where the kid got his gun from yet?'

Detective Inspector Dowell got his face in order. 'I'll give you three seconds to step away from the car, son. And about a minute after that to get off the estate.' His Scots accent was as tough as tyre rubber.

Ignoring him, Garvie looked past Dowell to the other man, impeccably uniformed, who sat nursing a bandaged arm.

'Inspector Singh. Nice to see you again.'

Singh just looked at him.

'Good luck with all this, by the way,' Garvie said. 'Think you'll need it.' He paused. 'Looks to me like it might be tricky.'

Out of sight, they loafed round the estate. It was, as the media had reported, semi-derelict. The layout was as simple as a noughts-and-crosses board: four cross roads at right angles within a rectangular perimeter, half a dozen lots between intersections. The roads, wide enough for trucks, were pitted and cracked, the verges bald and studded with industrial litter. Some of the buildings were brick, some prefabricated. All were run down, most unoccupied. There was a wholesale timber merchant still operating, a couple of car workshops, the warehouse and the lock-up; the rest of the buildings were disused. Although it was adjacent to the ring road, just south of the sewage plant and only a twenty-minute walk through fields to the edge of Limekilns, the whole place felt remote, its quiet broken only by the occasional freight train going by on the nearby goods line with a tortured-metal noise of squeals and clunks. It was one of those places that seem apart from everything else, separate and lost.

'Lovely, isn't it?' Smudge said after a train had gone by. 'I think my eardrums are bleeding. What the hell was the Gimp doing out here?'

Scanning round, Garvie said nothing. Smudge said, 'OK, let's look for clues.'

They went round the perimeter wire, kicking their way through drifts of litter, keeping an eye out for the police, Smudge giving a running commentary on his thoughts.

'This Magee must of abducted him somehow, I reckon, drove him out here, where it's nice and deserted, bundled him out of the car, up the road there into the lock-up, and bang. Like an execution. There's a witness saw most of it, apparently.'

Felix said, 'What about the camera, Smudge?'

'What camera?'

'CCTV, by the entrance. We just passed it. Police haven't said anything about a car.'

'Maybe they drove in a different way.'

'There is no different way. It's the only entrance. That's right, isn't it, Garv?'

Garvie said shortly, 'No other way for a car.'

They walked on in silence until they came to a hole in the fence.

'Wait a minute, I get it now,' Smudge said. 'They didn't come in a car, they came on foot. Magee pushes him through this hole here in the fence, drags him up the road there, bundles him into the lock-up and—'

'Assuming he gets past the SAFEWAY,' Felix said.

'What do you mean, SAFEWAY?'

'Security.' Security was one of Felix's main areas of expertise. 'SAFEWAY systems, Smudge. Multi-discipline hardware and software, wireless and hybrids. Not top of the range, like the SECO at that warehouse up there, but they're all right. Only problem is, they don't come with Smash and Crash. If you can find the control panel in sixty seconds after kicking in the door, you can just switch them off. And usually they're in the most obvious place. Another thing,' he said, warming to his theme, 'two o'clock's the perfect time to break in. Police shifts change then, see. Plod just wants to go home. Even if the alarm goes off, you can race the police response, beat him every time.'

Smudge looked disgusted by this sudden large amount of technical information. 'In other words, Magee probably could get past it, which is what I said. You got to remember, Felix, this was murder. No one was racing anything. So, to get back to what I was saying: he pushes him through the fence, drags him up the road, smash-and-crashes through the alarm hybrid thingy, bundles him into the—'

'Course,' Felix added thoughtfully, 'once you're in you've still got to get through the internal security doors. They can be a bugger. Though to be fair, with a bit of advance warning, you can fix them with a piece of thin card Blu-Tacked in the right place to the inside of the door frame. Cuts the current, see?'

'Fascinating,' Smudge said. 'You should run a school club: Science for Thieves. Anyway, as I was saying before I was interrupted: he pushes, drags, smash-and-crashes, bundles, Blu-Tacks, etc. and . . . bang. Classic execution really.'

They walked on, past a car workshop and a defunct fresh-fish wholesaler, still advertising on a faded wooden board WORLD'S FINEST SEAFOODS, STATE OF ART PREMISES and FREE PARKING, until they were back at the entrance, and Smudge said to Garvie, 'You're a bit slow today. Didn't you spot nothing?'

Garvie shrugged. 'No more than the obvious.'

'Go on then.'

'Five big sheets of cardboard against the back wall of one of the workshops.'

'Yeah?'

'Neatly tied carrier bag full of empty soup tins under the fire escape.'

'So?'

'Half a dozen flattened cans of Special Brew thrown in the bush next to it.'

'Yeah. It's called litter.'

'Someone sleeps rough here. He eats cold soup from tins and drinks Special Brew and sleeps under cardboard to keep warm.'

'Yeah, course. Obvious. So?'

'The witness mentioned by the police is almost certainly a vagrant.'

'OK. And?'

'His testimony is likely to be vague and untrustworthy and won't stand up in a court of law. So, as I said to Singh back there, it's going to be tricky.'

'Yeah, well. They're saying it's straight up. They got the guy already, remember.'

'Not being rude to them, Smudge. But they don't know how to think.'

Lighting up, they loitered by the gate, waiting for it to be too late to go back to school before lunchtime. Felix speculated on the contents of the lock-up units. Smudge gurned up at the CCTV camera until he cricked his neck.

Leaning against the gatepost, he said reflectively,

'I tried to talk to him once, the Gimp. Couple of years ago. Saw him on his bench, and I went over, gave him some old chat about the weather or something, I forget what, and he just stared at me. Just stared, on and on. Like I was the weird one.'

Felix and Garvie gave Smudge a look.

'No, but. He didn't say *anything*. Just looked at me. And I was like, *I do not know what you are thinking*.'

'And is that an unusual experience for you?'

'I can read people. Not the Gimp though. That's my point. The Gimp was . . . I don't know. I don't know, see, because I couldn't read him.'

As they stood contemplating Smudge's insight the police Humvee came quietly along the road on over-large tyres and stopped alongside them. The window went down and Inspector's Dowell's face appeared, as before.

'Why aren't you three in school?'

Smudge and Felix looked modestly at the ground.

'Doctor's note.'

'Study leave.'

Dowell looked at Garvie, who had said nothing. 'You?'

'Field trip.'

'To an industrial estate? Studying what?'

'Police competency. Anthropology, special option.'

Dowell's eyes locked onto Garvie's. His face changed colour around the edges. 'Tell you something, son,' he said in a low growl. 'I'm going to remember you.'

Garvie shrugged. 'Yeah, well. I'm going to try to forget you.'

There was a moment when Dowell seemed to reach for the door handle, but his in-car radio came on, and he gave Garvie a last stare, wound up the window and pulled away down the rutted driveway that led to the main road.

'Got a death wish, have you?' Smudge said to Garvie. 'The man's a nutter. Didn't you see his eyes? Didn't you hear what he said?'

'He said he was going to remember me.'

'No, he didn't. He said he was going to make it his business to seek you out and hunt you down and crush you into tiny bits of human rubbish. For a bright boy, sometimes you really don't pay attention.'

'He's right, Garv,' Felix said. 'Now he's clocked us. Best place for us is a long way from here.'

Garvie considered this.

'Let's go,' Smudge said.

They turned to go out of the gate and Garvie turned the other way and began to walk back down the access road towards the cordoned-off lock-up.

Smudge and Felix looked after him, baffled. 'What are you doing? That's like *the wrong way*.'

'Should've realized earlier,' Garvie said over his shoulder. 'How much they need my help.'

7

He opened the door of the Ford and slid into the passenger seat and sat there looking at Singh, who took no notice but carried on impassively reading his notes. After a moment a muscle twitched in the policeman's cheek.

Without looking round, he said evenly, 'What are you doing in my car?'

'This your car? You're kidding!'

Singh remained silent.

'It's not a very nice car. It's not as nice as that car you had before.'

Turning sharply, Singh glared at Garvie, who gazed back at him innocently, and at last the policeman swallowed his fury. He shook his head, almost laughed.

'No one else! Only you! Only you could barge in here and say something so . . . so . . . Well? What do you want?'

Garvie said, 'I can help.'

Singh rearranged his bandaged arm and put his face in order. 'No,' he said. 'You can't. I told you before, a crime is not a game. It's not a puzzle for bored school kids to try to solve.'

Garvie didn't reply. He nodded at the cordoned-off

area in front of the car. 'You've wrapped it all up nicely, I'll say that for you.' He paused and went on. 'It said on the news you'd been called out to an alarm going off at a warehouse somewhere. Up there, I suppose.'

Singh glanced sideways, nodded briefly.

'But you came down here to investigate. Must have seen lights on or something.'

Singh said nothing.

'You found the Gimp downstairs, and got hold of Magee up there?'

Silence.

'Come on, man. You can at least describe the layout for me. I could find that out anywhere.'

Singh sighed. 'There's a lobby through the entrance, a room behind that, and then the corridor to the lock-up units.'

'One of which is owned by Magee.'

'How do you know that?'

'Why would they meet in a place he didn't have access to? He wouldn't want to waste time finding the alarm control panel or mucking about with thin card or Blu-Tack, would he?'

Singh looked at him, nodded at last. 'You're right.'

'And is that where you found the Gimp? In his lock-up?'

'Pyotor was in the communal room behind the lobby.'

'To which any of the lock-up owners had access?'

'Yes.'

44

'What sort of people are they, the lock-up owners?'

Singh hesitated and closed his mouth.

'Doesn't matter. Easy to find out. Not the very rich. Small traders, I'm guessing. Mechanics, shop-keepers, parts dealers, that sort of thing. What about upstairs?'

'It's not used. Condemned, actually. The whole place should have been pulled down years ago.'

'So what's up there?'

'Nothing at all. Just rubbish.'

'And an armed maniac called Martin Magee.'

'Actually . . .' Singh fell silent.

'Come on. Keep going. You were doing so well.'

'Enough now, Garvie. Stop with these silly tricks. I'm not saying any more.'

'You might as well. This is the exciting bit. Detective Inspector finds murdered boy, legs it upstairs and overcomes the killer. It's a straight-up case, isn't it? There's even a witness saw Magee dragging the boy in there.'

Singh said nothing.

'All right, tell me this. Was the Gimp's gun loaded?'

Singh's eyes flicked onto Garvie and off again.

'Course it was. He was a very thorough boy. But that's the odd thing, isn't it? That's the whole difficulty right there.'

'What is?'

'The Gimp was armed, but the person who's meant to have shot him wasn't. Magee wasn't armed at all, as you were about to tell me.'

Singh stared at him in silence. 'This is ridiculous. You're just making assumptions. Besides,' he added, 'we haven't got all the forensics back yet. We don't know the facts ourselves.'

'I'm just making the obvious deductions. Which is what you'll have been doing yourself.'

Singh said nothing.

Garvie went on. 'If the gun was Magee's, he'd have been charged straight away, and he hasn't been. You're still looking for the murder weapon, aren't you? That's what all this is about.' He gestured at the cordoned-off area. 'And I don't suppose your witness is very reliable either,' Garvie said. 'Those vagrants drink too much.'

Now Singh sighed. 'We're going to have to release the information, so I suppose it doesn't matter if I tell you. He swears he heard the boy talking in Polish, but he can't identify Polish from any other language. He says the boy was wearing the Marsh Academy uniform, but he never describes it the same way twice. He's even confused about whether he heard the shots before or after he saw them in the street.' He clicked his tongue. 'It's very frustrating.'

'There you go then. You need my help.'

'You can't help me, Garvie.' He corrected himself. 'I will not allow you to help me.'

'Why?'

'You know why. Because I won't put you at risk.'

'That it? Anything else?'

'Yes. Because I don't trust you.'

Garvie said nothing.

'Listen to me,' Singh said. 'You lie to people. You do what you like. Wherever you go, you cause chaos. If I allowed you get involved in a high-security case like this, I would have to answer for you. Why would I take that risk?'

Garvie said nothing.

'Tell me,' Singh said. 'Why should I trust you?'

Garvie thought. 'I can't think of any rational reason.' He thought further. 'No, none.' He looked at Singh. 'Do it anyway.'

Singh looked at him. He said softly, 'What do you even know about trust?'

Garvie had no answer.

Singh pondered. 'How old are you?'

'Sixteen.'

Singh nodded. 'When I was sixteen, I took *amrit*, the Sikh vows. Making my commitments. Before the ceremony I asked my father what I would get in return. He laughed. It wasn't a purchase, he said. It was a leap of faith. It was a dedication. Five years later I entered the force, I took on the police code. I dedicated myself to the service. It's not what you get for yourself, Garvie, it's what you give.'

He looked at the boy hard, but Garvie's face was blank. A memory came to Singh, a stubborn boy standing silently in front of his guru on a ground of orange dust under a blue sky. A boy who hadn't always done what he was told. Frowning, he shook his head. 'Anyway, I won't do it.'

Garvie said, 'Listen, you've got to stop being emotional about it. It's in your best interests to trust me. I'm just being logical.'

Now Singh turned angrily in his seat. 'In my best interests? I trusted you last time. And look at me now!'

Garvie said nothing.

'Don't you understand?' Singh said. 'Why do you think you saw me in the patrol car last night? Why is Inspector Dowell leading this investigation, not me? I've been disciplined, Garvie. Because of you. All the things that happened after you got involved in the investigation into Chloe Dow's death, all the irregularities, the mess that you caused, they all were used against me. You made enemies of the top people, and they couldn't punish you so they punished me. I'm the only Detective Inspector in the service doing night shifts. What do you say to that?'

Garvie said nothing to it. He took a piece of paper out of his pocket and scribbled on the back of it. 'Here.'

'What's this now?'

'My number. Call me if you need help.'

Singh snorted. 'Well, I'm not giving you mine.'

'No need. You gave me your card before; it's easy enough to remember: *City Squad Police Centre, Service House, 30 Cornwallis Way GX1 4SH, direct line 0888 274987, mobile 07020 061417.*'

Singh controlled himself. 'The problem with you, Garvie, is you don't know how to think. The issue here isn't memory or logic. It's *trust*. You can't put that in one of your mathematical equations.'

Garvie shrugged. He got out of the car, shut the door and tapped on the window.

Sighing, Singh wound it down. 'What now?'

'I'll give you something for free. Just so you know you could have trusted me. You're overlooking the most important thing.'

'What's that?'

'His violin.'

'His violin?!'

'Yeah. His gun must have been in the case. So where was his violin? That's the question you should be asking yourself.'

Singh wound up the window. Through it he watched Garvie Smith walk away through the late morning sunshine and shadows. Then he closed his eyes and rested his fingertips against the lids.

8

In the kitchen of Flat 12 Eastwick Gardens, Garvie's mother sat facing him.

She said, 'You don't care, do you, Garvie? That's the truth.'

The principal feature of the kitchen was a steamed-up window. Some of the steam extended beyond the kitchen into the main room, which contained two easy chairs, a sofa covered in a red cotton throw piled up with big green cushions, and in the fireplace a small group of papier-mâché sculptures of women dressed in yellow-and-orange shawls, brought over from Barbados where Garvie's mother grew up.

'You don't even think. Do you?'

The secondary feature of the kitchen was the spicy-hot smell of bajan fish stew. Uncle Len and Aunt Maxie and their toddler son, Bojo, were coming for supper.

'You don't care what happens to you, you don't think about your future, you don't . . . Look at me, Garvie, when I'm talking to you. I'm right here. Don't ignore me.'

Garvie's mother was rarely ignored. She had a voice like a reversing truck. Ever since Garvie's father went back to Scotland – just after Garvie was born – she'd been sole carer, like thousands of other single mothers, only bigger and louder.

'Well?'

He blinked and stirred slightly, as if until that moment he'd been asleep with his eyes open. 'Well what?'

'I'm asking you. How did it go?'

'Fine.'

'Which subject was it?'

'Biology. I think.'

'Biology? Even I know Biology's next week.'

'History then.'

His mother's eyes narrowed and her voice thickened dangerously. 'You took an exam this afternoon, and you don't even remember what it was?'

'Now I think about it, maybe it was Geog.'

'You did take an exam, right?'

'You can call the school and check.'

'I already did. Written French is what it was. According to Miss Perkins, you turned up ten minutes late and agitated to leave half an hour early.'

'Oh yeah. I remember now. I'd finished.'

'Used up all your French, had you?'

As she spoke the door buzzer went and Garvie got up to let his aunt and uncle in downstairs. When he turned back his mother was still glaring at him.

He said sweetly, 'Do you want me to give the coo-coo a stir? You know Uncle Len doesn't like it overdone.'

Garvie's mother contemplated this with the sort of expression people usually reserve for junk mail stamped *Congratulations*. 'All right then,' she said at last. 'But this conversation isn't over, Garvie. Later.'

Uncle Len, senior pathologist for City Police, was a large man with a genial, crumpled look magnified by bifocals. His colleagues knew him as steady and dependable, sometimes inconveniently vocal about police failings. Away from work, he liked to wear Hawaiian shirts, listen to calypso and drink rum punch. Late in life he had married the much smaller, much younger Maxine, also from Barbados, a social worker with a flair for fashion, and shortly after that Bojo had arrived, now three years old, a velvety sphere of smooth dark skin and dimples, with an inexplicable fondness for his 'uncle' Garvie, and in fact the only member of Garvie's family who wasn't always on his case.

In the kitchen Garvie mixed his uncle a rum punch.

'How was the exam this afternoon, Garvie?'

'Good. Written French. *C'était bon*. That's French. At least I think it is. How's the Gimp case?'

'You know I can't talk about police work. And his name, by the way, was Pyotor.'

'You were there yesterday morning.'

'That's just a guess, I assume. You would have been in school.'

'And you'll have done the preliminary autopsy by now. I guess.'

Uncle Len said nothing, tasted his rum punch, nodded his approval.

'So you know the cause, mechanism and manner of death.'

'Which I can't divulge.'

'Cause, gunshot wounds to the chest.'

Uncle Len was silent.

'Mechanism, blood loss. Not sure what the technical term is.'

'Exsanguination,' Uncle Len said before he could stop himself. 'Damn.'

'And manner, of course, homicide.'

Uncle Len peered enormously at Garvie through his bifocals. 'I know what you're at. You get nothing more out of me.'

'That's all right. I was just wondering, though. There are two main questions, aren't there? Where did Pyotor get his gun from, and where did his violin get to?'

For some time Uncle Len stared at Garvie, and Garvie stared sweetly back.

'I know what you're doing,' Uncle Len said at last. 'You think it's like Chloe's murder. You think you can get involved, stir things up, annoy the police.'

'It's not my fault if the police really need my help.'

'Listen to me, Garvie. I don't say the service doesn't sometimes need help. I don't dismiss what you did last time either – some of what you did anyway. You're smart, and you showed it. But Pyotor isn't Chloe. You weren't Pyotor's friend, were you? You've no reason to involve yourself. If you want to show how smart you are, I suggest you concentrate on passing your exams. You know how much that would please your mother.'

Garvie looked properly concerned. 'I'm sure you're right, Uncle Len. Thanks.'

'Besides,' his uncle went on, 'this isn't a case you want to get mixed up in. It's going to be a lot trickier than people are expecting.'

'Because that knobhead Dowell's in charge?'

Momentarily Uncle Len's face betrayed his feelings about the knobhead Dowell, but he controlled himself. 'I've got nothing to say about that man. Nor about what's happening to Raminder, which is an absolute disgrace if you want my view. No, I mean that there are all sorts of things going to get stirred up here. Racial things. I'm thinking of the Polish community and the feeling there is here against them.'

'So don't you think the police need some help?'

'Not from you. Anyway, luckily you don't speak Polish.'

Garvie frowned. 'True. Still, I'd be interested to know, just out of curiosity, if Pyotor's gun had been fired or not.' He looked sweetly at his uncle.

For some time Uncle Len was silent. He said at last, 'You like technical information, don't you, Garvie?'

Garvie thought about this. 'Some,' he said at last, warily.

'OK then. This is what happened. It's all you need to know about Pyotor's death. Four high-velocity bullets entered the right side of his chest between the second and fifth ribs, tearing through the pectoralis major, causing cavitation, shearing and compression through all the soft tissue they encountered, penetrating the superior, middle and inferior lobes of his right lung and crushing the thoracic section of his spine before exiting through the latissimus dorsi muscle in his back. Do you understand what I'm telling you?'

Garvie was silent.

'I'm telling you that Pyotor Gimpel was a boy with a body exactly like yours. That his body was ripped apart by someone firing bullets into it. That he suffered and died. OK?'

Garvie nodded.

'OK then. Now I'll have another of those rum punches which you make so well.'

After Uncle Len and Aunt Maxie had gone, and Bojo with them, Garvie's mother sat alone on the sofa with a last drink, staring into the fireplace. Calypso was playing low on the stereo. Garvie was in his room, finally doing some revision. She sipped her drink and sighed as she thought about her son. When, many years earlier, she'd been informed that he had the highest IQ ever registered in the country, she'd been, among other things, worried. She'd heard that abnormally clever children often find it hard to make friends with 'ordinary' kids, that they put themselves under pressure to make unfeasibly quick intellectual progress and are prone to develop obsessions with their academic subjects. She choked slightly on her drink. Probably half of Garvie's friends couldn't even spell their own names. His ambition at school had been to avoid intellectual progress at all costs. His obsessions ran to loafing around, staring into space and, lately, smoking that stuff. The only sensible thing for him to do was stay on at school to study maths, but to do that he had to pass at least five of his eleven exams, which he seemed to prefer to fail or avoid altogether.

She cocked her head and listened. Silence from his room. Perhaps, she thought, he really was revising. On the other hand he might just have fallen asleep – though in fact he didn't sleep much, just lay on his bed staring up at the ceiling. An odd boy. It was extraordinary how much of a stranger he had become to her. There were people who found him charming, she knew. His uncle, who ought to be stricter. Girls. There was something unusual about Garvie that appealed to them: the slouch maybe, or the wise-cracks, the rudeness even, or the mixed-race combination of coppery skin and blue eyes. But to his own mother he was an enigma. Could she even trust him any more?

She listened intently to the silence from his room.

Perhaps she should give him the benefit of the doubt after all. The business with Chloe Dow had irritated the hell out of her, it was true, but there was a part of her that felt proud of him. She knew his attitude was mostly for show. He hid himself out of his own pride. With a little rush of tenderness, blinking, she remembered him when he was young, warmer and more open, a delicate child with a sunny smile, quick to show his feelings, his happiness and his fear, laughing at his uncle, quietly holding onto her hand as they passed a dog in the street, his little phobia. In those less complicated days he knew he needed her. Now he pretended he didn't – and she no longer knew him. She listened to the silence from his room as she finished her drink. Perhaps he was revising after all. Getting to her feet, she went quietly over to his bedroom door and peered in.

He was lying on his back on his bed with his phone up to his ear, grinning and whispering. 'Alex, mate,' he was saying. 'Yeah, good, thanks. Thursday, yeah? Usual place, usual time?'

His mother stepped through the doorway and positioned herself solidly in a way that suggested she was filling her lungs. Without showing any sign that he'd seen her, Garvie quietly put his phone in his pocket and put on an air of studied innocence.

'That your friend Alex Robinson?'

'Yeah.'

'The boy who lived in a squat in Limekilns?'

'Yeah but—'

'The boy who's always in trouble with the police?'

'Well, once or—'

'He's not in prison at the moment?'

'Not at the moment.'

'He's at large again, supplying drugs to the community?'

'Yes to the first question, no to the second.'

'So you weren't talking to him about a deal?'

'No. Really not. Alex has changed. He doesn't deal any more, at all. In fact, and it's a bit weird for everyone, he's gone all anti-drugs. He's cleaned himself up completely.'

'You surprise me'

'I'm surprised myself.'

'And why would he do that?'

Garvie thought about this. 'Her name's Zuzana,' he said at last. 'With a Z.'

'OK. It's a nice name. Where's she from?'

Garvie hesitated. 'Poland. As it happens.'

'And it was her you were talking to him about?'

'Yeah, it was, actually.'

'Why?'

He shrugged, gave her one of his infuriating blank looks. 'No reason.'

They looked at each other, Garvie wary, his mother suspicious. He sensed a lecture, something about her not knowing who he was any more. She wondered where to begin. This was how it generally happened, him settling back to concentrate on the ceiling, her fixing her gaze to concentrate on him.

At last she opened her mouth. 'You know, Garvie,' she began, 'there are times I think I don't know you any more . . .'

9

The music room at Marsh was kept locked at all times. Apparently all those instruments that ought to be in a museum were valuable.

Felix, crouching at the door, straightened up at last. 'There you go,' he said with a modest professional pride.

Glancing down the empty corridor, they went in together. It was a big room smelling of wax: a piano in one corner, stacks of orange plastic chairs down one wall and shelves of music and books round the others. A messy desk stood under the single window.

Felix opened another door at the far end marked STOCK ROOM and went in with Smudge.

'Here they are, Garv,' Smudge called. 'Plus every other instrument that's ever been made in the history of the world, looks like.'

Garvie was leafing through a sheaf of papers headed STOCK LIST. 'All right,' he said. 'How many?'

After a longish silence, Smudge called back, 'Seven.'

Garvie frowned. 'Are you sure? Count again.'

Smudge reappeared, holding a violin. 'Actually, I'm all right up to ten,' he said.

Garvie kept frowning. 'Odd,' he said.

'What's odd?'

'Or clever,' Garvie murmured. Smudge passed the violin to Garvie, who glanced at it, turned it over rapidly in his hands and gave it back.

'Thought you wanted to examine it.'

Garvie nodded. 'I did. Chipped round the edges. Diagonal scratch across the front, top right. Small brand on lower rib, capital letters M and A. Label pasted inside, "Gustav Klee VL100 4/4 Maple and ebony, reference number 245833X".'

Smudge held the violin up to his eye and squinted inside it, slowly reading to himself, his mouth moving. 'That's right, actually,' he said at last. 'What now? Any other instruments you want us to count? We can see how many French horns they've got. That'd be fun.'

Before Garvie could reply the door of the music room opened and a man came in looking bewildered.

'This door was locked,' he said.

He had sandy hair and wire-rimmed glasses and a pale beard. He put his hand in the pocket of his grey jacket and pulled out a set of keys, and looked at them amazed.

'It certainly should have been locked,' Smudge said. 'Don't you realize how valuable these old things are, sir?'

Mr Merryweather, the famously easy-going and sarcastic head of music, crossed the room and put his briefcase on his desk. Catching sight of Felix emerging from the stock room, he frowned again.

'Fricker,' he said. 'I might have guessed. And you, Smith. What are you doing with that violin?'

Garvie said, 'I was thinking of having lessons, sir.'

'You? You're the idlest boy at the Academy. I imagine you'd rather step on a tack.'

'And I was wondering,' Garvie went on, 'if I'd need my own violin, or if the school provides them.'

'An idle boy after idle information.' He resumed his habitual sneer. 'I suppose that's not surprising in itself. Well, some students have their own instruments, of course. The school has no instruments of its own – these are the property of the county music service, though they're registered to us, and we have use of them, to loan to students and so on. They're all identifiable, by the way, Fricker,' he said to Felix. 'No resale value.'

'They got labels in them,' Smudge said helpfully. 'Somebody Key.'

'The label is immaterial, Howell. Labels can be removed.'

Garvie said, 'They're all branded "MA", for the academy. You can't remove a brand.'

Mr Merryweather looked at Garvie. 'That's right, Smith. Though why you're interested I can't imagine. Anyway, I must press on. I've been held up for nearly two hours by the police about this ghastly business you've heard about. They seem to have locked down the whole school. You'll have seen the new security at the gates. Now they're camped out in the senior common room. I suppose it's because it happened so soon after Chloe.'

'Did the Gimp have a county-music-service violin?' Garvie asked.

'No. Pyotor had his own.' He looked at Garvie. 'Funny. One of the policemen asked me that.'

'Guy in a turban, I expect.'

Mr Merryweather stared at him a moment. 'You do seem to know a lot of useless stuff, don't you, Smith? Pity you can't take an exam in it, instead of in French and Geography and all the other subjects you know nothing about. Guy in a turban is right. Polite enough. The other was just a bully, if you want to know. He did most of the interview.' He peered closely at Garvie. 'Perhaps you know *him* too.'

'Big, bald head. Face the colour of putty.'

Mr Merryweather nodded. 'You *have* been getting into trouble.'

Garvie said, 'Good at the violin, was he? Pyotor.'

'I assume you're being serious now, Smith.'

'Yeah, I am, actually. Thing is, I never saw him without it.'

Mr Merryweather looked at him a moment, considering. Then he sat down and briefly put his head in his hands, and when he looked up his face had changed. His voice was different too, when he spoke, free of sarcasm. 'He was the best young violinist I ever saw,' he said softly. 'None better.'

The three boys looked at him.

Smudge said, 'A natural, then?'

'No, actually. He worked hard, he practised. In a way he was the most technically proficient of all the violinists I've worked with. But to get above a certain level you have to have a feel for the music. As you suggest, Smith, he had an obsessive streak. At first he was too mechanical – he played as if he was ticking off notes in a list.'

'Bad with people, good with lists,' Smudge said, attempting a wise expression.

'Yes. Don't do that with your face, Howell, you'll find you'll need surgery later in life. The point I want to make is: something had happened; he'd developed I don't know what, an instinct, a feeling. He had the solo part for our current piece, and was doing it very well. Very well indeed. It was a breakthrough. And now . . .' He shook his head. 'A ghastly business, as I say.'

Garvie said, 'Get on with the other violinists, did he?'

'No, he didn't. Ignored them mainly. Bad with people, as you said, Howell. Although . . .' Mr Merryweather thought for a moment. 'Listen. This'll tell you something about Pyotor. Once a week we have orchestra practice after school. Two weeks ago, after practice, he stayed behind to see me. Had something important to tell me, he said, very solemn. "All right, Pyotor," I said. "What it is it?" "You haff to give me detention," he said. You know how he spoke.

"What on earth are you talking about?" I said. Turned out the second violinist had handled Pyotor's violin, and Pyotor had taken exception to this and there'd been a scuffle of some sort. Not just a scuffle, in fact. Pyotor had pretty much gone berserk; I found that out later. Anyway, he wanted me to suspend the other boy, for "unpermitted usage" – he must have looked it up – and to give him, Pyotor, detention for fighting. He'd brought with him a piece of paper he called a "confession", stating exactly what he'd done. He also wanted the other boy to sign something saying he'd never touch Pyotor's violin again. It was all very strange. I suppose he liked things to be pinned down, made clear. When I talked to the other boy it was clear he just wanted to forget about the whole thing. Not Pyotor. He wanted the boy to be punished, but he admitted that he had to be punished too. Logical, I suppose, but definitely peculiar. Of course, he was very attached to his violin. That was Pyotor. He was, as I'm sure you know, rather disconnected from other people.' He sighed. 'Poor kid. God knows what his grandparents are going through. On top of everything else, those policemen were on their way to interview them.'

'Grandparents?' Smudge said.

'Yes. Pyotor lived with them in Strawberry Hill somewhere. Don't know what happened to his parents. Sad story, I expect.'

The school bell sounded, an always-accidental noise, like an alarm clock going off at the wrong time, and Mr Merryweather looked at his watch.

'Joy unparalleled,' he said. 'Elementary composition with 10F. By the way, if I find anything now or afterwards out of place in these rooms I will report your presence here today first to Miss Perkins and second to the bald-headed policeman with the face the colour of putty. And Smith?'

'Yes, sir?'

'I'm putting you down for violin lessons, am I?'

'Not sure now, sir. Orchestra sounds like a bear pit to me. Can't stop to chat, though. Got an exam.'

'Well, you better hurry then. The bell's gone; it'll have started.'

Garvie squinted at the clock above the door. 'Yeah. Quarter of an hour ago, I think.'

'Good God, boy, why didn't you say?'

But Garvie had already gone. Smudge, as he passed the teacher, tapped the side of his nose and said, 'Good with people, bad with exams.'

'You need to watch yourself, Howell,' Mr Merryweather said, as he turned to the mess of his desk. 'One day you are going to need serious amounts of therapy.'

10

The squad room at the police centre was noisy, phones buzzing, emails pinging, printers droning, competing conversations across twelve desks making a joint combined noise as vague and endless as traffic. Every few minutes the door slammed as a distracted patrol officer came thumping in, calling out to his colleagues for attention. Ignoring it all, Singh sat stiffly at a makeshift desk in the corner, with a keyboard on his lap, around him a zone of antisocial exclusion as much his invention as everyone else's. By force of will he did not let his concentration break, rapidly typing up his report, from time to time glancing at his watch. At last he stood, briskly checked his uniform and made his way across the squad room and into the corridor, leaving behind the general commotion and a few specific titters. Moving in his usual tightly wound manner, he went past Armoury and Evidence Storage as far as Meetings 1 and took the staircase to the first floor, negotiating his way across the open-plan admin section. *Only your actions shall go with you*, he said to himself, *your actions cannot be erased*, feeling the ambiguous comfort of Guru Granth's saying. With carefully neutral expression he reached his old office in the corner of the wing, glanced at the name on the door – DETECTIVE INSPECTOR R. DOWELL – knocked and went inside.

Standing in shirtsleeves in front of the operations board, Dowell stopped what he was saying and raised his eyebrows at Singh, who said quietly, 'The chief said it was OK to join the briefing once I'd finished the report on the corner-shop break-ins.'

Dowell nodded at a chair at the back.

There were three other people in the room: Detective Sergeant Mal Nolan, timeworn steel-haired veteran of Serious Crime; Inspector Doug Williams, a juvenile homicide specialist from out of town; and Detective Sergeant Darren Collier, a small, squat man with a grey over-mobile face, Dowell's closest friend. None smiled at Singh as he picked his way past them to sit at the back.

'Media,' Dowell said. 'As I was saying. You've seen the headlines; you know what they're like. It's the second kid killing in Five Mile in two months. The first investigation skewed it for us. It was too slow, too chaotic.' His eyes flicked briefly towards Singh. 'We do this one fast, and we do it well. I want you on-message twenty-four/seven. I don't need to tell you, the scum will rip us apart if they get the chance. We play their game, but we play it better, we play it harder, and we win big. Speed is our priority here. All leave cancelled for the duration. Any problems with that?'

There was a murmur of denial.

Is this what I was like when I was up there? Singh thought. He caught Dowell's eye and held it.

Dowell said, 'The press think it's an open-and-shut. I don't need to inform you they're wrong. We have major difficulties. Witness statement inadmissible. No link between perp and victim. No motive. Seriously. What we have is a mess: a kid who never went out of his house except to go to school, and a man without a gun or a motive, in the same improbable place at the same time in the middle of the night. We have to build this case from the ground up.'

He paused and looked at them. 'Let's get to it then. Mal, what have you got for us on Magee?'

Mal Nolan summarized her report. Martin Magee, twenty-eight years old, was a habitual criminal with a police record and a total of three years served in two different facilities for armed robbery and aggravated violence. 'He runs a sham garden-clearance business,' she said, 'but consistently seeks out criminal opportunities.' He had been in the city since January and had already come to their attention.

Singh said, 'He's helping us with enquiries into the corner-shop break-ins.'

'It's in the report,' Nolan said without turning.

Collier asked, 'What's his story?'

Dowell said, 'He has a crib in Limekilns. Says he couldn't sleep, took a walk, found himself in the industrial estate and heard shots. He went into the lock-up, found the kid breathing his last, heard us arrive, panicked and hid upstairs. Obvious bull, and he doesn't attempt to hide it either. Totally unco-operative in interviews. If we need to mix it up I'll be looking for help.'

Singh opened his mouth and Dowell looked the other way at Collier.

'Darren? You up for that?'

'Sure,' Collier said.

'OK. Doug, tell us about the kid.'

Doug Williams said, 'Pyotor Gimpel. Not your normal underage. His medical and social-care records are in the file. As you can see, he was on the spectrum, certified Aspi. No record of any sort of trouble. No social circle at all. A loner. Strictly private. Had a highly disciplined, narrow daily routine. As Bob says, when he wasn't at school – either for lessons or orchestra practice – he was at home. Not only is there absolutely no link with Magee, there doesn't seem to have been any oppor-tunity for the kid to ever encounter him. But he did, obviously, in a place he seems never to have known existed before, let alone visited.'

'Abduction?' Mal Nolan said.

Dowell said, 'For which he got out of bed in the early hours of the morning and dressed himself neatly in his full school uniform?'

There was silence.

'It gets worse,' Dowell said. 'Here's the big news, just back from forensics: the gun retrieved from the scene wasn't the murder weapon. Turns out it wasn't Magee's either. It was in the possession of this boy Gimpel, and was almost certainly carried by him to the lock-up in his violin case.'

There was another, longer silence while they absorbed this.

'So here's the thing,' Dowell said. 'The world assumes the kid's an innocent victim, but for all we know he went to the lock-up to kill Magee.'

Collier said, 'He's a sixteen-year-old Aspi. How could he have got hold of a gun?'

'Not on the market,' Dowell said. 'He found it, or he stole it. The question is where? But the bigger question,' he went on, 'is what the fuck? What made this kid tick? He didn't think like other kids; he didn't act like them. He did the unexpected.'

There was again a short silence while people flicked through the file.

Singh said quietly, 'But, of course, he was also just a kid. And we shouldn't rule out that what he did was just what someone else would have done.'

Ignoring him, Dowell ran through key directives and appointed tasks. There was the ongoing search for the missing murder weapon out at East Field, there was further research on Magee and associates, and there were the interviews with Pyotor's family and at Marsh Academy, all big areas needing detailed work done fast.

'What we need to work towards now is the link between perp and victim. How did they end up together in that lock-up? Was there a prior connection between them? I want that boy's schedule laid out in detail. I want the school turned over. Any questions? Let's get to it.'

Singh said, 'There's a possible hate-crime angle. He was Polish and—'

'In the file,' Dowell said. 'Along with the others. We're not treating this as a hate crime, or any other sort of crime, yet. We don't have enough to go on. It's part of our thinking, going forward. OK?'

'I meant, shall I assist in that area? My training—'

'Give support to Darren then. Time permitting. You know what the deal is here. Your priority is the corner-shop breaks-ins. What's the news from Strawberry Hill?'

'I've talked to Stanislaw Singer, who runs it.'

'Report done?'

'Yes. But I'd like to re-interview him. There are some oddities. According to Stanislaw—'

'What about the transcript of the Gimpels' interview?'

'Almost finished.'

'Do that next.'

Singh nodded.

Dowell was chatting to Collier and Williams, and Singh followed Nolan out of the office and went alone back through the open-plan, downstairs to the squad room.

11

P olice Interview Transcript. Not for Briefing.
Location: Interview Room 3, Cornwallis Police Centre.

Interviewers: Detective Inspector Dowell: pop-eyed, shiny-faced; Detective Inspector Singh: quiet, watchful; police translator Jan Nowicki: crop-haired, expressionless.

Interviewees: Zbigniew Gimpel, Bogdana Gimpel: pale, hesitant.

Note: all questions from inspectors Dowell and Singh, and all responses from the Gimpels, are via the translator.

DI SINGH: Thank you for coming in again. We realize how difficult this is for you both. We'll try to make the process as bearable as possible.

DI DOWELL: My colleague here, Detective Inspector Singh, is going to conduct this interview. I have to be somewhere else. I just want to ask if you've given any more thought to the question we asked you last time. Simply this: what was Pyotor doing on the estate that night?

ZBIGNIEW GIMPEL: We don't know. We've thought about it a lot.

DI DOWELL: You said he went to bed as usual at nine thirty.

ZBIGNIEW GIMPEL: Yes.

DI DOWELL: And when you went to bed yourselves at ten you were sure he was in his room, asleep.

ZBIGNIEW GIMPEL: Yes, yes. We told you already.

DI DOWELL: But four hours later he was on the estate.

ZBIGNIEW GIMPEL: We can't explain it.

DI DOWELL: Well, he must have gone there for a purpose.

ZBIGNIEW GIMPEL: We keep saying, we don't know what happened. Pyotor wouldn't have had the idea to go there on his own. Perhaps this man tricked him in some way. Perhaps he was forced.

DI DOWELL: You told us before there was no connection between the suspect and your grandson.

ZBIGNIEW GIMPEL: We don't know of any.

DI DOWELL: So how did he trick him?

[*Silence*]

DI DOWELL: Why did he trick him?

ZBIGNIEW GIMPEL [*silence*]

BOGDANA GIMPEL: Because he was *polski*!

ZBIGNIEW GIMPEL: Hush, Dana.

BOGDANA GIMPEL: You know it's true! Racism, that's what it is, and it's got worse and worse. Especially with all these Asians moving in. You know what they're like!

DI SINGH [*coughs*]: Well. I can assure you that all motives are being investigated, including racial ones.

74

DI DOWELL: Wait a minute. Listen to me, listen. I don't want you to think about the suspect's motives. Do you understand? I want you to think about Pyotor. That's your job here. We believe that for some reason he left your house in the middle of the night and went to the industrial estate. We need to understand why. And you need to help us because we know your grandson didn't think or behave normally. Without your full cooperation, I can tell you that this enquiry cannot proceed quickly. Do you understand?

ZBIGNIEW GIMPEL: We understand.

DI DOWELL: Detective Inspector Singh will talk to you now. Let me remind you that this interview is being videoed and recorded in transcript, and that the avoidance of full disclosure is a criminal offence. [*Noise of chair being scraped, footsteps, a door opening and closing*]

DI SINGH: Are you OK? Is there anything you want? Mrs Gimpel?

ZBIGNIEW GIMPEL: She will be OK. Dana, Dana, hush now.

DI SINGH: I'd like to ask you about Pyotor. General questions. What sort of boy was he?

ZBIGNIEW GIMPEL [*sighs*]: You know he had difficulties.

DI SINGH: Yes. We've received information from school services about his autism spectrum disorder.

BOGDANA GIMPEL: Why do they always bring that

up? Even now he's dead! Why can't they stop labelling him? Not normal? Of course he was normal. He was just different.

ZBIGNIEW GIMPEL: Dana, please. She does not believe these things. But you are right. He had difficulties. He was always very quiet, anxious. He did not understand people very well. People are too slippery. He was precise, he liked things to be definite, to have their proper names, like labels. It made him feel secure. He used to give people names too – he gave himself names – but of course it's not the same with people.

DI SINGH: Did he have friends?

ZBIGNIEW GIMPEL: No. He kept to himself. He was different before Ania moved out, I think. His mother. After she went he seemed to . . . I don't know how to say it. To shrink.

DI SINGH: How old was he when she left?

ZBIGNIEW GIMPEL: Five. Not long after we left Poland. His father had never been around. But then Ania remarried and began another family, and it wasn't possible for Pyotor to move with them, and he became . . . different. More shut up.

DI SINGH: Did he see his mother at all after that?

ZBIGNIEW GIMPEL: Sometimes. They were in touch. She has a new baby, and we heard just a few days ago that the baby is ill – seriously ill, I'm afraid. Pyotor was concerned. It upset him, actually. He became preoccupied with it. He was like that; he developed obsessions about things.

DI SINGH: Let me ask you about Pyotor's likes and dislikes. You say he spent a lot of his time on his own. What did he do?

ZBIGNIEW GIMPEL: He liked routines, to do the same thing every day. To eat the same food, to watch the same television programme. And play the violin, of course. He didn't like new things, unexpected things. It made him anxious, angry even.

DI SINGH: Did he have any special interests? Any hobbies?

ZBIGNIEW GIMPEL: He liked the computer.

DI SINGH: Doing anything in particular?

ZBIGNIEW GIMPEL: I don't really know. Games, I think.

DI SINGH: Anything else he liked to do?

ZBIGNIEW GIMPEL: He liked to take photographs, with his phone.

DI SINGH: Photographs of what?

ZBIGNIEW GIMPEL: I don't really know. I know he saved them on his computer.

BOGDANA GIMPEL: He had started to go to gym class at school once a week, at lunchtimes.

ZBIGNIEW GIMPEL: It surprised us. He didn't like it much, poor boy. But we were pleased. He was too sedentary. We'd been trying to persuade him to take more exercise. Suddenly he agreed. I don't know why.

BOGDANA GIMPEL: But his greatest love was music.

ZBIGNIEW GIMPEL: Yes, music was the thing he liked best of all. You could almost say he lived for his violin.

BOGDANA GIMPEL: He had a special talent. He could have easily been a professional violinist.

ZBIGNIEW GIMPEL: He was good, it's true.

DI SINGH: He played for the county youth orchestra?

BOGDANA GIMPEL: First violinist. Solo parts. There was no one like him. The best in all the county.

ZBIGNIEW GIMPEL: He was rehearsing a new piece with the orchestra. The concert is only next month. They were practising all the time, lunchtimes, after school. What they'll do now I don't know.

DI SINGH: You say he didn't have friends. No one in the orchestra?

ZBIGNIEW GIMPEL: No one we know of.

DI SINGH: So, apart from school and orchestra, he didn't see people, he didn't go out?

ZBIGNIEW GIMPEL: That's right. Let me think. Well, he went recently to the Juwenalia parade, you know, organized by the Polish youth club here.

BOGDANA GIMPEL: And he had extra maths tuition once a week at school, after orchestra practice. He had his exams coming up. Pyotor was very good at maths. Exceptional. I think he would have gone to university to study it. He was such a bright boy, such a . . .

ZBIGNIEW GIMPEL: Dana. It's OK. Here, take this. Blow.

DI SINGH [*pause*]: I have to ask you something else now, something difficult. I'm sorry. About the gun that was found at the scene. The only identifiable fingerprints on the gun are Pyotor's. Its position suggests he'd just dropped it. Although we're waiting for more forensics information, we are fairly certain it was inside Pyotor's violin case at some point. Could it be possible he'd somehow acquired this gun and taken it to the industrial estate?

BOGDANA GIMPEL: Are you as stupid as the other policeman? Where would Pyotor get a gun? Why would he have it? Obviously it belongs to this man, this Magee. He must have shot Pyotor with it and put it in Pyotor's hand.

DI SINGH: But it isn't the murder weapon. It hadn't been fired.

ZBIGNIEW GIMPEL: There's another gun?

DI SINGH: We believe so.

BOGDANA GIMPEL: You don't know? You haven't found it? You see, I told you, they're idiots, Zbigniew, we'll never find out what happened to him, we'll die not knowing—

ZBIGNIEW GIMPEL: Please, Dana, enough now. Stop it.

Singh read no more. For several seconds he sat perfectly still and upright in front of the screen, almost as if at prayer, oblivious to the hubbub of the squad room around him. Then, without glancing round at the others or showing any sign of nervousness, he attached the file to an email message and sent it to his home address, and immediately deleted the sent record.

12

The Academy had been named after a local marsh, a spongy bit of which remained in the yellowish rough pasture at the edge of nearby Marsh Woods. Haphazardly arranged in three blocks – A, B and C – its buildings were brutally functional: three boxes of jaded grey glass cheaply brightened here and there by plastic panels in Day-Glo colours. There were two sports fields, called Top Pitch and Bottom Pitch, and two gates, also Top and Bottom. The less dutiful of the teachers referred to the school as Bog Towers. The students seldom dignified it with a name other than 'school'.

Morning bell had gone, the playgrounds were deserted; in the gym, under the coldly watchful eye of Miss Perkins, three dozen exam candidates were opening their History papers. Outside, by Bottom Gate, exam candidate Garvie Smith finished one Benson & Hedges and started another, glancing from time to time at his watch. The policemen stationed on the gate at arrival time had disappeared inside the school. He gazed coolly at the huge pile of commemorative flowers that had heaped up on the verge, objects such as soft toys and miniature Polish flags, and messages under flaps of clear plastic written in felt-tip, left by pupils, the result of class projects organized by the teachers. He wondered how many of the commemorations were from people who had ever spoken to the Gimp. Sometimes he glanced at the nearby bench where the boy used to sit. He remembered him sitting there, violin on his lap, staring into space or taking random pictures with his phone. He also thought about him lying on his back in a concrete room, his pectoralis major ripped open, the three lobes of his right lung punctured, the thoracic section of his spine crushed.

He'd just flicked away his cigarette butt and turned towards the school when a voice came from down Wyedale Road, and he turned back.

A boy in T-shirt and jeans ambled up to the gate. He was big, toned and good-looking with a clean jaw and grown-out twists and a habitual scowl: Alex Robinson, school athlete and reformed drop-out. They touched knuckles.

'Looking good, Alex.'

'Feel good. What's up?'

'The usual. Nothing.'

'That's the thing with you, Garv. You need to get busy.' He cracked a smile and his whole face came out of shadow. Garvie nodded, relaxed. It was a good day for Alex Robinson. Garvie had known Alex all his life, a simple guy with a justified reputation for physical toughness and straight-forward if sometimes misdirected feelings, a sweet nature clouded by occasional dark moods and an unpredictable temper. Of all Garvie's friends he was the one with the skills and strength to be a real athlete, a professional. But things kept getting in the way. Girls for instance. Alex was one of the galaxy's great romantics: intense, deep, soulful, inexhaustible. He was never not in love, and it didn't always go well. With Chloe Dow it had gone very wrong. After she dumped him he'd dropped out of school, mixed with crazies, squatting in a condemned house up in Limekilns, doing deals out at East Field and Pike Pond. When Chloe's body had been found in the pond he'd lost control completely. That too was in his nature: periods of single-minded fury in which he listened to no one. But just two months later, with the suddenness typical of his character, he put it all behind him, there was sunshine after cloud, light out of darkness, all thanks to the appearance of a girl called Zuzana Schulz.

It was good to see him smile again.

'Got a question for you, Alex. East Field industrial estate.'

'What about it?'

'You used to deal there sometimes.'

Alex's scowl returned. 'Those days are done. I don't deal. I don't smoke that stuff. I turned myself round, Garv. You know that. You know why.'

'It's cool. This isn't anything to do with deals. Just a point of information. I want to know about a vagrant sleeping rough out there.'

'Why?'

'He's talking to the police about the Gimp. Claims he saw stuff, but can't get his story straight. His patch must be on that road in front of the lock-ups. Ever come across him?'

Alex thought for a moment. 'Yeah, think so. Secretive type. Name of Vinnie. Old white guy with a grey beard. Real crackerjack. He used to hide along there.'

'Thanks, man.' Garvie glanced at his watch and up the drive towards C Block. 'She coming then?'

'She'll be here. She's got frees all morning.'

Garvie lit up again. 'Seeing as we're waiting, got another question. About Khalid.'

'Khalid at Jamal's? I don't see him.'

'I was in there the other day. He's having some sort of psycho meltdown.'

'He's been in meltdown all his life, that boy.'

Garvie nodded. 'Yeah, the break-ins making it worse, maybe. Says he's got money worries.'

Alex shrugged.

Garvie said, 'I'm just wondering. What would someone desperate as that do to get some quick cash?'

Alex looked at him suspiciously. 'Where you going with this, Garv?'

'Just there's a rumour going round he's putting up storage for someone.'

'For who?'

'For Blinkie.'

Alex glared at him. 'OK, OK, enough. I told you I don't want to talk about all that.'

'You used to be tight with him.'

'I don't have anything to do with Blinkie no more, Garv. You know that.'

'It's OK, man. He's still dealing though, right?'

Alex shrugged. 'I heard he was out of it. But I don't know.'

'You think he's into something else? What?'

'I don't know.'

'Come on, Alex.'

'Garv! Serious, don't get me mad. I'm telling you. I don't know what this interrogation is about, but I don't do any of that shit no more. I don't talk to Blinkie, right? I don't see Blinkie. I don't know what Blinkie's up to. Got that?'

'I got it.'

'And by the way, don't ever call him Blinkie – it flips him out big time.'

'It's cool, man. Hated to see you with him anyway, worst-dressed man in Five Mile. Even his monster dog wears a goldy-looking chain.'

'Whatever. What I'm telling you is, I don't know *anything about all those people.* I turned myself round. I found someone, right? You don't know what that means, I know. But I found the person I been looking for. My soulmate.'

'Yeah, I know. Zuzana. With a Z. You told me. Once or twice.' He looked again at his watch. 'She's late. And I'm busy. I've got a violin to find.'

'You getting musical?'

'I'm getting impatient.'

'She'll be here. You just wait for this.'

They waited.

'She hasn't been in the city that long, you said.'

'Few months. Met her at a track event at Strawberry Hill Academy. She's in the sixth form there.' He smiled. 'It's like she turned up just when I needed her.'

'Yeah, you always were known for your speed. And she lives in Five Mile?'

'Best of all. In that flat back of Jamal's. On her own for the next few weeks too: her parents are in Poland doing something, her sister's on holiday somewhere. It's sweet, Garv.' He smiled again.

'And she's definitely Polish?'

'You got a lot of questions. Yeah, she's from Poland. Why?'

'Just asking. I mean, this whole thing, you and her, it's been so quick. How well do you know her?'

Alex stared for a moment. Then he put his big hand against his big chest. 'I know her here, Garv.'

'All right, then, Mr Romeo. Just one more question.'

'What now?'

'Can you trust her?'

Alex's face went back to shadow. He stared at Garvie a long time, and Garvie looked back at him. 'I don't know what you mean, Garv,' he said evenly, 'but it doesn't even matter. The answer's yes. Got that? Yes.'

Before Garvie could reply a call came from down the lane, and they both turned, and a girl walked towards them out of the sunlight.

13

Walking lightly on black pumps, wearing black trousers and a grey sweater, she came all the way up to them and smiled. Her hair was black and glossy, her skin pale, almost white, and she looked at Garvie with a pert, lit-up expression as if she'd just thought of a funny comment and was about to tell him. Her lips parted and showed white teeth. Her nose, Garvie noticed, was strong and irregular, with a bump in the middle, and her eyes were large and dark and shining, as if somehow magnified. It gave them a mesmerizing and unnerving effect, which confused him as they exchanged greetings and started to talk. Dropping his gaze, Garvie was briefly aware of the tightness of her clothes.

She wasn't what he had expected – though he couldn't now remember what he had expected.

'I do not go to *polski* church, to the *sklepy* in Strawberry Hill,' she said. 'But, yes, I speak Polish. English and Italian too. So?'

It was ridiculously hard to pull his eyes away from hers. He became nonchalant. It seemed a way of keeping things normal. He was aware too of Alex watching him.

'I need someone who speaks Polish to talk to the

Gimp's grandparents.' Groping in his pocket for a moment, he brought out a piece of scribbled-on paper and handed it, nonchalantly, to Zuzana.

'What's this?'

'List of questions for you to ask them.'

'You don't think I'm capable of asking my own questions?'

'Those are the questions I need answers to.'

'Are they sensible questions?'

'They're the right questions. After you ask them, you can ask your own if you like.'

'Very kind. Is there anything else you want me to do?'

'Yeah. Write down the answers so you don't forget them.'

'Anything else?'

'Yeah. Let me know what time you're going to see them. And tell them you'd like to go to the funeral and bring one or two of Pyotor's friends.'

'Of course. Anything particular you'd like me to wear?'

Garvie carefully kept his eyes off what she was wearing. She was smiling at him. Out of the corner of his eye he saw Alex grinning too. 'Listen, I do my own thing. This is the help I need. You can say yes, or you can say no. Up to you. I'm assuming, by the way, your Polish is up to it. Otherwise we can forget the whole thing.'

She had a smile he couldn't pull himself away from. He was aware of his nonchalance fraying at the edges. Keeping her eyes fixed on his, she said slowly,

'*Jesteś palantem i nie wiem dlaczego tracę na Ciebie czas.*'

Yes-tesh pal-an-*tem* nee-*eh* vem de la *jego* . . . The words made a caressing sound in his head like the sliding of water over stones. 'Fine,' he said. 'You don't even have to tell me what it means.'

'It means *You are a dickhead and I don't know why I'm wasting my time on you.*'

Alex guffawed.

Garvie dropped his cigarette butt and ground it out.

'You have not told me yet why you do this.'

'No reason.'

'Really?'

'My own amusement.'

'Oh yes. Doing your own thing. But why are you interested in Pyotor?'

He shrugged.

She looked at him with those cool, dark eyes.

'There's not much else going on at the moment,' he added.

'Only exams.'

'I just want to find out what happened.'

'Why?'

''Cause the police are too stupid to find out.'

'And you will?'

'That's it.'

'Because you are so clever?'

'That's it.'

None of this was what he wanted to say, but he realized that only after he had said it.

Zuzana said, 'But you need my help. Not so clever then.' She was looking at him still with those big, amused eyes, and with an effort he glanced away again.

'He's clever,' Alex told her. 'Photographic memory, the whole bit. Just a bit weird. You get used to him.'

'Good-looking too,' Zuzana said slyly. 'Is that why he is so cocky?'

Alex laughed. 'Garvie? Garvie never gets the girl.'

'But I don't think much of his reasons for getting involved in all this. Perhaps I won't help him after all.'

Garvie said, 'Look, I don't need reasons and neither do you. Reasons don't matter. Facts matter. The Gimp got shot. His violin is missing. His grandparents speak Polish. That's what I work with.'

She looked at him evenly.

'OK, you don't have reasons,' she said at last. 'But I do.'

He hesitated. 'What do you mean?'

'I knew Pyotor.'

Now he hesitated. 'You knew the Gimp? I didn't know that.'

'You didn't ask.'

He glanced at Alex. 'Information I had was, you'd only just come here. How did you know him?'

'I came here January. Since then I go to the youth

club Juwenalia meetings every week. I knew Pyotor, I know Bogdana and Zbigniew.' She was no longer smiling. 'So I will help you, for their sake. And also because you obviously need it.'

Garvie looked all round for something to rest his eyes on, and eventually found his watch. 'All right then. Got to go, got an exam.'

She looked at her own watch. 'It will have started by now, I think.'

'Yeah.'

'You didn't forget, did you? Not with your photographic memory.'

'I tend not to need the whole time.'

'Of course. You're too clever.'

To Garvie's relief his phone rang, and he turned and began to walk away up the drive.

'Felix, mate. Yeah. Got a small job for you . . . Nah, simple for a boy of your abilities . . . Yeah, that's the place . . . No, I'm good. I'll ride with Abdul.'

Zuzana and Alex watched him go.

Alex said to her, 'I know what you're thinking, babe. He's strange, right? But all the time I was homeless, he was the only one who came by. Serious. He's got my back.'

She frowned. 'Why's he interested in Pyotor? It doesn't make sense. Why does he want to find out all these things? What is he really up to?'

Alex shook his head. 'It's just, like, his thing. Working stuff out. It's not Pyotor he's interested in.

He doesn't really do people, not like that.' He looked at his watch and down the lane. 'Got to go, babe, before they spot me and stick me in a lesson.'

'I thought you had a school day today.'

'Can't.'

'Where are you going?'

'Nowhere special. Just stuff I've got to do.'

'Alex!'

'Nothing like that. I told you. All that's done with. I'll give you a ding when I'm done.'

Zuzana anxiously watched him walk away. When he had disappeared she began to read the questions Garvie had written down for her. After a while she sighed, shook her head and began to bite her lip.

14

The bus from Five Mile to Strawberry Hill only takes ten minutes. It goes from outside Jamal's, south down Pollard Way, across Town Road into Cobham Road, Strawberry Hill's main drag, and up the hill past shops and filling stations as far as the tower blocks. There are three towers, so tall they can be seen from anywhere in the city, vast grey Stickle Bricks ridged with walkways, sequined with satellite dishes, standing in a concrete pool called The Plain. To the east, towards Limekilns, are the modern maisonettes, cheap boxy houses and prefabs. Along the tree-lined streets rising to the west are the older brick terraces, now subdivided into flats.

The Gimpels' flat was dark and cramped: half a dozen rooms on the second and third floors separated off from the rest of the house, made darker and more cramped by the bulky ornaments and heavy Polish furniture standing stolidly in the gloom like cattle at the end of day. The old woman came in from the kitchen with a glass mug of raspberry tea, and Zuzana waited until she had settled herself in the upright armchair at the side of the fireplace before beginning to talk.

*

Location: front room, Flat 3, 25 Strawberry Rise;
    dark; bitter smell of gas and old carpets.
Interviewer: Zuzana Schulz: polite, pale, pert.
Interviewees: Bogdana Gimpel, Zbigniew Gimpel:
    tired, shabby, sad.
Translation by Zuzana Schulz.

ZUZANA SCHULZ: *Dziekuję za zaproszenie.*

BOGDANA GIMPEL: *Nie ma za co.*

ZUZANA SCHULZ: Thank you. I won't ask you how you are. I know.

ZBIGNIEW GIMPEL: We can't understand what has happened to us. It seems to get worse and worse. Today we hear that this man, this Magee, is a well-known racist. Polish people in Heeley, where he came from, tell us this. Dana has talked to them.

BOGDANA GIMPEL: It doesn't surprise us. Only the police are surprised.

ZBIGNIEW GIMPEL: Dana is very upset about it.

BOGDANA GIMPEL: This place! For a long time now we are not welcome here. Stanislaw's shop has been broken into four, five times in the last few months. We get nuisance calls. Notes pushed through the door. Other things too. Stones have been thrown at the house; once they broke a window. Always we tell the police, always they do nothing.

ZBIGNIEW GIMPEL: It doesn't stop them coming to ask us more questions about Pyotor.

BOGDANA GIMPEL: The questions they ask! The fat one with the bald head. And the Asian. It's as if they don't know how to think. They seem to believe Pyotor brought this on himself.

ZBIGNIEW GIMPEL: They think he must have done something strange, something abnormal.

BOGDANA GIMPEL: And now the papers talk about him as if he was a freak.

ZBIGNIEW GIMPEL: 'Aspi Kid' they are calling him. You must have seen it.

BOGDANA GIMPEL: What they ought to be talking about is the racist abuse.

ZUZANA SCHULZ: He had abuse?

BOGDANA GIMPEL: So much. He was a good Polish boy, everyone knew that. He went to the Catholic church, he celebrated Easter at the Polish Club. Just last week at the Juwenalia parade that was broken up by those, those . . . [*Sound of crying*]

ZBIGNIEW GIMPEL: Hush, hush. It's all right, Dana. I'm sorry, Zuzana, it is very upsetting for us. [*Sighs*] Pyotor was harassed, it's true. With the school orchestra performance coming up, he was staying late for practice every afternoon, and we used to worry about him coming home on his own. Sometimes other boys picked on him. Once he'd been hit in the face, here. [*Points at his own face*] Slapped. He wouldn't tell us who had done it.

BOGDANA GIMPEL: Do you know what boys are like?

ZUZANA SCHULZ: Yes. Yes, I do.

BOGDANA GIMPEL: It's not just the abuse. Of course they played pranks on him. Jokes, that's what they called them. But they tried to get him to do the sort of stupid things they did themselves. They tried to corrupt him.

ZBIGNIEW GIMPEL: Dana, let's not exaggerate. 'Corrupt' is too strong.

BOGDANA GIMPEL: You never saw it like I did. He was a good boy, very trusting, always well-behaved, always told the truth.

ZBIGNIEW GIMPEL: It's true. I don't remember him ever telling a lie.

BOGDANA GIMPEL: But he had started to change. Just the last few weeks he got into trouble at school. Detention, can you believe it?

ZBIGNIEW GIMPEL: He was at that age, Dana. He was a teenager.

BOGDANA GIMPEL: There's more to it than that. One day he came home and asked me for money. Money! I couldn't believe it. Ridiculous. What did he want it for? And what next? Getting drunk? Getting into trouble with the police?

ZUZANA SCHULZ: Did he talk to you about these things? I know boys are so secretive.

ZBIGNIEW GIMPEL: Pyotor never talked to us much. He had difficulties relating to people.

BOGDANA GIMPEL: He was just shy. Why do you have to always make out it was an illness?

96

ZBIGNIEW GIMPEL: Whatever it was, he didn't have any friends.

BOGDANA GIMPEL: But he was happy. Until recently anyway. Until this harassment.

ZBIGNIEW GIMPEL: Perhaps. Sometimes it was hard to tell if he was happy. In fact . . . when he was younger it didn't seem to bother him to be alone. He didn't mind he had no friends. He used to call himself Pyotor-on-his-own [*Pyotor sam dla siebie*]. He liked names that described things properly. But lately I think he had begun to realize it was a sad situation, poor boy.

ZUZANA SCHULZ: When he was here, at home, with you, what did he like to do? How did he spend his time?

ZBIGNIEW GIMPEL: He did his homework, of course. He liked the computer, though what exactly he was doing on it I don't know. Games of some sort. Maths he liked. On Tuesdays he had extra maths tuition at school.

BOGDANA GIMPEL: He worked so hard, at everything. But his greatest love was music. His violin.

ZBIGNIEW GIMPEL: It's true. In fact I'd say . . . well, it doesn't matter now.

ZUZANA SCHULZ: What?

ZBIGNIEW GIMPEL: He loved his violin so much it made him almost anxious. He wouldn't let it out of his sight. I suppose that's just the way he was. In fact—

*

'What's that?' At the sound of the crash the old man flinched in his chair and looked about fearfully. His wife glared at him and he closed his mouth.

'You see?' she said to Zuzana. 'Just what we were talking about. This is the sort of thing they do!'

Her husband nodded grimly. 'What was it? A brick or something? Against the back wall upstairs. Did you hear the window go?'

'Do you think they've broken it?'

'I don't know, Dana.'

'Do you think they're still out there?'

'I don't know.' He looked anxious.

Zuzana said, 'It might be nothing. Let me go and check. Wait here.' She went out of the room into the narrow hallway and up the stairs. It was dim and quiet in the stairwell, her footsteps muffled by the thick and densely patterned carpet, and she crept up, listening in the silence, until she reached the landing above, where she found the light switch and went along trying the doors. The first was a bathroom hung with drying underwear, large and sturdy, the second a bedroom crowded with more of the bulky old Polish furniture she had seen downstairs. The third was sealed off with police tape, and she stood there for a moment looking, wondering what sort of things were behind the closed door, clothes that would never be worn again, books that would never be read, games that would never be played. Finally she went across to the landing window and looked out at the street below, gloomy yellow under streetlight and deserted. If there had been someone down there throwing things up at the house, they had gone now. Everything was silent. She checked the window itself: nothing broken.

As she went downstairs she took Garvie's list of questions out of her pocket and scanned it again, frowning. They were too pointed, too insensitive, too strange. *How often did he have temper tantrums? Where has he hidden his violin?* She pushed the paper back in her pocket and went into the living room, where the two old people were looking at her anxiously.

'You don't have to worry,' she said. 'I can't see any damage anywhere. I'm not sure it was anything at all. If there was someone outside, they've gone now.'

They looked at her balefully.

'Do you mind if maybe I ask you one or two more questions about Pyotor?'

The old woman put her face into her hands, and her husband put his arm round her, and Zuzana sat back down and waited.

15

In Pyotor's room Garvie and Felix relaxed as they heard Zuzana go back downstairs.

Felix was examining the window. 'It's these old sashes,' he said. 'They can slip, just like that. Very inconvenient. Nearly took my hand off. Still,' he went on cheerfully, 'told you we didn't need to bring a ladder. Amazing how often there's one just lying around. Soon as I saw that re-roofing job down the road I knew we'd be OK. Shall I start over here then?'

Already looking round, Garvie ignored him. The room was small and square and so tidy it gave the impression of being empty. The walls were white, the carpet brown. There was a single bed with a plain mustard-coloured duvet, a wardrobe dulled in patches where the varnish had peeled off, a chair, a small gate-leg table with nothing on it but a narrow frame of dust, and half a dozen shelves stacked with rows of folders and game boxes arranged with a sort of intense neatness by size and colour.

It was a room without happiness, without emotion of any kind.

Garvie opened the wardrobe door. One grey jacket, some grey trousers, a few white shirts, grey socks, white pants, black jumpers, two pairs of black shoes.

'Going to try some of them on, are you?' Felix said. 'Tell me if you are. I don't want to watch.'

Garvie ignored him. 'No patterns,' he said.

'Only wear patterns these days, do you?'

'No stripes, no spots, none of those stupid paisley shapes. Same everywhere. Plain duvet, plain walls, plain carpet. Patterns freaked him out.'

'Quite a lot of stuff freaked him, I'd say. Makes you wonder what was going on in his head. Looking at all this, makes you think it was just grey in there.' He sniffed. 'Good at maths, though, eh, Garv? You maths champs are robots.'

Garvie said nothing.

'Brain like a computer.'

'He was clever. That's what we've got to remember.'

'Fair enough. What are we looking for, by the way? Clues, stuff the rozzers'll miss? Gunpowder deposits, notes in invisible ink, cyanide pellets, that sort of clobber?'

He was looking at a row of official-looking cardboard packets arranged with typical orderliness along the windowsill. 'Cir-ca-din,' he said, slowly and tentatively. 'Mel-a-tonin, two mg, slow-release tablets. Abil-ify ari-pipra-zole, ten mg. What do you reckon?'

'I reckon he needed medication.'

'And they say you're a genius. I'll start over here.' Felix drifted towards the bin, grinning. All his life he'd been drawn to bins. They perked him up.

Garvie went through the shelves. Game boxes for *Assassin's Creed*, *Alcatraz*, *World of Warcraft*, *Haunted House*; three red folders marked ABA, EIBI and TEACCH, all empty, and one blue one marked ORCHESTRA containing a musical score for something called *The Lark Ascending* by Ralph Vaughan Williams, with pencil comments written in the margins at various points, all very neat and totally illegible.

'This is a bit disappointing,' Felix said, peering into the wastepaper basket. 'Nothing out of the ordinary here.'

'What sort of ordinary?'

'Tissues, apple cores, sweet wrappers.'

Garvie went over and peered in. He frowned and fished out a sweet in a green-and-yellow wrapper and stood for a long time looking at it.

'It's a sweet, Garv. You put it in your mouth and chew it.'

'Not been unwrapped.'

Felix gave it another glance. 'Yeah, well, you can eat too many of those things, do yourself a mischief.'

Garvie was sifting through the bin. 'There's a lot of them in here, none of them unwrapped. Don't you think that's odd?'

Felix had a closer look. 'Maybe he bought a load and decided he didn't like them. They look pretty nasty to me.'

'Look. They're in layers down the bin. He didn't

buy a load, he bought small amounts of them regularly. He just never ate them.'

'All right, if that's true it's a bit weird. But this is the Gimp, Garv. He was a bit weird.'

'He didn't buy them to eat. He bought them for another reason.'

Felix screwed up his face. 'What reason?'

Garvie didn't answer. He dropped the sweet back into the bin and stood there lost in thought. At last he moved away and started looking at the packets of tablets on the windowsill. Over his shoulder he said, 'When I went into Jamal's the other day, Khalid told me he was getting protection.'

'He's been telling everyone that. Hundred-and-sixty-pound mastiff from the Safeguard Kennels on the Limewalk Road. He's going off the rails if you ask me. He was done for gun possession last year, remember? There's security-minded and there's asking for trouble.'

'Why does he need it? 'Cause of the break-ins?'

'I guess. Unless it's true he's putting up storage for Blinkie. Alex would know.'

'Alex told me he doesn't.'

'I don't know, man. They used to be tight. Word was, Alex owed Blinkie.'

Garvie thought about that. After a while he said, 'What do you know about Sajid?'

'Khalid's kid brother? Nothing. Khalid gives him a hard time, apparently. You could ask Dani. His brother's in Sajid's class, I think.'

Garvie nodded. 'Good.'

There were noises downstairs, a door opening and closing, voices.

'Time to go,' Garvie said.

Felix nodded. 'Well? Did you find what you were looking for?'

'No.'

'Never mind. Can't win them all.'

'You don't understand, Felix. I was hoping not to find it.'

'Not find what, then?'

'The violin. It's missing. As I thought it would be.'

16

Dowell stood in front of the operations board, his pale face shining evenly. He had the exhausted, cheated look of a man who had spent the night trying to find an itch. He said, 'I have to be in a news shout in ten so let's keep it short. I said we wouldn't lose the message. We're losing the message.'

He gestured at his desk, where one of the morning's newspapers lay, headline uppermost – *Police Clueless about Aspi Kid*.

'Now's the time to take the message back. OK. Where are we with the murder weapon? Darren?'

'Nothing. The site's been searched. No sign of it.'

'Have it searched again. What about the gun the kid had? Where did he get it?'

'No leads as yet. We know it was stolen, that's all. We've hauled in all the local guys but we can't pin it on any of them, and they know it. Probably half of them have shifted a Webley in the last year, but they're not telling us who to, and the only names we get are the usual suspects.'

'What's your gut?'

'They don't know any more than we do.'

'Extend the search to Heeley. I want more traders

pulled in. Someone somewhere knows that gun. We need to know who had it before the kid. All right, what about Gimpel? Doug?'

'All the interviews confirm what we knew already. He's a typical high-functioning Asperger's kid, had difficulty with social relationships, a restricted range of interests. Borderline obsessive. Highly competent in mathematics and music. Some motor impairment, not serious. Anger management issues resulting in minor incidents, such as the one reported by his music teacher, but no history of violence. Extremely routinized: he did the same thing every day. Went to school by the same route, came home by the same route, watched the same TV shows, ate the same food, played the same computer games, went to bed at exactly the same time every day.'

'Opportunities for meeting Magee?'

'Nil. All his time over the last few months can be accounted for. Home, school, orchestra practice. That's it.'

'Didn't he have any friends at all? No one he saw socially?'

'No one. He didn't see anyone, he didn't go any-where. Literally. When he came home from school he stayed in.'

'He went to the industrial estate at two o'clock in the morning with a handgun.'

Williams was silent. 'Nothing in his history explains why he did that.'

Dowell chewed his lip. 'OK. Darren, where are we

with the school? You know how important it is, politically.'

'Our biggest team's on it. We've had a permanent presence there since day one. No one can be in any doubt how seriously we're taking it.'

He nodded. 'And the interviews?'

'Everyone. All the teachers, half the students, some of them twice.'

'Results?'

'Nothing. The kid turned up, went to his lessons, orchestra practice, whatever, and went home. He didn't get into trouble. He hardly ever talked to anyone.'

There was a brief silence in the room.

Singh said, 'What about his extra maths tuition? The Gimpels mentioned it.'

Collier said, 'Tuesday afternoons, after orchestra practice. Details in the file.'

'I couldn't find the name of the teacher. Was it his regular maths teacher?'

Collier hesitated. 'In the file,' he repeated.

Singh said, 'It's only a detail, but if everything else in Pyotor's schedule is accounted for—'

Dowell said, 'All right, all right. Darren, re-interview the teacher. Let's move on. What about the kid's computer? Doug?'

'The lab boys are looking at it now. Early reports are it's full of photographs.'

'Photographs of what?'

'Nothing. Everything. Whatever was in front of him. Standard obsessive behaviour.'

Singh said, 'Do we know where his violin is?'

They all turned to him. Dowell said, 'His *violin*?'

'Yes. It wasn't at the scene. I wonder because—'

'Have you checked the inventory of his room?'

'Yes. It isn't listed so—'

'Why does it matter?'

Singh hesitated. 'The gun was in the case. So the violin must have been somewhere else.'

'And the violin's important in what way?'

Singh hesitated.

'Listen,' Dowell said. 'I said at the beginning, speed's the thing. OK? We have to focus on the important stuff. Mal, any more on Magee?'

'A little. I said before, he's a regular. Registered as self-employed, doing odd jobs sometimes, mainly garden clearance, but he's done three years already, armed robbery and two counts of assault. He'll be in and out all his life.'

'I know his type. Small-time, violent with it.'

'And ambitious. A couple of years back he was questioned about a big job down south. A furrier's. Things went wrong. There was a death. No charges brought in the end, mainly because no one was willing to talk. He inspires fear.'

'He thinks he does. I'm getting bored of his sneers. Anyway, I'll handle him. You focus on his associates. OK, that's all. We know what we're doing. Anyone got anything to say? Good, then I'll—'

Singh said, 'Thinking about the hate-crime angle, I've been talking to the Polish community, here and elsewhere. There's plenty of talk about Magee.'

Dowell got ready to leave. 'OK, but I have to go. What's the gist?'

'They're very clear. Magee was an active racist.'

'Evidence?'

'So far, circumstantial.'

Dowell put on his jacket and began to look for his cap. Singh continued, 'But four of the five corner shops Magee robbed were Polish. The furrier's mentioned by Mal is owned by a Polish consortium.'

'OK. Anything else?'

'It's a common assumption among the Poles that he's an official member of an anti-immigration organization. He's been seen taking part in rallies. It's the same group that broke up the recent Juwenalia parade.'

Dowell paused at the door, nodded. 'Give me proper evidence then,' he said. 'Not all this circumstantial stuff. I want all the CCTV along the parade route checked and sorted.'

'OK. Understood.'

'By the end of the week.'

Singh nodded.

'After you've finished the corner-shop paperwork. And if I were you I wouldn't spend any more time thinking about violins. OK?'

Singh held his eyes, nodded again.

They sat in silence watching Dowell button his jacket and adjust his cap. As he went, he said, 'Last thing, everyone. This case gets solved. I've given my word to the chief. I don't break my word.'

Then he was gone. The mention of the chief seemed to impose a moment's fretful silence on the room, then Collier, Nolan and Williams began to talk among themselves, and Singh went without speaking out of the office and back to the squad room.

17

At ten o'clock the following evening as Singh sat alone at a monitor in Investigative Division, scrolling inch by inch through grainy black-and-white footage of a four-hour, eight-mile-long street procession, across town, in Eastwick Gardens, Garvie Smith lay in his bedroom not revising. It was a cool summer night, the dark blue sky so smooth it seemed to be coloured paper fitted neatly to the windowpane, and Garvie turned his head and stared at it without blinking.

An hour passed.

Garvie's mother began to get ready to leave for her shift at the hospital; Garvie could hear her opening and shutting her wardrobe door, taking her uniform coat from the chair. Soon she would go into the living room and hunt in vain for her keys, which were on the kitchen windowsill. Sure enough, after a minute or two, he heard her moving stuff around on the mantelpiece, rummaging in drawers, muttering to herself.

After a while he called out, 'On the windowsill!'

He heard her go across the room in the same firm, direct way she did everything. In a minute he would hear her come back the other way, equally firm, equally direct, and stand in his doorway to ask how much revision he'd done and what time his next exam was, and why he hadn't settled down to sleep already.

She duly appeared, considering him with a serious expression, which he returned with his usual impassivity. Something unspoken passed between them, some blend of irritation and love. She opened her mouth and before she could speak he said, 'Couple of hours on Geography. Half an hour Eng. Lit.'

After a moment she opened her mouth again and he said, 'Friday afternoon, two thirty, school gym. Mobile phones are not allowed in the auditorium.'

She regarded him with a long and searching look. 'If only you could be such a know-all *in the exam*. What about Special Maths? That's the one I'm really worried about. High level, Miss Perkins said. Gifted and talented students only.'

'Nearly three weeks off. It'll be fine. I'll wing it.'

'Wing it! I know your wing it. Your wing it has *nothing to do with flying*.'

She was looking at him in that sceptical way again.

'I can't stop thinking about that poor boy,' she said.

He could feel her watching him closely. He said, after a while, 'What poor boy?'

'You know who I mean.'

'Oh. The Gimp.'

His mother's face softened. 'Do you remember him when he was small, at nursery?'

'I never had anything to do with him. He was just around.'

'He never played with anyone. He just sat there looking like he was thinking sad thoughts. The only thing he used to do was put all the toys in rows. Line them up. And if anyone disturbed them he cried. He cried a lot. Not like a little boy. Like a grown-up, to himself.'

Garvie said nothing.

He felt his mother focus on him again. 'I'm surprised you don't remember.' Then she sighed. 'Don't stay up too late. You need a good night's rest. You should have settled down already.'

'Yeah, yeah.'

She narrowed her eyes. 'Don't even think of going out.'

'Course not. Don't worry about me. Off you go. Be good at work.'

She came across the room and kissed the top of his head, and he smelled the hot, dry smell of the iron on her uniform, medicinal odours of hairspray and hand gel, and then she was gone. He heard the flat door clicking behind her, her footsteps echoing like slow handclaps in the stairwell, the outer door closing with a distant *whump*, then silence, and he was on his own.

For a long time he lay there staring at the window. He frowned. He was fed up with people pestering him about the Gimp. *Did you know him? Didn't you know him? Why are you interested in him? Why do you care that some kid got shot? You don't care, do you, it's just a puzzle to you, isn't it, just a distraction from your exams?*

He thought about the Gimp. It was all very well spilling over with pity. Didn't he deserve a bit of justice too, same as everyone else? The Gimp had never needed his pity, and didn't need it now. Better to ask the interesting questions. What *had* the Gimp needed? Even better: what had the Gimp *wanted*?

Yeah, that was interesting.

Sighing, he got up, took his old leather jacket from the floor in the corner of his room and went out of the flat, down the stairs and through the little car park into Pilkington Driftway, deserted now and cool in the purple evening. The sky was blurred and thick. No stars. Five Mile didn't do stars. It was half past eleven, and he drifted down the street towards the shops, jacket zipped up, hands in pockets, shoulders hunched, his face blank. When he got to the corner of Bulwarks Lane he took out his phone and dialled a number.

'Singh here.'

'What's up, dude?'

'Who is this? Garvie?'

'Didn't wake you, did I? I assumed you'd be on your night shift.'

'I'm . . . Never mind. What do you want? Is it about Pyotor?'

'Just wondered if you'd got any more updates for me.'

There was a pause. 'Remember,' Singh said, 'that you promised to help me too. So far it's been all the other way round. You haven't even thanked me for the things I sent you.'

'Yeah. Truth is, I was surprised you changed your mind about that. And I've been a bit busy with exams. Though you've been busy too, probably, working nights, handing out traffic fines, whatever it is demoted coppers do.'

Singh made a noise of irritation. 'So what did you think of the material? The interview with Pyotor's grandparents, for instance?'

'All right. Some of it was even interesting.'

'Is that all you've got to say?'

'Don't rule out Magee just yet. All your problems might just be the result of one very simple thing.'

'What's that?'

'Police incompetence.'

Singh made an exasperated noise. 'The problem is time,' he said. 'We couldn't charge him with murder, so he was charged with resisting arrest in order to detain him for further questioning, but if we don't bring new charges soon we have to release him on bail. His lawyers are already pushing for it.'

'Good luck to your ace interrogator then. Oh, by the way, got a quick question for you.'

'Yes?'

'Does Jamal have a unit in the lock-up?'

There was a pause. 'Jamal who runs the store in Bulwarks Lane?'

'Yeah.'

'I don't know. Why do you ask?'

'Can you find out?'

There were more noises of irritation on the other end of the line. 'You know, Garvie,' Singh said, 'I'm risking a lot to pass on information to you. It's strictly against regulations.'

'Yeah. And I know what you feel about regulations. Beautiful things.'

Singh ignored him. 'I need something back, and I'm not getting anything.'

'Shocking, isn't it?' Garvie said 'But I've got to go now. Laters, man.'

18

By this time he'd drifted down Bulwarks Lane in the direction of the taxi rank where Abdul kept his cab and was standing across the street from Jamal's, closed now with metal grilles shuttering the windows. There was a faint light in a fringe around the curtained windows upstairs where the family lived. The shop was dark, the street deserted, and Garvie stood there alone, unmoving, like a figure in a photograph titled *Nightscape in the City*.

He lit a Benson & Hedges, puffed out a little smoke. At the back of the shop was the flat where Zuzana Schulz lived, and her image came into his mind, her black hair, wide mouth, her eyes – her eyes especially, not so much their size or brightness but the expression in them, the way she'd looked at him in that mocking, shining way, so difficult to read. He pictured her clearly, remembered the tone of her voice, the shape of her gestures – of her shoulders, her hips, her legs – but when he tried to *think* about her he just felt confused. He took a deep drag on his cigarette and frowned. She'd unsettled him. He was unsettled now to find himself thinking about her, hanging round outside her flat. The last thing he wanted to do was to fall for his best friend's girl.

Alex had turned himself round because of her, and Garvie was glad for him. He pinched out his cigarette, and was turning to go when he heard a faint noise from the other side of the street.

A tapping. He couldn't tell whether it came from inside the shop or behind it.

After a moment it came again. It had a secretive, insistent tone, like a coded message.

Discarding his Benson & Hedges, he crossed the empty road and went quietly down the unlit alley at the side of Jamal's to where it turned round the back of the building. As the tapping came a third time, now the unmistakable sound of knuckles on glass, he peered round the corner. The alley was dark. On the near side was the back door to Jamal's shop, on the other a brick wall with a wooden gate in it, slightly ajar, and at the far end the door to Zuzana's flat, darkly shadowed. Someone was standing there with his back to Garvie: a short guy wearing an outsized retro tracksuit and a Dirty Ghetto Kids Snapback. His Timberlands glowed like pumpkins in the dark. As Garvie watched, he knocked again on the door and moved back into the shadows, grinning to himself. After a moment he turned to look back down the alley, his glasses flashing in the moonlight, his idiot eyes blinking big and slow, and Garvie pressed himself against the wall.

Light came on in the flat and Blinkie's face withdrew. A silhouette appeared in the dimpled pane of the door, and Garvie tensed up, waiting for Zuzana to appear. But Zuzana did not appear. The door opened and Alex stepped out. He turned, scowling, and Blinkie stepped forward laughing and put his hand on Alex's shoulder, and they stood close together whispering. Garvie waited a moment but could hear nothing, so he took a risk and slipped through the shadows across the alley to the wooden gate at the far side and tiptoed through it, and stood at the gatepost, listening.

He heard Alex say, 'Forget it, man.'

He heard Blinkie say, 'Be nice to her,' in his strange reedy voice. 'Tell her it's all good. She going to love it.' His laugh was a wet crackle in the silence.

Then he heard Alex mutter, 'I'll call you. Don't call me.'

There was the sound of Blinkie fumbling in the pockets of his tracksuit, chuckling in the same cracked way, and Alex turned without saying anything and went back inside the flat, and Blinkie stood alone grinning to himself, lifting his face occasionally to look about him, blinking.

Garvie stood there, thinking. Alex had taken a risk getting mixed up with Blinkie once. But Alex had said all that was over.

As Blinkie turned to come back down the alley, Garvie slipped deeper into the blackest shadows at the back of the little yard, where he tucked himself into the side of an old metal wardrobe to wait for Blinkie to go past. Down the alley Blinkie's footsteps came nearer, and Garvie held his breath while he went by. But he didn't go by. His footsteps slowed – and stopped. There was silence. In the shadows of the yard Garvie listened to Blinkie listening on the other side of the gate. Then the gate slowly opened inwards, and Garvie saw Blinkie standing there, peering around blindly, blinking with his watery big eyes, cocking his head as if he was trying to smell what he couldn't see. There was a moment when he seemed to look right at Garvie, though his expression didn't change, a strange expression, unsmiling and unhinged, fish-like, predatory. The man closed his mouth briefly, it fell open again, then he turned and shuffled away.

Moments later there was another man's voice in the street, and an engine started up, a door slammed and a car with a pimped-out exhaust muffler roared away. Garvie stayed where he was. Ten minutes passed. Silence descended. Finally he emerged. He stepped out of the yard and heard in the night quiet-ness the faint sound of a man's crying in a room above Jamal's shop. Khalid's room. It came and went, a quiet baby-wail of mucus and despair, the loneliest sound in the world. He listened to it for a moment. Then he went out onto the street and walked slowly away down Bulwarks Lane, thinking.

19

Saturday morning, just after breakfast, Garvie and his mother went to his uncle's. His mother was going shopping with Uncle Len and Aunt Maxie, and Garvie was going to mind Bojo – in between dedicated periods of revision. That was the theory.

They sat all together in the front room, drinking coffee. Garvie said nothing, and his mother said nothing to him. Occasionally she gave him a strong look. Aunt Maxie and Uncle Len glanced at each other.

'Well, Garvie,' his uncle said, 'how did your exam go yesterday?'

Garvie considered this. 'Good,' he said at last. 'Very straightforward, thanks.'

'What subject?'

He considered this for a while longer. 'Geog.'

'I thought you'd dropped geography last year.'

Garvie glanced at his mother. 'Don't think so. Think I'd remember if I'd dropped it.'

In her position on the sofa his mother began to fill her lungs. It gave her an overloaded and unstable air.

'Yeah,' Garvie said, taking a risk. 'Definitely geography. I think.'

His mother spoke – to Uncle Len. ' "Geography",

yes. "Straightforward", no. "Good", almost certainly not. Quarter of an hour *before* the end of the exam I had Miss Perkins on the phone. Informing me my son appeared to have left the examination room. Was nowhere to be seen. Had left behind his paper with half an hour left on the clock. Which had surprised her, she told me, particularly because he'd turned up half an hour late and had only been in the room an hour for a two-hour paper.'

'I'd finished,' Garvie said.

'The point isn't to finish,' his mother said. 'The point is to pass.'

'Maybe I've passed as well.'

'Just went,' his mother said to Uncle Len and Aunt Maxie. 'Didn't ask, didn't give a reason. Just slipped away.'

'Didn't want to disturb anyone.'

'You disturbed them plenty. Formal warning given, enquiry to follow, possibility of automatic penalties. What is wrong with you, Garvie?'

Garvie rolled his eyes. 'It's only an exam. I don't see why everyone's so worked up.'

Garvie's mother eyes whitened and widened and threatened to detach themselves from her face, but she stopped herself from saying whatever it was she had in mind and breathed in and out for several seconds until she appeared normal again.

'Len,' she said.

Uncle Len gave her an anxious look. 'Yes?'

'I wonder if this would a good time for you to

have that chat with Garvie we talked about.'

'Chat? Oh. Yes. Garvie, give me a hand clearing away these coffee things, will you?'

In the kitchen, they faced each over the breakfast bar.

'I don't like doing this,' Uncle Len began, 'but you give your mother such a hard time.'

Garvie just looked at him.

'I shouldn't have to do it,' he said.

Garvie said nothing to that either.

'Stop staring at me – you know it makes me lose concentration. Listen. You think no one gets to tell you what to do, you think it's your life, you take the decisions. Yes? Well, you're right. So, let me ask you, what are you going to do next year?'

Garvie shrugged.

'Stay on at school? Leave and get a job? Go on the dole?'

Garvie shrugged again, and Uncle Len nodded. 'OK, Garvie. I'm trying to think, What would I do in your place? What would I do if I were not exactly stupid but lazy as all hell. I wouldn't want to be on the dole; you have to spend all your time applying for jobs you don't want to do. I probably wouldn't get a job either. Even good jobs are hard work for a really lazy person. I'd ask myself what subject I liked best at school, and I'd stay on, fully paid for, and spend two years doing that. I wouldn't have to work so hard if I didn't want to, and I'd still end up with an impressive-looking qualification. Of course, you'd have to pass at least some of these exams now to stay on. But, as I say–' he spread his hands – 'that's up to you.'

He sat back and looked at Garvie, and Garvie looked back at him. His nephew was unnervingly hard to read. For a minute neither spoke. Then Garvie gave a little shake as if coming out of a trance, and said, 'Uncle Len, did the Gimp have anything of interest in his pockets?'

'*What?* Have you been listening to anything I've just said?'

'Or anything at all really, even stuff you'd expect to find – you know, an apple, uneaten sweets, ammunition for his gun.'

'Garvie! What the hell is wrong with you?'

'I know, I know, it's confidential. Just tell me then when the personal effects are being returned to the family.'

'Tell you when the . . .' Uncle Len breathed hard. 'Why do you even want to know?'

'So I can go and look at them.'

Uncle Len snorted. 'Oh yes, of course – if you knew these people, which you don't; if it wasn't an invasion of their privacy, which it is; and if you spoke Polish, which luckily you don't. Anyway,' he added hurriedly, 'for all you know, the police still have them.'

Garvie sighed. 'You're always one step ahead of me, Uncle Len.' He got down from the breakfast bar and drifted over to the door and looked back.

'Don't worry,' he said. 'I'll tell her you gave me hell.'

Aunt Maxie had brought Bojo down and, avoiding his mother's eyes, Garvie went over and began to play with him. When he looked up, the others had all gone into the kitchen, and he could hear the low strain of voices through the shut door. They were talking about him: he could imagine his mother laying into Uncle Len.

He looked at his cousin, who knelt on the floor like a miniature colossus in scarlet dungarees among scattered dinosaurs and heavy-duty trucks, and sighed. 'Bojo, what do you think? Sounds to me like the personal effects have been returned already.'

Bojo put his fingers into his mouth and solemnly showed Garvie the wet remains of a chocolate finger.

Garvie nodded thoughtfully. 'But the violin isn't one of them. So where is it, Bojo?'

Bojo regarded Garvie placidly. He gave a little wave with the chocolate finger and put it back in his mouth.

'Think, Bojo. If you had a favourite thing, I mean something you couldn't eat, and you had to make sure no one found it, where would you hide it? Where would you hide it if you were a clever kid, a kid who always has a plan. Hmm?'

Bojo laughed till he choked and what was left of the chocolate finger slid out of his mouth and was lost in the carpet, and he began to look for it, making noises of outrage and distress.

Garvie's thoughts switched to Alex, and his frown deepened. His best friend had just joined the category of people he didn't understand. Why, now that his life was back on track, would Alex hook up with Blinkie again? What the hell was wrong with him?

The phrase echoed uncomfortably in his mind, in his uncle's voice. He thought of what Uncle Len had just said. He knew it made sense. If he was half as smart as people said he was, he'd put in the minimum amount of work to pass his exams and take the next two years off. He'd go along with it, all the stupid questions and answers. There must be something wrong with him, he thought – perhaps some actual medical problem – to make him think they were the wrong questions, the wrong answers. He just couldn't help thinking that the right questions, the important questions, were elsewhere. Briefly he thought of his mother. He knew how worked up she got. She couldn't help it. He promised himself that he would do everything he could to avoid upsetting her, no matter how many slightly shaky reassurances he had to give her.

When the others emerged from the kitchen they found Garvie and Bojo sitting stickily on the sofa with a new box of chocolate fingers.

'We're off,' Aunt Maxie said. 'Be good.'

Garvie's mother looked meaningfully at Uncle Len.

'Ah yes,' he said. 'Remember what I said, Garvie, about revision. What's your next exam?'

'Biology, written paper.'

'You sure about that?'

'Yes.'

'And when is it?'

'Monday afternoon.'

'Monday afternoon when exactly?'

'Monday afternoon at two o'clock.'

'And where is it?'

'Gym.'

'And you know where that is, and you'll be there on time?'

Garvie looked at him evenly. 'I'll be there,' he said. 'There is absolutely no need to worry.'

20

At half past one on Monday afternoon Garvie stood with Felix and Smudge in the cemetery of the Catholic Church of Our Lady of Perpetual Help in Strawberry Hill, the '*polski* church'. The cemetery was an isolated tangle of tilting tombstones and crumbling monuments surrounded by the high brick walls of the shopping centre and cinema. Beyond its wrought-iron railings was a line of a policemen, a crowd of journalists with their cameras and sound booms, and, further along, groups of well-wishers standing with flowers and mementoes. Behind them cars accelerated noisily up the hill, and other people went past talking and laughing, but inside the cemetery, at the far end, there was a hush broken only by the steady quiet chanting of the priest reciting the final part of the service that had gone on much longer than anyone had expected.

Behind the grave was a small group of black-suited mourners, middle-aged and elderly representatives of the local Polish community. At the priest's side were Zbigniew and Bogdana Gimpel, formal and bowed in their stiff mourning dress, and, beside them, a younger woman holding a baby, her wet face distorted by weeping, and, next to her, Zuzana, pale and quiet, in a dark grey skirt and jacket that made her seem slighter and smaller and more elegant than Garvie remembered. There was only one other person at the side of the grave, and he left it now and walked, as if irritably, to where Garvie, Felix and Smudge were standing a little way off. He was wearing full police uniform tight round the stomach and creased around the knees, and a peaked cap with a dribble of gold braid on the rim, and he got close up to Garvie and looked at him with menace before he spoke.

'Told you I'd remember you.'

Garvie gazed back at him. 'Met before, have we?'

'What's your name, son?'

'Smith.'

'Funny.'

'Depends on your sense of humour. My mother doesn't think it's funny.'

Unsmiling, Detective Inspector Dowell took in Felix and Smudge with his small, hard eyes. 'OK, let's do it all again. You.' He raised his eyebrows at Felix. 'It's a school day. So what're you doing at Peter Gimpel's funeral?'

'Personal friend.'

'And you?'

'Personal friend,' Smudge said. 'Quite close.'

Finally Dowell looked at Garvie. 'Personal friend too?'

'No.'

'Another field trip then.'

'No.'

'Sick leave maybe?'

Garvie shook his head.

'Why are you here then?'

'Related,' Garvie said. 'On his mother's side.'

Dowell's peaked cap seemed to vibrate slightly on the crown of his bald head. 'Polish, are you?'

'My great-great-grandfather was. Makes me six and a quarter per cent Polish. Though I'm sure you could have worked that out yourself.' He cleared his throat. *'Jesteś palantem i nie wiem dlaczego tracę na Ciebie czas,'* he said.

Before Dowell could respond, there was a noise from the graveside and they all turned. Pyotor's grandmother hung staggering on her husband's arm, shouting at the younger woman, who turned away as if to protect her baby and, face lifted in anguish, began to wail. Zbigniew Gimpel manoeuvred his wife to the other side of the grave and, tentatively, the priest continued his chanting, but Zuzana moved away and came up the path towards them.

'Here's another of my cousins,' Garvie said to Dowell. 'She's pretty much all Polish. She's come to collect me 'cause we have to get back now to put the kettle on. Good luck with the investigation by the way. I hear you've got everything sewn up.' And he went past the policeman and took Zuzana's hand and they walked away together down the path that ran around the outside of the church and through the gates.

When they had gone a little way Zuzana said, 'You can stop holding my hand now.'

He dropped her hand without looking at her, and they walked along the road round the corner into the pedestrian precinct, where they sat on a bench outside a betting shop.

'You can explain as well,' she said.

Garvie's hand still tingled where it had touched hers. A sort of embarrassment came over him. 'He's a policeman,' he said briefly.

'Yes, I noticed that.'

'But he's getting a bit too friendly. I had to get away. I'm not encouraging him,' he added. 'He must be the friendly type.'

When he glanced at her she was looking at him steadily.

'I'm glad to help,' she said.

'Yeah. Oh – thanks.'

She was looking at him as if trying to decide whether to say something else before leaving, or just leave, and he said quickly, 'In any case, I wanted to ask you a question. Like you said,' he added, 'I could do with your help.'

She looked amused again. 'What question?'

'What was all that shouting by the grave?'

Now she sighed. 'Pyotor's grandmother is angry with his mother. She says she abandoned him. It is true; she went to start another family. Pyotor still saw her but not too much. He thought about her a lot, though. I know this because his mother's new baby is ill. He needs an operation, and it can't be done here, only abroad, and it is very expensive. They have had a price given to them, and they can't raise the money. Pyotor was upset. He thought perhaps the baby might die. He kept asking Zbigniew and Bogdana how much money the operation would cost. For months he's been obsessed with it.' Her expression changed again and she looked at Garvie with brimming eyes. 'You see? How much sadness in his life.'

Garvie gave a brief nod.

She said, 'And how many people come to his funeral? You, Smudge, Felix. Is all.'

'I thought maybe Alex would be here as well.'

She gave him a little look of outrage. 'No. Alex doesn't come. You think Alex is Pyotor's friend? Are you? Is Smudge or Felix? Pyotor had no friends. He saw no one except at school and Juwenalia. No friends. No friends at all. This is sadness. You see now?'

Garvie sighed. 'Yeah, course.'

'He found all the world hard. Things happened and he did not understand why.'

She sat on the bench in her smart grey skirt and jacket with her hands folded in her lap. When she was serious she had a slight pout, he noticed. Her mouth softened and pursed, her chin puckered.

'How is Alex, by the way?' Garvie asked.

'Good,' she said shortly. 'But we are not talking about Alex.'

'No worries. Can't stop long anyway – there's something I've got to get to. Before I go, did you bring the answers to the questions I wrote down for you?'

She turned and looked at him a long time without answering. Finally she took several sheets of paper from her jacket pocket. 'I did not ask your questions,' she said.

'What?'

'No. They were too stupid. I asked my own questions; they were better. I record it for you. Here.'

Garvie sighed.

'Now you say "thank you", like a good boy.'

'Thanks,' Garvie said, 'sort of.' She gave him the papers, and he began to read.

'They are frightened people,' she said. 'I feel their fear. Zbigniew and Bogdana, they have been frightened a long time. They think people are against them, they think—'

He interrupted her. 'Orchestra practice was every afternoon?'

He showed her the paper, and she looked at it again.

'Yes.'

'Are you sure?'

'This is what Zbigniew said. Because of the concert so soon. Why?'

'Orchestra practice after school was once a week. His music teacher told me.'

'No.'

'Yes.'

Zuzana stared at him, her lips apart.

'I don't understand. Why would Zbigniew tell me every day?'

He looked at her a moment before answering. 'Because that's what the Gimp must have told him.'

They were both silent. Around them people went in and out of the shops, absorbed in their tasks.

'Pyotor lied to him?' she said at last. 'But he never lied, his grandparents told me.'

'Think of that then,' Garvie said. 'The boy who never told a lie lying about where he was four evenings a week. Looks like he didn't find the world that hard to understand after all.'

They were silent again, thinking.

'But if he wasn't at practice, where was he?'

'That's the question, isn't it?'

She was staring at him, her black eyes enormous, fixed on his, poised, as if she were about to say something, do something, unexpected, and he felt her strangeness again, her mysteriousness, felt it so strongly he almost got to his feet, but she put her hand on his, and he stayed where he was, as if she'd pinned him to the bench. Her eyes were shining.

'Something is wrong,' she said. 'We will find out what it is.'

'I am finding out,' he said. 'Thanks, though.'

She ignored him. 'I will go back and see Zbigniew and Bogdana again.'

'I can handle it from now on.'

'You? You don't know Zbigniew and Bogdana. You don't speak Polish. Besides,' she said, 'you are rude and difficult. I will see them.'

'Better if I see them. You can arrange it for me if you like.'

'We will see them together. Together we will find out what has happened.' She gave him a sly, interested look. 'I know there is something else you want to ask them.'

'How do you know?'

'It was one of the questions you wrote down. About his violin. At the end I asked.'

'And what did they say?'

'They don't know. They think in Pyotor's room.'

'It's not.'

'How do you know? The police have sealed his room.'

He said nothing.

'Then,' she said, 'it will be with his things from the lock-up. What are they called?'

'Personal effects. I don't think so.'

'Perhaps the man who killed him took it.'

'Pyotor wouldn't have let that happen. It was the most precious thing he had. He wouldn't have risked taking it there.'

She was looking at him again with that unreadable expression. He couldn't hold her eyes any longer, and dropped his gaze to where her hand still rested on his, and at the same time, matter of fact and decisive, she removed it, looked at her watch and stood up.

'We agree,' she said. 'I will arrange for us to see Zbigniew and Bogdana. Yes?'

'All right then. If you insist.'

'Any more questions?'

'Yeah.'

'What?'

'Ever heard of a guy called Blinkie?'

Her face creased in surprise. 'A man called what? Blinkers?' She laughed. 'No. Why?'

'Doesn't matter.'

'You think I know him?'

'Forget it.'

She looked at him and shook her head. 'You are strange. Now, it is two o'clock. There is the tea at the Polish Club.'

Garvie frowned and got to his feet. 'Actually, I've got to be somewhere.'

'It will be kind for you to come. There will be very few people.'

He shrugged.

She shook her head. 'It is curious. You are interested in Pyotor but you do not care about him.'

'Yeah, well. If I don't get going, there's other people going to think I don't care about them either.'

She frowned, and slowly began to smile. 'Ah, I understand now. You're late for another exam.'

He had no answer to that. He turned and went through the crowds, sauntering as if he had all the time in the world, then, when he got round the corner out of sight, began to run.

Zuzana watched him go thoughtfully. When he had disappeared, she took out her phone.

'Alex,' she said. 'Alex, *kochanie*. Call me, OK? I need to talk to you.'

21

The Marsh Academy gymnasium, like much of the rest of the school, was in the architectural style known as the Claustrophobic. Scaled down to save money, it was no more than two-thirds the size of a regular gym, too small for any sort of team sports. It stood in need of repair as well as modernization: one rack of wall bars was unsafe, there was a patch of damp blooming in a corner of the ceiling and the face of the wall clock, now showing five minutes to three, had long ago cracked, swung loose and fallen off. The glass roof was black with rain-crust, and even on a warm day the air was damp and itchy, as if the whole building had sweat rash.

Sitting at one of the temporary desks, Garvie Smith considered his surroundings as he held his hand in the air. After a few moments he clicked his fingers, and Miss Perkins, stationed in front of the metal roll-top door of the locker room, looked up. Her face changed when she saw who it was, and it continued to change as she walked down the aisle, eyes narrowing, her mouth disappearing, until she seemed only just in control of herself as she reached Garvie's desk.

'Yes?'

A small woman, neatly dressed, she gave an impression of bottled savagery; there was a hint of it in her voice below her compressed, minimal phrases. 'Queen Bitch' was the name given her by generations of students. Her teaching colleagues were not so kind.

'What is it, Smith?'

'Finished, miss.'

For some time she just looked at him. Then she turned to walk back to the front.

'All right to go then?' he asked.

She turned back and considered him again. She lowered her head and spoke quietly with her eyes fixed on his. 'You cannot go, no. You arrived half an hour late, and there is still half an hour to go. You will stay where you are. You will not speak again. You will come to see me in my office as soon as the examination has ended. You will spend the rest of the time available to you now thinking of reasons why I should not disqualify you from this exam, or bar you from all those you have yet to take.'

Her eyes were green, he noticed, with yellow flecks at the centre, unusual in a human. He watched her as she went back along the aisle towards the locker room, and settled himself in his seat, sighing, wondering how to get through the next thirty minutes.

He thought of a girl beautiful and smart, whose eyes were mesmerizing, whose expression was hard to read, whose help he did not need, whose soulmate was his oldest friend, but these were not comfortable thoughts.

He thought instead of his oldest friend whispering in the shadows with a funny-looking gangster he said he never saw, but that wasn't comfortable either.

Idly, he glanced at his exam paper, more or less complete, and open now at Question 5 (d) (i): *Red blood cells transport oxygen. Explain how oxygen is moved from the lungs to the tissues. (3 marks).* He did not think of this; he thought instead of the three lobes of his own right lung penetrated by a high-velocity bullet. *Describe what happens to your lung.* Your lung collapses, your respiratory tract fills with blood. *What happens to the blood in your lung?* It rises burning through the bronchi and trachea, emerging suddenly, in sneeze-like explosions shockingly brilliant in colour, from your gasping mouth. *What is the impact on your speech?* The ability to speak is lost, though perhaps there is no one to talk to. *What happens to your ability to play the violin?* The ability to play the violin is also lost, though you have already hidden it. *Why have you hidden it?*

He thought briefly about that.

Because they will look for it.

As the school bell went off, Garvie looked up. Through a crowd of students getting to their feet, he was dimly aware of the tiny inhuman form of Miss Perkins at the front of the hall. She made a gesture at her watch and exited the gym in the direction of her office.

140

Why will they look for it?

Another interesting question. One that deserved his immediate attention.

He got his stuff together and drifted out of the hall. Hesitating only a moment at the foot of the stairs, he turned towards the main doors, away from the corridor to Miss Perkins's office, and went out across the playground.

He was halfway to Jamal's when he got the call.

'Singh here.'

'What's up, dude?'

'I've just been at the grandparents' house. There was a break-in.'

Garvie hesitated. 'Oh yeah? Are you looking after all break-ins now, not just corner shops?'

Singh ignored him. 'They got into Pyotor's room.'

Garvie thought of Pyotor's room. Had Felix forgotten to close the window when they left? Had they put the ladder back in the wrong place?

'How did they get in?' he asked carefully.

'Through the window. One of those old sashes.'

'But how did they get up to the window?'

'It seems they borrowed a ladder from a re-roofing job nearby.'

'But –' and here he was genuinely puzzled – 'how could you tell the room had been broken into?'

Singh seemed puzzled in his turn. 'Well, because of all the damage.'

'Damage?'

'The whole place has been turned upside down.'

Garvie began to relax. 'Oh, OK. This break-in wasn't last week then.'

'Why would it have been last week? It was lunchtime today, while the funeral was going on. Neighbours heard the noise, but they were too late reporting it. The room's been ransacked. Half the furniture's trashed. They even ripped up some of the floorboards.'

'Damn,' Garvie said thoughtfully. 'I didn't think of the floorboards.'

'Garvie? Why is it I always get the impression you know more than you're telling me?'

Garvie ignored him. 'The old Gimps must be pissed off.'

'Mr and Mrs Gimpel are naturally very upset. They assume the break-in was racially motivated.'

'But you know better.'

'I have pointed out to them that only Pyotor's room was targeted. It's not vandalism, in my opinion; it's something else.'

'Course it is. It's a very bad sign is what it is.'

'What do you mean?'

'They're looking for it too.'

'Looking for what?'

'The violin.'

There was a pause. 'Why are you so sure the violin's important?'

'Think about it. *He* thought it was important. He never usually let it out of his sight.'

Singh considered this. 'So you think he hid it? Why?'

'So they wouldn't find it. Obviously.'

Singh made a noise of exasperation. He said, 'Well, if they were looking for it, I'm not sure they found it. It's not listed in our inventory of the room, which was done before the break-in. And if it was hidden, it must have been well hidden, or they wouldn't have taken the room apart like they did. The strange thing is that they were so . . . chaotic. Angry, or desperate, or just out of control, whoever they were.'

'Whoever they were it wasn't Magee.'

'No. Though he's a criminal, with convictions to prove it. And a racist, though it's harder to get the evidence. What we really need is a specific link between him and Pyotor.'

'Have you checked out the CCTV of the Juwenalia parade in Strawberry Hill last month?'

'Yes. I've spent time on that myself. We can identify Pyotor, but not Magee.'

There was a little silence. Garvie said, 'What about Pyotor's computer? The one he had on that little table in his room.'

Singh hesitated. 'How do you know there was a computer?' He paused again. 'How do you know there was a table?'

'Course there was a computer. And if there was a computer there was a table to put it on. I'm just being logical. What I want to know is, have you checked out his photo collection yet?'

'There's someone working on it now.'

'First thoughts?'

'Thousands of pictures of completely random subjects. The playground, the classroom, the street, his room. Literally thousands of them. What do they mean?'

'They mean he was a watcher.'

'But what was he watching?'

By now Garvie had reached Jamal's and he came to a standstill across the street.

'That's the question,' Garvie said. 'What did he see? But don't think about the detail yet. Think about the pattern. He logged all his pictures, right?'

'That's the extraordinary thing. They're all numbered and dated, in hundreds of separate lists.'

'Exactly. Check the numbers, find the pattern. Oh, by the way, did you find out if Jamal has a lock-up at East Field?'

'Yes, he does. And I'd like to know why you want to know.'

'I'll tell you as I soon as I know myself. You know what?'

'What?'

'You need to move faster. You'll have to release Magee soon, won't you?'

'His lawyers have been pushing hard. Successfully. Last week the magistrate put a limit on ongoing custody, two consecutive sessions of ninety-six hours, plus twenty-four for allowance of process. I don't know when that runs out exactly, but—'

'When did the magistrate set it up?'

'Last week. The day I talked to you. At noon.'

'Wednesday the twentieth. OK. Then he'll walk at twelve noon this Friday.'

'Well. It's something like that.'

'It's exactly that. You've got four days. Good luck.'

Singh made a noise of annoyance. 'You really don't care about other people, do you?' He was saying something else too, but Garvie cut him off.

He stood there for a moment, thinking, then crossed the road and looked in through Jamal's window. Old man Jamal came stumping on his crutches into the shop through the back door, carrying a cardboard box, which he slid with difficulty onto the counter before stumping out again. Ignoring his father, Khalid was talking on his phone, his intense face moving in jerks, and Sajid was sitting at the end of the counter playing on his laptop. Dressed as usual in his Marsh Academy basketball kit, white short-sleeved shirt and navy shorts, he was lost entirely in whatever game he was playing, eyes wide, face soft, like a little kid. A little kid at peace, a quiet little kid without a worry in the world. Garvie knew different though. He'd had a word with Dani and he knew there'd been a time, quite recently, when Sajid had been getting into plenty of trouble. Fighting, truanting. He'd been accused of stealing from the school office. But lately, suddenly, he'd calmed down, started to take his basketball more seriously; his grades had picked up. Some said Khalid had taken him in hand, though what that meant was anybody's guess. It wasn't just that Sajid was quieter; he was more nervous too. He wasn't out on the streets like he used to be. Khalid went with him to school in the mornings and picked him up from basketball practice, and shouted at him in the evenings (and, for some reason, Garvie reflected, cried to himself upstairs at night). Garvie stood there a moment longer, watching and thinking. Checking the time, he saw that he was already late home, but he pushed open the battered door and went in, and Khalid looked up, scowling, to greet him.

22

'Yeah?'

'Hey, man.'

'You want to buy something today?'

'Think I'll just browse a while first. You've got such lovely stuff.'

Scowling more deeply still, Khalid moved down the aisle towards the door at the far end, talking into his phone. 'Nah, man, not a customer. Just another kid likes to hang out in my shop. Yeah. Anyway, I told you before, three days tops. That's all you've paid for. Three days and you got to shift it, man.'

The door slammed behind him and it was quiet again. The shop was untidier than ever. On the floor was a stack of newspapers still in their plastic wrapping, the headline showing: *Gimpel Murder Suspect to Be Released*. Another newspaper ran with *Polish Protest March to Go Ahead*. Garvie looked over at Sajid, still playing on his laptop.

'How's it going, Sajid?'

Sajid glanced up, shrugged, went back to his game. The neckband of his shirt was loose around his neck.

'Going well then?' Garvie said.

Sajid still said nothing, his eyes fixed on the screen,

his fingers flickering. He sucked in his bottom lip and frowned.

Garvie looked at him thoughtfully for a while. 'He looks all right to me,' he said out loud. 'Bit silent. Of course, he could have lost his voice. On the other hand, the bruises on his neck are clearing up nicely.'

Sajid turned to him in alarm. He pulled at the neckband of his shirt. He opened his mouth and shut it again, and his eyes brimmed suddenly.

'Classic signs of anxiety,' Garvie went on. 'Wants to say something but frightened to.'

'I'm not supposed to talk to you,' Sajid said in a whisper.

He said no more. A door banged and Khalid came jogging down the aisle, pointing his phone at Garvie.

'That's it, yeah. Told you before, right. Coming in here jamming up my shop, not buying nothing, talking. Out!'

'I was just about to buy a pack of Rizlas,' Garvie said. 'Maybe two packs. That's five whole pence to you, man.'

'Out before I call the coppers. And you!' Sajid flinched when his brother shouted at him. 'You got ten minutes, then I want you in the back room doing your school shit. I don't know why this is going on. Don't know what I got to do, right? Got to ban everyone from my shop, is that it?'

Putting his hands above his head in surrender,

Garvie went out onto the street, and as he let the battered door swing shut behind him he heard Khalid already talking on his phone again.

The back room at Jamal's was part living room, part store room, cardboard boxes stacked along the walls and under the table and next to the chairs. It was dim and stale as if the curtains had been drawn shut for many years, and there was a crusty old smell of trodden-in curry and cat, and Garvie sat on a broken-down easy chair in the corner, squinting in the gloom, trying not to breathe the furred air and wondering if he had time for a cigarette.

Sajid came in and switched on the light and stood there with his mouth open.

'Come in, Sajid. Shut the door. Close your mouth. Let's have a chat.'

'How did you get in here?'

'Back door. Your old dad was having trouble humping all those boxes in and I gave him a hand so he could have a lie-down. That leg of his is still giving him gyp.' Garvie put out his hand. 'Here, have one of these. The Gimp's favourites.'

Sajid gave a lopsided smile when he saw the yellow-and-green wrapper. 'He hated them.'

'Course he did. They're horrible. I bet he was the only punter in Five Mile went for them.'

'Apart from Khalid, and he only carries them round to try to make people think they're nice.'

'There you go. But Pyotor bought a load every

time he came here, didn't he, to keep Khalid off his back?'

Sajid said nothing.

'Course,' Garvie said, 'he didn't come for the sweets, did he? Why don't you sit down and we'll have a chat? I'm sure Khalid won't mind. I won't even ask you anything about those bruises round your neck, so no one will ever need know about them.'

At last Sajid shut the door to the shop behind him, sidled in and sat down gingerly on the edge of a chair at the table, all the time watching Garvie with big, unblinking eyes.

'Hey, no need to go all worried on me. This is just a little chat. Don't you trust me? What do you think, I'm going to interrogate you like some big old detective inspector?'

Location: back room, Jamal's corner shop, Bulwarks Lane; dark, fusty, proximity of unseen cats.
Interviewer: DI Garvie Smith: tall, casual.
Interviewee: Sajid Baloch: small, big-eyed, nervy.

DI GARVIE SMITH: Khalid didn't like the Gimp hanging round here so much, did he?

SAJID BALOCH [*shakes head*]

DI GARVIE SMITH: He was here a lot, wasn't he? Playing *World of Warcraft* with you.

[*Silence*]

DI GARVIE SMITH: Come on, Sajid. I know Pyotor was a WoW freak; I've seen the boxes on his bedroom shelf. And I've seen you fooling around with it on your own in that sad, half-arsed way, like you don't know what to do any more. You played arenas together, didn't you? Ring of Valor and stuff.

SAJID BALOCH [*nods*]

DI GARVIE SMITH: Nearly every evening after school?

SAJID BALOCH [*nods*]: Not Tuesdays.

DI GARVIE SMITH: No. He had orchestra practice Tuesdays. Still, that's a lot of time you were hanging out together. What happened in the end? Khalid banned him, right?

SAJID BALOCH [*nods*]

DI GARVIE SMITH: We'll come back to that. Tell me about WoW.

SAJID BALOCH: It started in January. I was out in the shop playing a battleground game with this bunch of losers and every time we grabbed their flag we got killed. And he must have been watching me, 'cause suddenly he started telling me what to do. He was like, 'Buff him now,' and stuff, and next thing is, we'd got the flag and it was all done. So then we got talking about *WoW*.

DI GARVIE SMITH: The Gimp *talked*?

SAJID BALOCH: That's the thing. When he talked about playing he was, like, someone different. He said he'd been playing for a while, which I could tell, obviously. But when he showed me his account – man, he was 'Paladinski'!

151

DI GARVIE SMITH: 'Paladinski'?

SAJID BALOCH: Like, famous. In the Icecrown Citadel Raid. Got all the armour, tons of epic stuff.

DI GARVIE SMITH: OK. So he wasn't bad at it?

SAJID BALOCH [*smiling for the first time*]: He was the best! I never saw anything like it. And it was so weird, that he would play with me. I mean, I don't hang out with anyone from your year, and I don't know any kid his age would spend time with me. But Pete was . . . there was something about him. When he played, he wasn't weird any more. It was like, this was his world. And he was just really good to be with. He made a toon and we teamed up and started playing the arenas, two versus two. And no one could beat us. I mean, we didn't lose, in six months, not ever. We were the team, man.

DI GARVIE SMITH: I get it. So you spent all your time playing *WoW*.

SAJID BALOCH: Mostly.

DI GARVIE SMITH: Where? Not out in the shop.

SAJID BALOCH: No, in here, where no one would bother us. Khalid's on my case a lot of the time, so . . . You won't tell him I said that, will you?

DI GARVIE SMITH: I won't tell him.

SAJID BALOCH: So he's always going on about, finish your school work first, you can't play till you done your maths or whatever. So some of the time Pete helped me with that, you know, to get it done. The rest of the time, yeah, we were

152

just taking on those losers, beating everyone we played.

DI GARVIE SMITH: I get it. Tell me this, Sajid, though. Why didn't Khalid like him? I mean, the Gimp helped you with your school work, right? Your grades were going up. What's was Khalid's problem?

SAJID BALOCH [*long pause*]: Don't know.

DI GARVIE SMITH: I think you do. What did Khalid say when he banned Pyotor? I heard something about that.

SAJID BALOCH: Yeah, but that was all a mistake.

DI GARVIE SMITH: Remind me.

SAJID BALOCH: He said Pete'd been nicking stuff. [*Pausing*] I didn't think anyone knew about that.

DI GARVIE SMITH: I didn't. But I do now. What stuff?

SAJID BALOCH: His phone. It was a mistake though. Pete was always tidying stuff, putting it in some sort of weird order, like everything had to be in this pattern he had in his head. He didn't mean nothing, taking his phone. He just used to do it without thinking. Anyway, the phone turned up later.

DI GARVIE SMITH: Was it just his phone Khalid accused him of stealing?

SAJID BALOCH [*long pause*]: Yeah.

DI GARVIE SMITH: Sure?

SAJID BALOCH: Yeah, I think.

DI GARVIE SMITH: You sure? Are you sure Khalid

didn't accuse him of stealing something else too?

SAJID BALOCH: I don't know. I heard Khalid having a go at him a couple of times. Pete didn't like it. It made him weirder. His eyes used to get sort of puffy.

DI GARVIE SMITH: What did Khalid have a go at him about?

SAJID BALOCH [*shrugs*]: I don't know.

DI GARVIE SMITH: Yeah, you do.

SAJID BALOCH: I don't!

DI GARVIE SMITH: Was it about the phone, or something else? Come on, Sajid, trust me. What were they arguing about? What did you hear them say?

SAJID BALOCH: I don't know!

DI GARVIE SMITH: Hey, don't get all upset on me, Sajid.

SAJID BALOCH: I don't like these questions any more. Something about going to the police. I don't remember.

DI GARVIE SMITH: Who was going to go to the police?

SAJID BALOCH: I can't remember.

DI GARVIE SMITH: Was it Khalid? Did Khalid threaten to go to the police? I can always ask him if you won't tell me. Was it Khalid, Sajid?

SAJID BALOCH: No!

DI GARVIE SMITH: So it was the Gimp. The Gimp threatened to go to the police. I wonder why.

About something Khalid had done? Something Khalid was into?

SAJID BALOCH: I don't know! I'm telling you, I don't know!

DI GARVIE SMITH: OK, Sajid. I believe you.

SAJID BALOCH [*snuffling, eventually quiet*]: He's going to be proper mad with me now.

DI GARVIE SMITH: No, he isn't. Definitely not. Don't worry, I'm not going to tell him. Come on now. Here, dry your face. I've only got one question left.

SAJID BALOCH: I don't like your questions.

DI GARVIE SMITH: You won't mind this one. Did Pyotor bring his violin here?

SAJID BALOCH: He didn't go anywhere without that fiddle. It's funny, you know, 'cause—

There was a slam of a door somewhere from the back of the building and rapid footsteps and a power-drill hammering of claws on floor, then the door to the back room banged open, and Khalid lurched in behind an enormous mastiff panting and straining forward on a thick metal chain.

Sajid fled behind the sofa.

Khalid said nothing, and Garvie said nothing, just quietly and slowly got to his feet and stood there very still, and for a moment the only sound in the small room was dog-pant *thrapping* madly like the noise of a overloaded generator.

Garvie went white.

'Told you, yeah,' Khalid said in a hiss. 'This is Genghis, right.'

Garvie nodded slowly. 'Hi, Genghis,' he said. His voice was quiet and careful.

Khalid payed out the chain slightly, and Genghis strained a couple of feet closer to Garvie. As the dog reared up, he could smell its breath, foul as boiled body parts, coming out of its mouth in waves, and feel spittle flecking his cheeks when Genghis gnashed his teeth. Garvie did not look at Khalid. He made himself look at those teeth, concentrating on standing upright and making sure his voice worked.

'Well,' he said lightly, 'I'd love to stay and pet your new puppy. But I really have to go now.'

'Thing about you, yeah,' Khalid said, 'you think you know what you're doing. Thing is, you got no idea. So I'm telling you. Drop all this, yeah? 'Cause you getting into stuff you don't understand.'

'Well, I'll certainly bear all that in mind,' Garvie said, as he went carefully around the edge of the room to the door, keeping about a foot between him and the straining mastiff who turned with him, jaws snapping in regular wet chomps.

Khalid said, 'You should be thinking about yourself, not bothering other people. You're a waster, man. Everybody knows it. You got a lot of sorting out of your head to do.'

Finally Garvie reached the door. There was just one more thing. He turned back and pointed a finger at Sajid. 'Next time I ask you questions I want you to give me answers.' Before Khalid could react he went through the door and closed it behind him. For a moment he couldn't move. Then he was staggering outside in a rush and vomiting at the side of the alley. He made it to the bench on the street and sat there gulping air, wiping his face with his sleeve. A white-haired old lady stopped and looked at him, and he made reassuring gestures with his hands.

'I'm OK. I just really don't like dogs.'

She nodded sympathetically. 'I have a Peke,' she said. 'The little shit.'

At last his legs felt normal again, and he got up and began to walk home.

He didn't mean nothing, taking his phone? That was interesting. But was it just Khalid's phone he took?

He walked on a bit further, thinking.

Something about going to the police? Why? What had the Gimp seen Khalid do?

He crossed the road and went on.

Waster? Sorting out your head? He stopped with a look of disgust on his face, and at that moment a text came through on his phone from his mother. It said *Where r u?!*

He looked at his watch. He was a couple of hours late home, give or take. Sighing, he pointed himself towards Eastwick Gardens, and after a few reluctant paces he got another message, from Alex.

Call me.

He called him. 'Alex, mate.'

'We need to meet.'

'I'm a bit pushed now. I just got a—'

'Got to see you, Garv, and it's got to be now.'

Garvie frowned. 'OK then.'

'Usual place in twenty.'

'All right, all right. At least tell me what it's about.'

There was a long pause. 'Think you know,' Alex said.

'Course I don't know. Tell me. What you want to talk about?'

'Zuza.'

Garvie hesitated. 'What about her?'

Alex said, 'You remember the question you asked me? Can I trust her?'

'Yeah, but—'

'That's what it's about then.'

'Yeah, but wouldn't it be . . .'

Alex had rung off. Garvie reluctantly turned round and went back along Bulwarks Lane, past Jamal's, towards Old Ditch Road and the kiddies' playground.

23

The kiddies' playground was almost unrecognizable in daylight, small and cluttered and unexpectedly childish. There was even a child on the swings, looking so out of place Garvie had the urge to ask him what the hell he thought he was doing there. He went instead across the grass, carefully avoiding a dog-walker, to the other side of the playground and sat on the little roundabout.

He thought about Alex. He regretted now asking him whether he trusted Zuzana. Trust was a pretty basic formula to most people, to Garvie in particular, but to Alex it was a whole complicated drama of emotion. Alex was paranoid: the slightest wrinkle in a relationship flipped him sideways. Garvie asked himself cautiously what might have made Alex flip now. Something Zuzana had done? Something Alex had imagined she'd done? And why would Alex want to talk to him about it? Reluctantly Garvie gave this some thought. He'd hardly seen Zuzana himself, very few times anyway, and never secretly, and it was only because Alex hadn't been around that Garvie hadn't mentioned any of it to him. This line of thinking only produced a sharp but confused feeling, very physical, located somewhere between Garvie's chest and his throat. He couldn't help remembering what Zuzana had said to him the last time they had met – 'Together we will find out what happened' – and the words – particularly the word *together* – rang awkwardly in his mind.

He started when he heard his name called out and, looking up to find Zuzana standing in front of him, stared at her dumbfounded. She was wearing grey leggings and a T-shirt, very tight. He thought for a second she was a weird hallucination.

Then she laughed. 'I could not believe it when they told me this is where I will find you.'

He hastily looked all round the field, and at his watch, and round the field again, and when he'd done all this Zuzana was still standing in front of him, and Alex, nowhere to be seen, was still just about to arrive and find them there together. His brain seemed to slow down almost to a standstill. 'What are you doing here?' he said at last. He did not say 'Where's Alex?' He did not trust himself to mention Alex.

She regarded him with that mocking, amused look again, and he felt himself flush. 'Do you want me to give you a push?' she said.

In distraction he looked beyond her to the edges of the field. 'Actually, I haven't got much time.'

'I was not being serious.'

'I knew that,' he said after a moment. He got off the roundabout.

'I have something to tell you about Pyotor.'

'OK, but it has to be quick. I still don't understand why you're here,' he added.

'I met Mrs Gimpel and she told me they have had a break-in.'

'I knew that already.'

Zuzana raised an eyebrow. 'She is very upset.'

'Course. Look, if that's all, I'll catch you in a bit, 'cause I'm—'

'I have arranged for you to meet them.'

That got his attention. 'All right. When?'

'In a few days. They will tell me. Also I know now they have the personal effects. The police have returned them. No violin. I asked. But you will want to see the other things. And —' she looked at him – 'I think you will want to see where Pyotor lived.'

His brain began to work again. 'Yeah, that's right. In fact I want to see where he did his homework.'

'His homework?'

'He didn't do it in his room. No schoolbooks there.'

She looked at him curiously. 'How do you know that?'

He ignored her.

She said, 'There is something like a desk against the wall in the living room. Big. Old-fashioned. I think they must have brought it over from Poland. It has a sort of cover. Perhaps that is where he did it.'

He nodded. 'That's where we need to look.'

'That is going to tell us where he was four evenings a week?'

He shook his head. 'No, I already know that.' He said it before thinking and looked up startled when she grabbed his arm.

'You know where he was?'

'Yeah.' He hesitated but only for a second. 'Jamal's.'

'*Jamal's!*' Her grip tightened on his arm.

'Yeah. You think that's weird?'

'No, of course not.' She removed her hand. 'But it is right where I live. What was he doing there?'

He explained.

'It was all about the game, see,' he said. '*WoW – World of Warcraft.*'

There was a long pause while she looked at him. Her eyes went soft and she began to nibble her bottom lip. He could almost see her thinking, though her thoughts were hidden, and he felt, once again, how unreadable she was.

'Was it really?' she said at last.

'Yeah. It was, actually.'

'Or was it about Sajid?'

He frowned. 'What do you mean?'

'It sounds to me as if Pyotor had made a friend.'

It was obvious, of course. He remembered Mr Merryweather telling them how well Pyotor was playing his solo – as if he was feeling the music for the first time; and Sajid saying Pyotor helped him with his homework; and Pyotor lying to his grandparents about where he went, knowing they didn't like Asians.

Zuzana was looking at him. 'This is what I think. It was all about friendship. I know what sort of boy Pyotor was. He never had a friend before. No one his own age took him seriously. No one his own age would have played that game with him. But Sajid did. Sajid liked being with him.' Her eyes were locked on Garvie's. 'For Pyotor it was all new. Think of it, Garvie. His feelings. It was a big change for him. Very big. It was like –' and now her eyes flicked away from him, as if suddenly embarrassed – 'it was like falling in love,' she said.

They looked at different parts of the park. Her phone went and she looked at it and sighed.

'Alex. Wants to know where I am. Says he's about to meet someone.'

Garvie skipped backwards away from her and glanced all around him.

'What are you doing?'

'Nothing. Bit of cramp.' He scanned the field anxiously.

'Alex has been acting strange,' she said. 'Jealous. He thinks I go off, meet boys.'

'Yeah, well,' he said. 'That's news to me, I didn't know that, he's never said anything about it. He wouldn't, it's got nothing to do with me. Anyway, good talking, but I've really got to get on, so catch you later.'

'What are you doing now?' she said. Garvie was behind the climbing frame, looking around in all directions.

'Not doing anything. Nothing at all. Don't you have to be somewhere?'

She looked at him. 'And you think Pyotor was weird,' she said. Turning briskly, she walked away across the grass to the gate on Old Ditch Road at the same time Alex as came into the field through the gate on Somerfield and made his way rapidly towards Garvie.

24

A lex said, 'Who was that with you just now?'
'With me? No one, man. Just some kid.'
'Some kid?'

'Some kid's mother. Told me to get off the roundabout.' Garvie held his pose of absurd nonchalance
next to the climbing frame, and Alex stared at him
fiercely, but before he could speak, Garvie said, 'You
got a problem, man.'

'I know it.'

'Yeah. But it's not what you think it is.'

Alex hesitated. 'What?'

'You want to talk to me about trust?'

'That's right, Garv.'

'Well, I want to talk to you about trust.'

'What?' Alex stood there confused.

Garvie said, 'You've not been straight with me,
man. You told me you weren't seeing Blinkie.'

Alex set his jaw. 'I'm not seeing Blinkie.'

He stared at Garvie through narrowed eyes;
breathed heavily through his nose; began to bite his
lower lip.

Garvie sighed. 'Alex, mate, don't ever get into the
habit of being interrogated.'

'What do you mean?'

'You've got a tell like a burglar alarm. Whenever you lie you stare at me for exactly three seconds and start chewing on your bottom lip.'

'Bullshit!' Alex stared at Garvie; began to bite his lip; put his hand up to his mouth in confusion.

'You've been doing it since you were nine years old, man. You're not going to stop now. I know you're seeing Blinkie.'

Alex's eyes popped. He shook his head wildly. 'You don't understand.'

'What I want to know is, are you dealing again?'

'I told you, I don't deal no more. Blinkie doesn't deal either. For all I know.' This time he didn't bite his lip.

'So why's Blinkie coming round to see you?'

There was a long pause.

'He's not,' Alex said. Again, no lip biting.

'What's he doing then?'

Alex heaved a tremendous sigh. 'He's coming round to see Zuza!'

Crushing his fists into his eyes, he paced up and down on the playground tarmac and Garvie stared at him in amazement. He laughed out loud.

'Blinkie? Now I know you're crazy. Blinkie fell out of the ugly tree, man. He's got idiot eyes, dude. He's a mouth-breather. Blinkie! Come on, man, give her some credit.'

Alex just looked grim. 'He's been coming on to her. I know he likes her.'

'Who knows what he likes? He's so high on all

that coke, his brain's all cranked out. The point is, Zuza can't possibly like him.'

Alex said nothing. He couldn't, his lips were too tightly shut. He gave a big bitter shrug.

'Alex! Think about it! Where's the attraction? Some silly dealer in a nylon tracksuit going around with a big dog on a leash like some cartoon warlord, doing stupid shit like cocaine.'

'Ex-dealer,' Alex said.

'All right. Ex-dealer. In a nylon tracksuit, going around, etc., etc. Is it the car she likes?'

'It's not about the car.'

'Man, he's hopeless. You know all this. You know it better than me. Don't do it, man. You're cocking your leg on the wrong tree.'

Alex stared at him a long time.

'It was you, Garv,' he said quietly.

Garvie started. 'Me? I didn't do anything. I've hardly seen her,' he added.

'You started me thinking.'

'What, about trust? You've got the wrong end of the sandwich, man. I just meant—'

'You asked me how well I know her. Got me thinking. I know nothing about her. It's like we've just met.'

'You have just met, you idiot. You'll get to know her. Listen, I've got to be honest: you're out of line. It was the same with Chloe. Yeah, yeah, I know you don't want to hear that. But seriously, when it comes to commitment you're like Mr Hundred-and-Fifty-

Per-Cent. You feel too much. Take it down a notch, man. It's sweet, isn't it? You told me yourself. Don't let jealousy wreck it.'

Alex turned away with a sigh. 'I don't know why I'm asking you, anyway, Garv. It's not like you know anything about girls. It's just . . .' Groaning, he bowed his head and put his face in his hands.

Garvie put a hand on his shoulder.

'Hey. Listen to me, pal. You can trust her, I'm sure of it. Seriously. You've got nothing to worry about. Except your own sanity, of course.'

Alex scowled; nodded.

Garvie's phone rang and he looked at it; winced; cut it. A second later a text came through from his mother. *Been waiting 2 hours. Get here now.*

'Listen. Got to amble. Been good talking. Sort of.'

He and Alex parted at the gate to Old Ditch Road. For a moment he watched his friend going off towards Bulwarks Lane and Zuza's flat. He thought about Alex talking to Blinkie outside her door. He thought about Zuza too. Then, deliberately, he stopped thinking about her. He turned and went the other way, towards another tricky conversation.

25

Location: kitchen, Flat 12 Eastwick Gardens; airless; steamed-up, claustrophobic, conducive to guilt.

Interviewer: Garvie's mother: solid, humourless, determined.

Interviewee: Garvie Smith: pale, evasive.

GARVIE'S MOTHER: She was here. Waiting for you nearly an hour. Now she's gone.

GARVIE SMITH: Who?

GARVIE'S MOTHER: Miss Perkins.

GARVIE SMITH: She was here? What, in our flat?

GARVIE'S MOTHER: That a surprise to you?

GARVIE SMITH: It would be a surprise to anyone. The general assumption is she goes straight back to her coffin the moment school ends.

GARVIE'S MOTHER: Don't fool with me, Garvie. She told you to go and see her in her office after your exam was over. What happened?

GARVIE SMITH [*striking forehead*]: She meant after the exam *this* afternoon?

GARVIE'S MOTHER: Garvie, I don't want to do things slowly. You understand? She left this.

GARVIE SMITH: What is it?

GARVIE'S MOTHER: Take a look.

GARVIE SMITH: Something to do with sixth form? Looks a bit technical. Probably best if I read it in detail later.

GARVIE'S MOTHER: I'll summarize for you. You need to pass five exams to stay on at school.

GARVIE SMITH: OK, I'll bear it in mind.

GARVIE'S MOTHER: Let me be clear. Since your chat with Uncle Len you told me you want to stay on. You don't want to get a job. You don't like the idea of going on the dole.

GARVIE SMITH: Yeah, that's right. I'll stick with that.

GARVIE'S MOTHER: You have eleven exams, right?

GARVIE SMITH: Well, I never actually counted them up but—

GARVIE'S MOTHER: You missed the Maths because of all that trouble with Chloe Dow. Since then you've taken five. You were ten minutes late for written French and wanted to leave early. You were late for spoken French, late for History, and late for Geography, and Geography you just left when you felt like it. Biology today, it seems you arrived half an hour late and wanted to leave half an hour early. What have you got to say?

GARVIE SMITH: I think you're being a bit unfair, to be honest.

GARVIE'S MOTHER: Why?

GARVIE SMITH: I didn't leave Geography when I felt like it. I felt like leaving it a lot earlier, but I stayed on out of a sense of—

GARVIE'S MOTHER: Don't play games with me, Garvie. I'm not going to argue with you. I'm telling you: you want to stay on, you have to pass five exams. You don't pass them, you don't get to stay on. Do you understand? You don't stay on at school, it's a whole different set-up. You're out looking for an apprenticeship. You're paying rent to me.

GARVIE SMITH: I get it. You're not listening to me.

GARVIE'S MOTHER: I'm not listening to you because I don't trust what you tell me! All right, let me calm down. Now, give me something worth listening to. How many exams do you think you've passed so far?

GARVIE SMITH: Well. Not Maths, obviously. I mean, I missed that one. Written French I could have passed. Maybe. You know, if the examiner gets where I was coming from. Spoken French too. Not sure about History or Geog., to be honest. Really not sure. Biology, I've got to say, I think it's very unlikely.

GARVIE'S MOTHER: OK then. Let's be cheerful and say you've passed two so far. You've got another five and you've got to pass three of them. One of them is that Special Maths. Three out of five. Sound easy to you?

GARVIE SMITH: I think so.

GARVIE'S MOTHER: That's because you don't know how to think. My advice to you? Do some revision.

GARVIE SMITH: All right then.

GARVIE'S MOTHER: What's your next exam?

GARVIE SMITH: Eng. Lit. I can definitely pass that.

GARVIE'S MOTHER: Sounds to me exactly the sort of subject you'd struggle with. Have you read any of the books?

GARVIE SMITH: You can get a lot out of a title. You know what?

GARVIE'S MOTHER: What?

GARVIE SMITH: I really wish you trusted me, just a little, just now and then.

GARVIE'S MOTHER: Trust, Garvie, is just a word to you, just something you say. What I hope is, one day you don't get a big shock when someone you trust lets you down. OK, tell me again, when's Eng. Lit.?

GARVIE SMITH: Wednesday.

GARVIE'S MOTHER: And you know where it is, and what it's about, and what you need to take with you?

GARVIE SMITH: School hall. Eng. Lit., unit one. 1.30 p.m. You will need no other materials. Time allowed one hour. Use black ink or—

GARVIE'S MOTHER: Enough. You remember all that, OK. But what you need to remember is, if you don't turn up it's just harder for you to do what you yourself want. Think of that, Garvie.

26

Wednesday lunchtime found Garvie in Cornwallis Way at the edge of the business district. Cornwallis Way was a short, wide, semi-developed road between the new tower blocks of insurance companies and banks on one side, and old brick factories and yards on the other. It began confidently enough with a shiny new building in glass and chrome on the corner, but quickly lost its mojo in a half-hearted row of mid-sized concrete offices, petered out pathetically into vacant lots of cracked asphalt and weeds and ended abruptly, with a sort of two-fingered defiance, in the graffiti-covered wall of a long-vanished brick warehouse. The last building on the left, number 30, was the least attractive in the street, a scaled-up piece of post-industrial packaging, in ribbed concrete a shade of Old Magnolia, squatting like a space invader on splayed rough-cast legs above an underground car park. A row of steel anti-terrorist bollards separated it from the pavement, and all the windows were smoked glass. Above the entrance was a fluorescent blue sign: CITY SQUAD POLICE CENTRE.

Garvie had ridden down with Abdul, who'd dropped him at the corner and taken off again in nervous haste. Abdul had a healthy fear of City Squad, known for their strictness in dealing with taxi drivers' registration papers. Garvie went under the blue sign into the lobby and told the receptionist he had an appointment to see Detective Inspector Singh.

She told him to take a seat.

He sat in the far corner between a woman and a man with a tattoo of an eerily similar-looking woman on his forearm. At the other side of the room a dealer called Bennie was sitting holding a soiled paper towel to his face. Garvie avoided eye contact; Alex had told him once Bennie didn't like being looked at. Positioning himself in his usual horizontal slouch, hands in pockets, Garvie concentrated on the ceiling and thought about Alex. He could under-stand him thinking Blinkie was coming on to Zuzana: the man was dangerously unplugged from reality. But he couldn't possibly think that Zuzana might go for Blinkie. Alex might be the most jealous human being alive, but he wasn't stupid. On the other hand, Garvie didn't credit him with the cunning to use the story as a cover. It was puzzling and that was odd in itself, because generally Alex was the least puzzling person he knew. On the whole, though, he was worried. He knew that if Alex got picked up dealing again the police wouldn't cut him any slack.

Every few minutes a constable came in to collect someone, escorting them back through the security door into the police area. The door made a swishing sound as it opened and a heavy *whumph* as it closed behind them. A bugger to get through, according to Felix. Garvie put his hands in his pockets and felt for the card and Blu-Tack he'd brought with him. Then he went up and spoke to the receptionist again.

'We're just locating him now,' she said.

'Thought he had an office.'

'Inspector Singh's based in our squad room. But he's in a meeting. Won't be long.'

Garvie didn't have long. Eng. Lit. was due to start in an hour, and it would take him half an hour to get back to school. Back in his seat, he thought about the conversation with his mother. She was right; not that he would have admitted it to her. Passing five exams was the smart thing to do. Making the effort to pass six was obviously a gross waste of time but only passing four would be a blunder. Besides – and this was an uncomfortable fact he didn't often confront – he didn't actually want to upset her. He didn't like seeing her upset. It was irrational, a bit like his thing with dogs, but he couldn't help himself.

Bennie was collected and escorted away. The woman and man next to Garvie had long since left. Hands in pockets, he walked up and down until he came to rest by the security door. There was only one other person left in the lobby, and after a while a constable came in and escorted him into the police area too – Garvie helpfully holding open the door for them – and then Garvie was alone. He moved away from the door and went back to the receptionist.

'Can you page him or something? It's important. And I do have an appointment.'

'I'll try again.'

'Tell him it's about the violin.'

'Violin?'

'It's a musical instrument.'

She stared at him.

'Goes under the chin. If you saw it you'd recognize it.'

She turned away with a sour expression and spoke on her headset, and when she looked round again the boy must have gone back to his seat in the corner because he was nowhere to be seen.

In his office Detective Inspective Dowell stood in front of the operations board in an attitude of betrayed disbelief. He had been talking about the media. There had been a report in the press about the Polish march the previous night descending into violence, the result – it was claimed – of inadequate policing; also a report about the persistent failure of the police to bring timely charges against guilty criminals; also a general report about police inefficiency.

He held up a newspaper. 'How about this? *School blames police for disorder.*' Marsh Academy had made complaints about the disruptive effects of the police presence – at the same time as parents were demanding greater security for their children.

'Open season on law enforcement,' he said. '*And why not?* What have we given them?'

Apart from his breathing there was silence in the office. Uneasily they began their review of the case. There was more work to be done in every area. At the lock-up, where the murder weapon still hadn't been located. In the black market, where guns were traded. Among the Polish community, who insisted that Magee was an active racist responsible for previous hate crimes. Their first priority, however, was the work to be done at the school. It was the result of the investigation's one positive development. They had belatedly discovered that there was no record of any school personnel giving Pyotor extra maths tuition on Tuesday afternoons.

Collier summarized. 'We've double-checked. No teacher at Marsh knows anything about it. But a member of the cleaning staff saw Pyotor leaving school premises late one Tuesday. We're going through the school CCTV now. So far no sign of him anywhere inside the buildings, but twice he shows up exiting through the bottom gate. He was at school at that time, and we don't know why. What was he doing? Was he seeing someone? It's totally out of character for him. This could lead somewhere.'

Dowell said, 'Supplementary budget's been approved by Higher. We're getting new men from Central to cover off the extra tasks. It's important we push this. I want good news fast. As of now, it's our best lead.'

The chief himself had given an update to the press,

and a request had gone out to the public asking for anyone with relevant information to come forward immediately.

'So give me progress,' Dowell said.

Singh asked, 'Do you need any assistance? Is there anything more I can do?'

'No,' Collier said.

Dowell moved on to review the investigation going on in Heeley, where interviews with Magee's former associates and multiple gun dealers had so far yielded no results.

Singh interrupted. 'By the way, I've been wondering why Magee left Heeley to come here.'

Dowell said, 'I think that's clear. The heat got too much for him down there. He'd pulled too many jobs, was too well-known. Obvious thing for him was to leave.'

'Yes. But why come here?'

Doug Williams said, 'The city profile's perfect for a type like Magee. Good opportunities.'

'Correct,' Dowell said. 'Standard career move for a guy like that.'

Before Singh could respond there was a knock on the door and a young constable looked in. 'Message for Inspector Singh,' she said. 'Your twelve thirty appointment's waiting.'

Singh frowned. 'I don't have an appointment.'

'Been waiting in the lobby, sir. Says it's important. About the violin,' she added.

Singh hesitated, then got to his feet, the

embarrassed object of attention, and went across the office to the door.

'*Violin!*' Dowell muttered as he passed.

He went at speed down the stairs and along the corridor past Communications, Records and the café area – and abruptly stopped. Retracing his steps, frowning, he walked back to the café and went with an incredulous expression between the tables to a chair in the corner, where Garvie Smith was sitting with his feet on a table sipping a coffee.

'You've been ages,' Garvie said.

'What are you doing here?'

'Just popped in to give you a hand. That's the deal, isn't it? It's not because I feel sorry for you,' he added.

'But how did you get into this area?'

'Walked along the corridor same as you.'

'How did you get through security?'

'Well, I'd been waiting so long.'

'What do you mean?'

Garvie gestured vaguely. 'In the end they just sort of waved me through. Can't stop, though. I've got an exam to get to. Can we make it quick? Do you mind?'

There was a silence in which Singh seemed to be exerting an effort to control himself. 'Come with me,' he said at last.

Leading Garvie away from the café, he went briskly to the staircase, down to the interview rooms below, and along the corridor to a door badged INTERVIEW ROOM 2. He punched in a twelve-digit code and they went into a narrow room with a bank of screens along one wall, each showing a different angle of the same empty room.

'That must be the interview room,' Garvie said, looking up at the screens.

Singh nodded.

'Get to it through that door?'

There was a door at the end with a red light above it.

Singh nodded again.

'And this is, what, the monitoring room?'

Singh ignored him. He said, 'Look. Before we start, I don't want you coming here again. Do you understand? Because I'm in the squad room now there's nowhere here I can meet you. It only makes things more difficult for me. Just now,' he added, 'I was in a meeting.'

Garvie shrugged. 'Fine. Your call.' He paused. 'Got a question for you about the Juwenalia parade.'

Singh settled himself in his seat. 'I told you. No sign of Magee.'

'But you picked out Pyotor?'

'Yes. He was easy to identify. At the edge of the parade the whole time, by himself. For four hours he doesn't seem to even speak to anyone else.'

'You sure?'

'Yes, I'm sure.'

'And no one speaks to him?'

Singh shook his head. 'He was a loner. He did things alone.'

'He went to orchestra. He went to Juwenalia, even if he didn't speak to anyone.'

'He didn't speak to anyone at orchestra either if he could help it. And I've checked the records for Juwenalia each year. This year was the only year Pyotor went: just to the parade, nothing else. His grandparents had encouraged him to go. Otherwise he would have stayed at home by himself, as usual.'

'Can I see the Juwenalia records?'

Singh produced printouts from his folder and Garvie scanned them.

'Attendees for the last ten years,' Singh said.

'Yes, I see.'

'Pyotor's name isn't on any list except this year's.'

'Yeah, I see that too. I wasn't looking for Pyotor's name, though.'

Singh frowned.

Garvie said, 'But I didn't really come in for that. I wanted to talk about Pyotor's weekly schedule.'

'Good,' Singh said. 'In fact, we've just made a discovery. Pyotor told his grandparents he was having extra maths tuition at school every Tuesday after orchestra practice – but the school know nothing about it.'

Garvie shrugged, and Singh looked at him in surprise.

'It could be important.'

'I wouldn't bother if I were you.'

'We are bothering very much. We know already that he was at school at that time, and it's beginning to look like he met someone there. Nothing to do with maths. Nothing to do with orchestra.'

Garvie shrugged again.

'We have extra manpower to speed up the process of viewing the CCTV and conducting the interviews, not just at the school, but in the area in general. A public request for information has gone out in the national media.'

'I really wouldn't bother.'

'Why?'

'It was me.'

There was a pause then.

Singh said quietly, 'What?'

'Me. I was giving him a bit of help with the Maths exam coming up. We used to meet Tuesdays up there on Top Pitch where it's convenient to smoke. Sorry. End of. Let's move on.'

Singh was pale. 'Why didn't you mention this before?'

'You didn't ask. What am I, psychic? Anyway, luckily for you, you've just made another breakthrough.'

'No, we haven't.'

'You're about to. Sadly, it's come to light that interviews aren't Detective Inspector Dowell's strength.'

'What do you mean?'

'It didn't register with him when Mr Merryweather told him orchestra practice after school was once a week.'

Singh frowned. 'Practice was every evening. Pyotor's grandfather told me himself quite clearly.'

'Only because that's what Pyotor told him.'

Singh hesitated again. 'But if he wasn't at practice . . . then where was he?' he said at last.

'Jamal's, as it happens.'

'Jamal's!' Singh's face seemed to stop momentarily, and start up again. 'What, every evening? How do you know this?'

Garvie explained all that Sajid had told him, and Singh sat and listened, and when Garvie had finished he remained silent for several minutes.

Then he said, 'OK. We missed it. We need to rethink.' He thought. 'Why would Pyotor threaten to go to the police?'

Garvie shrugged. 'You know Khalid better than me. You must have been talking to him about the break-ins.'

'Yes. He has made a great many complaints, as you can imagine.'

'So what do you reckon?'

'Let me think.' Singh thought. After a while he began to speak. 'So . . . Khalid accuses Pyotor of stealing his phone.'

'Correction. Khalid accused Pyotor of stealing things, including his phone.'

'OK, OK. Then the phone reappears, so perhaps Pyotor had just put it somewhere, tidied it, like Sajid said.' He looked at Garvie questioningly.

'Could be.'

Singh pondered. 'But was there *something else* Khalid thought Pyotor stole? That's a question. OK. Something maybe he couldn't shout about. Something Khalid didn't want anyone to know he had in the first place. Let me think about that. What did he tell you, about protection? He said he was getting protection, right? Meaning the dog.'

'Not quite. First he said he'd *got* protection. Then he corrected himself, said he was getting it.'

'Ah. OK. So he had protection. Then he didn't have it. This is before Genghis arrived.'

Garvie nodded.

'Last year,' Singh went on, 'Khalid was cautioned for unlawful gun possession. It wasn't the first time, and we didn't think it would be the last. So let us say he had a gun. He *had* protection. And then he didn't. That's what you think, isn't it? You think Pyotor stole Khalid's gun. That's why Khalid got Genghis.'

'Where else would the kid get a gun? What does Uncle Len say?'

'Preliminaries were incomplete. We haven't had the full report yet.' Singh fell silent again. 'But there's another question. Pyotor might have stolen Khalid's gun, but it was Pyotor who threatened to go to the police. Why?'

'Pyotor was a watcher. He saw where Khalid kept his gun. Whatever Khalid was up to, he would have seen that too.'

'So he saw something, something he didn't like, something that frightened him, made him angry. He stole Khalid's gun, he took it and went to the lock-up, where Jamal has a unit. What goes on at Jamal's? What goes on in that unit?'

Garvie shrugged again. 'You'd have to ask Khalid. Only, if I were you, I'd go easy on him. He's definitely the nervous type.'

Singh nodded. 'He has a temper also. We've had complaints about his treatment of his brother.'

Garvie looked at his watch, cursed and got to his feet. 'Got to shoot. Got an exam. Don't want to be late. What? What are you looking at me like that for?'

'You know, Garvie, all this time you've never used his real name. It was always "the Gimp". Now it's "Pyotor". And you were helping him with his schoolwork.'

Garvie scowled as he got to his feet. 'Doesn't matter what I did. Doesn't matter what he's called either. If I were you, I'd think less about what he was called and more about what he did.'

'You don't need to tell me that.'

Without waiting for Singh, Garvie went out of the room and jogged down the corridor and up the stairs to the main drag on the ground floor, where he unexpectedly encountered Detective Inspector Dowell coming the other way.

Dowell's malevolent face went from passive to active.

'Hello, son.'

'Can't stop,' Garvie said, moving round him.

Dowell blocked him off. 'Late for another funeral?' he said.

'There'll be a funeral if I don't get moving.'

Dowell nodded. He stopped a passing constable. 'This boy says his name's Smith.'

'Sir.'

'How many other Smiths his age do we have on record?'

'Couldn't say exactly, sir. A few hundred.'

'Could get confusing. We need to sort this out. Escort him to my office.'

'Sir.'

The constable took hold of Garvie's arm. Not in a friendly way.

Garvie said, 'Seriously, man, I'd love to chat, and I hear how good you are at it, but I'm late. Got a cabbie picking me up to take me to an exam.'

Dowell nodded again. 'Well, you're going to be even later now, aren't you?'

27

At six o'clock the next morning twelve police officers wearing the black uniforms and helmets of the Counter-Terrorism Unit and wielding semi-automatic carbines kicked in the unresisting door of Jamal's corner shop on Bulwarks Lane and charged inside, all identifying themselves as law-enforcement officials at the tops of their voices above the noise of cascading shelves and imploding refrigerators toppled in their wake. Joining other counter-terrorist colleagues who had simultaneously forced entry at the back, they kicked down another (unlocked) door and rushed shouting up the narrow stairs to the tiny landing above, where they jammed together, thrashing about with their weapons, still bellowing instructions for calm and order.

In the back seat of the chief constable's car parked across the road, Detective Inspector Singh sat pale and grim, listening to the noise. Screams came from upstairs; there was a crash as something heavy fell over and a big pop of glass as a window exploded. A shot rang out, and a muscle in Singh's cheek twitched.

'Sir,' he began.

The chief constable raised his hand. 'We don't take risks with suspects who may be armed,' he said.

'No, sir.' Singh sat there imagining the headlines on the hoardings outside Jamal's the next day.

Gradually the noise inside the building abated, the general uproar shrinking to the sound of a child crying and a shrill voice complaining about bandits, abruptly silenced.

The chief added, without turning round, 'This is your initiative, detective inspector. I'm only here to observe. I hope it yields results. This case has been short on results so far. I've asked Detective Inspector Dowell to let you handle the interview.'

'Thank you, sir.'

'It's possible, of course, you may find the suspect uncooperative,' the chief added.

'Yes, sir.'

'I'm expecting you to prevail.'

A few moments later two policemen dragged a young man of South Asian descent out onto the pavement. He was wearing shorts and a T-shirt fouled with blood, and he struggled raggedly against the men as they frogmarched him towards the emergency response unit. For a second, in the middle of his struggling, he looked across the street to where Singh waited, and their eyes met. Then the policemen got him under control and manoeuvred him like an inconveniently sized box into the cage in the back of the van.

Two hours later Khalid and Singh faced each other again, in Interview Room 1 in the basement of the police centre in Cornwallis Way. Khalid was still dressed in shorts and T-shirt. His face had changed though. One eye had been replaced by an unnaturally smooth and glossy purple bump and the other had sunk into a watery red socket. One of his earlobes seemed to have come loose. His forehead had developed an unorthodox extension above his nose, and his bottom lip was inflated to twice its normal size.

'Khalid,' Singh said quietly. 'How are you feeling?'

Khalid said nothing. It was not immediately clear that he was capable of speech.

Location: Interview Room 1, Cornwallis Police Centre: echoey, over-bright.

Interviewer: Detective Inspector Singh: tired, cautious.

Interviewee: Khalid Baloch: pummelled, maddened.

DI SINGH: You've been seen by the on-duty medical officer, I hope?

KHALID BALOCH [*silent, glaring with one eye*]

DI SINGH: And you've exercised your right to contact your lawyer?

KHALID BALOCH [*silent; glaring; blinking*]

DI SINGH: OK. Listen. I've been asked to speak to you, Khalid, about issues relating to the murder of the schoolboy Pyotor Gimpel. I know this isn't a good moment, I know you're upset, but

I urge you to cooperate, OK? It will make a material difference to the investigation. Do you understand?

KHALID BALOCH [*silent, glaring, blinking, twitching*]

DI SINGH: We can take our time. Let me know if you need anything. Glass of water? OK then. The first question I want to ask you concerns—

KHALID BALOCH: Take our time? Material difference? What about *Got your head kicked in by a bunch of robots*? What about *Bust up your shop*?

DI SINGH: Khalid, I—

KHALID BALOCH: What is it? Is it 'cause I'm getting burglared all the time it's all right for the coppers to join in, beat me up as well?

DI SINGH: Khalid, please—

KHALID BALOCH: I got my pie cabinet all smashed, yeah? I got my big Williams done over, right? The multi-deck, man, nearly new off of eBay! What about all the shelving? What about all the stock? What about the *door*? Put a couple of hundred into new locks last week – now I got no door left! What I got is damages I can't pay for, right? What I got is full refurb, yeah? *Six o'clock in the morning*, man, I hadn't even brushed my teeth! Now I'm not even sure I still got all my teeth.

DI SINGH: Khalid, please, let me—

KHALID BALOCH: Think I got insurance? You think I'm that dopey?

DI SINGH: I'll make sure you get legal advice, OK? To help you make the appropriate claim. Do you understand? To help you decide if you want to make a formal complaint.

KHALID BALOCH: Formal complaint! I know what your formal complaints is.

DI SINGH: But there are some important questions I have to ask you first. So, now, please. Thank you. As you know, Pyotor Gimpel was murdered on the night of Friday eighth June. I want you to tell me what you know about it.

KHALID BALOCH: You having a laugh? Is that it? Comedy capers, is that what this is?

DI SINGH: Where were you during that night?

KHALID BALOCH: Nowhere, man.

DI SINGH: You were at home? Who can corroborate that? Your father? Sajid?

KHALID BALOCH: You're not listening, man. This murder, yeah? I don't know nothing about it, right?

DI SINGH: Tell me about Pyotor then. We know he spent a lot of time at your shop, in the evenings, with Sajid. And that you had an argument with him. You accused him of stealing.

[Silence]

DI SINGH: We know all this, Khalid, so you might as well be straight with me. I want you tell me about Pyotor.

KHALID BALOCH: This is all bullshit, man. You don't know what he was like.

DI SINGH: What was he like?

KHALID BALOCH: No sense of whose is whose is what. He'd just take stuff, know what I mean?

DI SINGH: What did he take?

KHALID BALOCH: My phone is one thing.

DI SINGH: He stole your phone?

KHALID BALOCH: I got it back, right? But only after I told him.

DI SINGH: Did he take anything else?

KHALID BALOCH: He was just weird like that, is all I'm saying.

DI SINGH: Khalid, did he take a gun from you?

KHALID BALOCH: *Gun?!* Gun now, is it? All this is bullshit, man. I want that lawyer you talked about.

DI SINGH: OK, Khalid. By the time the lawyer's here we'll have got the forensics from the gun Pyotor had at the lock-up. If it was yours, we'll know.

[*Silence*]

DI SINGH: If you withhold this information now, you're putting yourself in a very difficult position. I won't be able to help you.

[*Silence*]

DI SINGH: Think of your family, Khalid. Think of Sajid.

KHALID BALOCH [*weeps*]: This is such bullshit, man. Got the shop trashed, yeah? Got beat up, right? Now I get hit with this. All right, he stole a gun. You picking on me for having a gun when I'm getting burglared all the time, when what you should be thinking of is why that weirdo kid wanted it.

DI SINGH: When you found out he'd taken it, you challenged him, didn't you, and he threatened to go to the police?

KHALID BALOCH: You don't understand nothing. He was so weird, that kid.

DI SINGH: What did you say to him then? Did you tell him to meet you somewhere?

KHALID BALOCH: Nah, man.

DI SINGH: Did you tell him to meet you at your lock-up?

KHALID BALOCH: Nah, man. I swear.

DI SINGH: What goes on at your lock-up, Khalid? Do you run storage for dealers in the city?

[*Silence*]

DI SINGH: We have a warrant, and we're going in today. Before we find whatever's in there, you should tell me what the situation is.

[*Silence*]

DI SINGH: All right, Khalid. We'll find out for ourselves. In the meantime I want you to tell me what happened at your lock-up that night.

KHALID BALOCH [*holds head, weeps again*]: Nothing! Nothing, I swear. It's all bullshit. You don't understand. All this burglaring. Abbu gets his leg broke. I'm getting all these phone calls. I got all this going on, and I can't do it no more, I can't . . . [*Weeps, bangs desk*]

DI SINGH: Take it easy, Khalid.

KHALID BALOCH: How many times the shop's been done? Four, five times the last two months. What are the police even for? I can't even get them on the blower, then there's like thirty of them busting up my shop. You think that's one of them coincidences?

DI SINGH: Khalid, calm down! What are you saying?

KHALID BALOCH: I'm saying about Sajid, I'm saying about Abbu, I'm saying about working! Man, I'm working hours I didn't even know they had. And look at me here with my face all out. You don't even know what it's like to be skint. I can't go on. It's just bullshit. [*Weeps, noise of desk being kicked*]

DI SINGH: Calm down now.

KHALID BALOCH [*stands, screams*]: *You think I'm not calm?*

DI SINGH: Enough. We're going to take a break.

KHALID BALOCH: *You think I don't know what calm is?* I can see. I got eyes. It's not me you should be on at! It's him! That weirdo kid. You should be asking yourself what did he want the gun for, that's what you should be asking. What weirdo stuff did he want it for? If it wasn't for him none of this would've happened! [*Weeps, then silence*]

28

*L*ocation: kitchen, Flat 12 Eastwick Gardens:
stale, early-morningish.
Interviewer: Garvie's mother: grim in her badly
fitting dressing gown, tired.
Interviewee: Garvie Smith: dishevelled in shorts and
T-shirt, braced for the worst.

GARVIE'S MOTHER: I talked to Uncle Len when I got
back from my shift last night. He told me what
happened.

GARVIE SMITH: Right. I just want to say—

GARVIE'S MOTHER: So you were kept at the police
station all yesterday afternoon?

GARVIE SMITH: Yeah, but—

GARVIE'S MOTHER: And you missed your exam
completely?

GARVIE SMITH: Yes.

GARVIE'S MOTHER [*long silence, deep and
unreadable*]

GARVIE SMITH [*equally long silence, wary*]

GARVIE'S MOTHER: And now you think I'm going to
grill you as usual?

GARVIE SMITH: Yes, that too.

GARVIE'S MOTHER: Well, I'm not.

She got to her feet and went over to the window and looked out at the sky, still pale and unripe-looking so early in the morning, and after a while she put a hand up to her face and brushed below her eyes with her fingertips. Garvie stayed where he was, watching her.

'I can explain,' he began at last, and fell silent.

'I know you can,' she said. 'And I can tell you why you're wrong. And then you can tell me how I'm being unfair. We've done it so many times I can probably tell you word for word what we'll say, you and me both.' She turned from the window and shook her head. 'Forget it, Garvie.'

She came back to the table and sat down opposite him and looked at him carefully, her face very close, her eyes sad and damp.

'I don't think we need to do that bit any more,' she said quietly.

This was different. He hadn't seen her like this before, so quiet and tired, as if all her usual spirit had been beaten out of her. It was hard to look at her, and hard not to look. He dropped his eyes and took a breath.

'Look at me, Garvie,' she said, and he made himself look at her again.

'Whatever it is you've been doing, it's not what you should have been doing. But I'm done with telling you what to do. Get this now.'

She was silent a moment and, looking at her, for

almost the first time in his life he could not tell what she was going to say.

'I'm asking you,' she said.

Garvie just stared.

She put her hand across the table and took hold of his. 'I'm begging you. Please. Please, Garvie, do this for me. God knows there are all sorts of sensible reasons why you should do it anyway, but you know them all already. Do it because if you don't, I'm telling you, you're going to make me so unhappy. OK?'

It was a shocking moment, unlike other moments; it hardly seemed connected to their ordinary life. Garvie wanted to tell her to stop it, to shout at him as usual, to tell him what she was going to do to him if he didn't get his shit together. But he didn't say anything, wasn't sure he could.

She squeezed his hand.

'I've been thinking,' she went on, 'this overtime I've been doing, it means a bit more money coming in. I was thinking, maybe when the exams are over we could go away for a few days. Have a little holiday. We haven't done that for a long time. You can decide where we go.'

Still he said nothing. He had nothing to say to this. She blurred as he looked at her.

'Of course,' she said softly, 'maybe you wouldn't want to go with me. That's OK. I could give you some money so you could go with a friend. It's not much to offer but it's a treat.'

Garvie took a breath, managed to nod.

'OK then. Enough. I've said my piece. You get ready for school now.'

He got to his feet and stood there, looking at her wet, defeated face.

'Mum,' he said in a whisper.

'It's OK. You go on.'

'Mum.'

He couldn't say anything else.

'Go on,' she said again, but he came the other way round the table and hugged her silently.

'Enough,' she said, at last. 'You'll be late.'

And finally he went.

29

The day was fine. It got hotter; by late afternoon the whole illuminated summer package was on display, even in Five Mile. Sunshine and trees, breezes and flowers. At four o'clock the sun shone strongly on the ring road and the car plant, on street and shops. It shone on the newspaper hoarding outside Jamal's convenience store advertising the new headline of the local evening edition: *Dawn Raid Ends in Chaos*. It shone too on Top Pitch at the Academy, where Garvie Smith lay on the thick green turf, smoking gloomily with Felix and Smudge.

Smudge said, 'No point in fretting now. It's gone, mate. Get over it. Wasn't your fault DI Psycho-Killer kept you in interrogation all afternoon.'

'I wasn't interrogated, Smudge.'

'Threw you in the dungeon, whatever. What does Queen Bitch expect? As excuses go, I think it's pretty safe. I'm sorry, Miss Perkins, I was wrongfully detained by the police, my lawyers are acting on my behalf, I'll let you know how the case develops.'

Garvie ignored him. Miss Perkins had not in fact been impressed by his reason for missing his Eng. Lit. exam. He didn't think about that, however. He thought about walking to school that morning past Jamal's and seeing the corrugated sheet of metal across the doorway, the squares of cardboard taped to the broken windows, the handwritten sign that said CLOSE TO FURTHER NOTICE. He'd seen Sajid's face at an upper window gazing out at nothing, and a few minutes later he'd had a call from Singh. Very brief, very uptight. There had been an altercation at the police centre, Singh said: Khalid had resisted detention and was currently in hospital. Simultaneously the police had entered his lock-up in East Field industrial estate and found it full of second-hand toys which Khalid had been collecting on behalf of a charity providing for homeless children in the Middle East.

'He'd been scared to tell us because he'd heard of a friend who worked with the charity before, who'd been investigated under the Anti-terrorism Act.'

Unfortunately, Singh had added, Dowell had now instigated an investigation into Khalid on exactly the same grounds. Headlines had already appeared on the internet: *Murder Suspect a Jihadist.* In the meantime Jamal had confirmed that Khalid was at home on the night of the eighth, and Khalid was officially no longer a suspect, nor even helping police with their enquiries. Many papers still ran stories on the mystery of Pyotor Gimpel's extra maths tuition, for which no tutor could be found. Hundreds of responses had been received to the official appeal for information, though none had yet proved useful.

Singh had concluded his call to Garvie with an instruction: 'Do not attempt to contact me again about this matter. Ever.'

It was a mess. Worse, it felt like *his* mess. He remembered what his mother had said: that whatever he had been doing was not what he should have been doing.

'We did warn you,' Smudge said. 'You can always tell them by their eyes, the nutters.'

Garvie sighed. He thought about his encounter with Dowell the previous afternoon. It had given the policeman enormous satisfaction. He'd left Garvie to stew for an hour or so before summoning him into his office to give him the benefit of his wisdom. He'd had seen it all before, naturally, he knew exactly what advice to give to a young man without aims, confused and troublesome, like Garvie. To hear him talk you'd think he'd been on earth for centuries, vampire-like, all-seeing, all-knowing: there was nothing in human nature that surprised him any more. Smudge was right: the man was obviously a nutter. A useful one, though. He'd made it very clear that if Garvie persisted with the Gimpel case he, Dowell, would personally make sure Garvie was taken by secret-service jet to an unknown army base on a foreign island thousands of miles away and interrogated for the rest of his active adulthood at the public expense.

Garvie sighed again. None of this was what really upset him.

He lit another Benson & Hedges, lay on his back staring blankly at the blameless blue sky and thought about his mother.

This was what really upset him.

She was putting her trust in him. He remembered, in unwelcome detail, their conversation in the kitchen, her badly fitting dressing gown, her wet face, the way she looked at him, the way she took hold of his hand. She was putting so much trust in him she was letting him decide for himself what to do.

Smudge was telling Felix how he'd aced Eng. Lit., and Felix was saying he didn't think Smudge could even spell Eng. Lit. let alone tell him what it stood for, and, tuning out their voices, Garvie lay there thinking about trust. You can't put trust in a mathematical formula, Singh had said. It was true that trust seemed a lot more complicated than it used to. Singh didn't trust him. Alex didn't trust Zuza. What about Sajid and Pyotor – what bond of trust had existed between them? He concentrated. Could his mother trust him? For her sake, could he drop all the Pyotor stuff and pass some exams instead? That's what he wanted to do. It was just that . . . as soon as he began to think about Pyotor he felt something tantalizingly close, a detail he couldn't quite get hold of, the key to the whole problem. If only he could get hold of it, everything would fall into place; then someone else could do the rest, even Singh. He knew what the detail was. The violin. Or not exactly the violin: the space where the violin should be, the emptiness in the hands of a boy who sat on a bench in a school playground looking at Garvie with that familiar impassive expression.

A boy sitting on a bench. His mother sitting at the table. Two images in his mind.

He flicked his cigarette butt across the grass. Enough was enough. He would forget about Pyotor, forget about Khalid and Sajid, forget about Alex and Blinkie, forget about Zuzana too, in other words go home now, straight away, at once, and put in the smallest effective effort necessary to pass three exams. As soon as he had thought this he felt better and got to his feet.

And that was when he heard his name called.

She came up the slope of grass with sunlight in her hair, smiling as she came.

Smudge waved. He said in a low voice to the others, 'Zuza's been getting a bit friendly, boys, but it's cool, it's OK, I'm handling it. You know I'm not going to let Alex down, right? The important thing's for me not to encourage her.'

'Babe,' he called as Zuzana reached the top of the slope, 'I've got to dig that whole slinky thing you've got going there. It's powerful, girl. I mean, I don't know if I'm strong enough to handle it.'

'Hello, Smudge. Hello Felix.' She looked at Garvie. 'It's good I find you here. I thought maybe I had to walk over to the little children's playground.'

'We're here,' Smudge said. 'Here we are. Garvie's with us.'

Still smiling, she took Garvie to one side. 'I have heard from Bogdana. We can go now to see the things the police have returned. Come.'

Garvie shook his head and she frowned at him.

'It's no good,' he said. 'Sorry.'

'But they have things to show us. His clothes. His bag. They do not want to keep them, but if we go now we can see them before they are thrown away.'

He hesitated.

'They have his phone, though something has happened to it.'

'What?'

'I do not know. We must look.'

He hesitated again. 'Do they have the violin case?'

'Yes, that too.'

She smiled at him. She leaned in towards him and took his cigarette from between his fingers and took a drag herself, squinting at him through the smoke, and gave it back. Her face was close to his; it seemed very precise in the bright sunshine, her lips crisply shaped, her eyes dark, her skin pale against her black bobbed hair. Her chin was so neat and pure he didn't know whether it would break rocks or shatter if he touched it with a fingertip. He imagined himself touching it. She pointed it at him.

'Come. It is the right thing to do. For Pyotor. But we should go now or everything will be lost.'

Behind him Smudge was saying something but he

wasn't listening. For a moment he fought against himself, and they all stood watching him.

'Let's go then,' he said, and they went down the slope together.

30

They got off the bus at the stop by the tower blocks and walked westward across The Plain into a street lined with old trees and tall terraced houses, their front doors encrusted with buzzers and numbers, their small front gardens concreted over, over-flowing with stringy city-weeds and multi-coloured wheelie bins.

Garvie had said nothing since they left the Academy. Now he turned to Zuzana and said, 'You're going to do the talking, right?'

'Yes.'

He nodded. 'Good.'

They walked on. 'They must be feeling bad,' he said after a while.

If she was surprised at this unexpected touch of concern, she didn't show it. 'They are the same. They need our sympathy.'

'Yeah, course. What can you say, though, about something like that?'

'I can give them our good thoughts. I can tell them again how sorry we are for their loss, what a good boy Pyotor was, how hard it must be for them, and—'

'Yeah, yeah, I know. What I meant was, what will you say *in Polish*?'

Now she was surprised. She looked at him blankly.

'I want to hear what it sounds like.'

'You are a strange boy,' she said.

'Yeah, well. Humour me.'

So, as they walked under the dusty plane trees, through the litter and weeds, she began to speak – *Bar*-zum me *sheh*-gram sto-*vo*-du – and an expression came into his face as if the language or the way she spoke the language both soothed and mystified him – though when, after a few minutes, she stopped, he said nothing at all, gave no sign that he'd even been listening, and she shook her head at him in silent bewilderment as they went on together, crossed into a third road, Strawberry Rise, and arrived at last at the Gimpels' flat.

Pyotor's grandfather met them in the hallway. He nodded at Garvie and they followed him silently up the stairs to the second floor, their footsteps echoing on the bare boards. All the way up there was a smell of old rain and pets. At the door of the flat, Bogdana stood waiting. To Zuzana she seemed smaller than before, dark-faced. It was clear that she had been weeping. Without saying anything, she turned from them and moved away slowly, unsmiling, through the cluttered, curtained living room to her chair, and turned back to face them, where they stood awkwardly together in the half-light of the dim room, and there was a moment when no one seemed to know what to do.

Making a great effort, Bogdana smiled hesitantly

at Garvie and said, '*Dziękuję za przybycie.*'

Zuzana opened her mouth to answer, but Garvie stepped forward and said, '*Bardzo mi przykro z powodu Twojej straty, Dana.*' He briefly put his hand over his heart.

There was a moment's astonishment, not least from Zuzana.

'*Wiem jam jest Ci trudno,*' he went on in a quiet and respectful voice. '*Pyotor był dobry chłopak.*'

Bogdana took both Garvie's hands in hers. '*Tak, tak,*' she said. '*Twój chłopak jest bardzo uprzejmy,*' she said to Zuzana, smiling.

Zuzana blushed and frowned. 'Yes, but he's not my boyfriend,' she murmured.

Garvie went on gracefully. '*Pyotor był wspaniałym muzykiem i genialnym matematykiem. Duma dla szkoły, dlatego wszyscy będziemy za nim ogromnie tęsknić. Chciałbym ci pomóc, jeśli tylko potrafię.*' He finished with a little bow, and there was a flourish of gestures from Bogdana, who went into the kitchen to make raspberry tea, and, before he joined her, Zbigniew took Garvie's hand and shook it silently, over and over, before he went to help with tea.

Garvie and Zuzana sat side by side on the old upright settee with the bag of personal effects which the Gimpels had put out for them.

'What?' Garvie said, catching her eye.

She was looking at him critically. 'So. You are pleased with yourself.'

He shrugged.

'You show off your famous memory. This is why you wanted me to speak Polish for you.'

Garvie said nothing.

'But you do not know what it means. You did not *mean* any of it.'

He shrugged. 'If they like me it'll be easier to find out from them what I want to know. I'm just being logical.'

She did not stop looking at him. She began to frown. 'Wait. There is something I do not understand.'

He glanced at her, found her staring at him, puzzled, and glanced away again. 'Yeah? Don't let it worry you. I'm just a big show-off. We've got stuff to do.'

'But—'

'Listen.' He turned to her. 'My advice to you: focus. Don't get distracted. Don't fuss. Don't get sentimental. Right. What's in the bag?'

He took the clear plastic hold-all from her and they began to go through it. The Gimpels had not touched Pyotor's belongings since the police had delivered them, and showed no sign of wanting to see them now. They had told Zuzana that they were going to destroy the things; they held too much pain. The police had destroyed the clothing already, in fact. In the bag there were only the school bag, the violin case and the things that Pyotor had carried in his pockets. Garvie began to examine them rapidly.

In the school bag were an exercise book for English homework, a textbook entitled *Supporting Advanced Mathematics*, the *Little Oxford Dictionary* and a pencil case containing pens and pencils, a rubber, a pencil sharpener and other bits and pieces. The last entry in the exercise book was a essay headed *In My Room*, which began: 'My room is square, it has one door and one window.'

He handed it to Zuzana and she began to examine it. 'Look how neat his handwriting was,' she said.

Garvie was already sorting through the things that had been in Pyotor's pockets. He glanced in turn at a balled-up tissue, latchkey, hair comb and membership card for the Polish Youth Society and put each of them back in the bag.

'He was neat all over,' he said, turning his attention to a mobile phone, now in pieces held together by an elastic band. 'The interesting thing is that he'd torn out three pages from the exercise book. That's not something a neat boy would normally do.'

Surprised, she examined the book, holding it up to her eye and running her finger along the gutter of the pages. 'It is true. But why?'

Garvie ignored her. 'His phone's been stamped on.'

She looked at it. 'To stop him calling for help?'

'Or destroy what was on it.'

'What was on it?'

'Nothing was on it any more. He was too careful for that. But look.' He held out the remains of the phone, a splintered pulp of plastic. 'The person who did this had a temper on him all right.'

He began to examine the violin case. He turned it over in his hands, held it up to the light, weighed it in his hands.

'What are you doing?'

'Nothing useful. It's not the case I'm interested in. But unfortunately the violin isn't here.' He examined the inside of the empty case, felt along the lining, held it upside down and shook it. 'Unless I'm being unusually dense.'

'Where is it then?'

He ignored her again. 'Listen. In a minute the Gimpels are going to come and ask if we want to see Pyotor's room. Tell them yes.'

She pursed her lips, frowned. 'You like this, don't you? Playing the detective, giving orders.'

'I'm just trying not to waste time. Look, here they come. Tell them you've seen Pyotor's story about his room in the exercise book, you can tell how happy he was living here with them.'

Zuzana gave him an irritated look, but as Bogdana and Zbigniew came into the room with the tea things she spoke to them.

Bogdana nodded and became upset.

'His room is not the same,' Zbigniew said, 'since we had the break-in. It has upset Dana.'

Weeping, Bogdana took hold of Zuzana's arm, talking loudly.

'She wants us to see his room,' Zuzana said over

211

her shoulder to Garvie. 'To see what the racists have done to it.'

They went out to the stairs and up to the landing, where Garvie had a sudden and surprising fit of coughing. He clung to the banisters, eyes streaming, and Bogdana patted him on the back, talking to Zuzana.

'She says Zbigniew will get you a drink of water.'

'It's OK,' Garvie croaked. 'I can get it. I don't want to make Mr Gimpel go all the way back downstairs. Tell her—' and he smiled winningly through his coughs – 'she's much too good to me.'

He left them on the landing, Bogdana watching him go with maternal concern, and went back down to the kitchen, ran the tap briefly and jogged into the living room, where the desk was.

It was a tall, old-fashioned piece of furniture with a slatted roll top. Dark wood polished almost red. The top was locked. Garvie tugged at the handle twice, peered critically at the big old keyhole and sighed. Fishing a piece of oilcloth from his pocket, he unwrapped the tension wrench and half-diamond pick Felix had loaned him. He put the short end of the wrench into the plug of the lock, prodded the pick in underneath and felt around with the end of it to find the pins of the lock shift. The roll top slid up with a softly rhythmic sound and he began to search through the compartments and shelves inside, listening out for noises from the floor above.

31

When Garvie and Zuzana left the apartment an hour later the Gimpels gave them slices of apple cake – *szarlotka* – to take with them, and said their goodbyes wistfully. Bogdana held on to Garvie's hand, talking in Polish and patting his cheek.

On their way back through the streets Garvie said nothing for a long time. He seemed barely aware that Zuzana was with him. In the end she took hold of his arm and stopped him on the pavement.

'Now you must explain. You are being funny with me.'

'What do you mean?'

'I can't trust you. You have been keeping secrets. When you spoke Polish to Bogdana you said something strange. I have realized what it is. You told her Pyotor was *genialnym matematyk* – an excellent mathematician.'

'So?'

'You did not hear me say this. How did you know to say it in Polish?'

Garvie looked at her a moment. 'It's what Pyotor wanted me to call him when he solved a problem.'

'Solved a problem?'

'When I was helping him with his maths.'

She stared at him. '*You* were the one? The one they talk about in the newspapers? The one they try to find?'

Garvie shrugged. 'I didn't ask them to look for me.'

'I did not think you knew Pyotor. But you were with him every week.'

'It's not a big deal.'

She frowned. 'Why did you help him?'

'He was having trouble with vector notation.'

'Did he ask you for help?'

'I offered.'

She made a baffled face. 'But you do not do things for other people. You do them only for your own amusement. You told me this.'

'Yeah, well. I made an exception.'

She thought about this. 'Who did you tell about this help?'

'Why would I tell anyone?'

'Did your mother know?'

He looked at her in surprise. 'You think I tell my mother what I'm doing?'

'You kept it secret? She will think you were out drinking and smoking at the kiddies' playground.'

He shrugged.

She clicked her tongue. 'You are very strange. Much stranger than Pyotor. Now you tell me properly: what happened when you were with him? What did he talk about? Did he seem upset? Did he say anything suspicious?'

Garvie held his hand up. 'Listen. You're getting too emotional. It wasn't like that. We didn't talk. He did the problems, I showed him where he'd gone wrong, that was it.'

'But you must have learned something about him.'

'I learned he wasn't a fool,' Garvie said shortly.

He turned then, and they walked along in silence until they had come out of the tree-lined streets, crossed the road to The Plain and reached the bus stop underneath the tower blocks.

'OK,' she said. 'Now you tell me what happened in the flat just now.'

'What do you mean?'

'Glass of water! I am not stupid. What were you doing?'

Garvie took three sheets of paper from his pocket and handed them to her.

'Where did you get these?'

'From that desk thing in the living room. Where he did his homework.'

'It wasn't locked?'

'Not for long.'

'You have stolen them.'

'Yeah.'

'Why?'

'They're the pages he tore out of his exercise book.'

'But why did you take them?'

'Read what he wrote.'

She read. She put her hand up to her mouth.

'Yeah, that's right,' he said.

'What does it mean?'

'Obvious, isn't it? He was practising.'

'He was practising . . . a confession.'

'Trying to get it right. His English wasn't that great. Same thing, over and over, see? With variations. Practice runs. Look what he wrote: *I, the undersigned, confess . . . I promise to cease and desist what I have . . . I, the undersigned, promise to stop . . .* He was trying to get it to sound proper – legal.'

'He was going to confess . . . to something bad. Why?'

'He thought that if you did something wrong you ought to fess up to it and promise not to do it again.'

'But what had he done?'

Garvie stayed silent.

The Five Mile bus appeared at last, and they got on it and went to sit upstairs at the front. Evening sunshine lit up the dusty windowpane in shifting light-filled cloud patterns as they swayed out of the shadow of the towers and back down Cobham Road.

For a while they said nothing. Then Zuzana said, 'You tell me nothing. I will think it for myself and you tell me if I am right.' She took a breath. 'Nearly every evening Pyotor went to Jamal's to play games with Sajid.'

'Correct.'

'And while he was there something happened. He saw it.'

'Correct. But what?'

'I don't know. Something bad. Am I right?'

'Yes. But you've got to ask yourself: bad for who?'

She thought about that. Her eyes widened. 'Bad for Sajid! He saw something bad happening to Sajid. Or going to happen.'

'Yes. So what would he have done?'

'He would have tried to stop it. Even if . . . even if he had to do a bad thing himself.'

She looked at Garvie, and after a moment he nodded.

'What would he have done?' she asked.

He hesitated. 'He would have stolen a gun,' he said at last.

She put her hand on his arm. 'The gun they found at the lock-up? It wasn't Magee's?'

'It was Khalid's.'

'Pyotor stole it from Khalid. And he put it in his violin case.'

'And he took it to the lock-up.'

'And then he . . .' She looked at him. 'What?'

'Obviously that's what we have to find out.'

'How?'

He shrugged. 'Usual way. Ask someone who knows.'

'Who?'

He said nothing. He had said too much.

He sat there silently as the bus trundled past the Strawberry Hill shops, ignoring her questions.

'Garvie? You are being funny with me again. Tell me, what is it you are thinking?'

He was thinking of quadratic equations. Quads can be fiddly. $45x^2 - 74x - 55 = 0$. $40x^2 - 483x + 36 = 0$. That sort of thing. Three coefficients, lots of different permutations. Tricky. You can factorize them, you can graph them; either way it takes a lot of time and you've got to be really careful. Or you can forget all that and just use the quadratic formula. The formula solves all quadratic equations stone-cold dead. Not interesting, not elegant, just one hundred per cent practical. He thought of Pyotor and his violin and Khalid's gun. He thought of his mother and her dressing gown and her wet face. He thought of Alex and Blinkie and Zuzana's back door at midnight. He thought of Zuza, and at last he thought of Zuza and him together. All those tricky coefficients, all those fiddly permutations. And he thought of the formula that would solve them all.

'Don't want to be rude,' he said, 'but I can handle it on my own from here.'

She stared at him. 'No. No, you can't.'

'Best you're not involved, really.'

'You need me.'

'In fact, I'm not even sure I can be bothered to take it any further myself. I lose interest in things very easily.'

'What are you talking about?'

He shrugged.

She said fiercely, 'If I was not here, you would not

218

see the Gimpels, you would not find these papers.'

He could feel her looking at him hard, an imagined pressure on his face almost as physical as the touch of her hand, but he continued to stare through the window at the road in front.

'What is it?' she said. 'You think you can't trust me?'

Now he felt awkward. He didn't want to think about trust. He said quickly, 'It's not about that, it's not about Alex or anyone else, it's about . . .' He forgot what it was about, if he had ever known. '. . . doing my own thing,' he said, immediately wishing he hadn't.

The sudden sneeze-like noise she made startled him, and he broke his concentration on the road ahead and looked at her in confusion. She was laughing. At him. It was the prettiest laugh he had ever seen. Her nose wrinkled, her eyes scrunched up, her lips parted to show the pink tip of her tongue, she laughed for sheer fun. She laid her head on his shoulder and continued to laugh.

'What?'

'So funny. Always to do your own thing. For your own amusement, yes. Like a little boy who just wants to be left alone to play with his toys.'

He scowled.

She sneezed with laughter again, holding onto him as if to stop herself falling off the seat. 'And why,' she said when she could, looking at him mockingly, 'do you talk about Alex?'

'I didn't,' he said, remembering at the same time that he had.

'You think Alex can't trust me? You think I can't trust Alex?'

'No, I—'

She looked at him suddenly with great seriousness, her eyes black and steady. 'Listen. Do not think about Alex. Stop thinking about him, please. For me.'

When he said nothing, she went on. 'I am myself. Do you understand? I am free to do what I need to do.' She took hold of his hand. 'Without me you will fail. Believe me.' She lowered her voice. 'You think I don't know what you are like. Pretending always to be so cold.' She shook her head. 'I know,' she said. 'I start to think Pyotor knew.'

Her face seemed very close to him, and very beautiful, and expressionless, and he had one of those moments in which he could not read her, did not know what she was going to do – argue with him, walk away or stare him to a pulp.

'You can trust me,' she said softly. 'I will show you how to do this.'

He got to his feet clumsily. 'I'm getting off here.' She held his gaze as he hesitated, her mesmerizing eyes dilated.

'You agree?'

At last he shrugged. 'All right then. Not my fault if . . .'

'If what?'

He looked away from her smile, wincing as if it were a too-bright light. 'Doesn't matter.'

'Good. Tell me what you want me to do.'

'Remind me how many languages you speak.'

'Three. Why?'

'Pick up a six-pack of Special Brew and meet me at midnight outside Jamal's. And bring a torch.'

Then he was gone, leaping lightly into the stairwell as the bus juddered to a halt at the end of the Bulwarks Lane.

32

By moonlight the industrial estate was a mass of silhouettes and shadows. It loomed behind the wire fence like an abandoned city, dark and empty. It had taken them a quarter of an hour to walk down the lane from the sewage plant, where Abdul had dropped them, as far as the main entrance.

'Not that way,' Garvie said.

'Why?'

'CCTV. We're going round the side. There's a hole in the fence.'

A night breeze streamed through the scrub as they found the path and went into the darkness, Zuzana in front of him, a wavering shade tethered to a beam of torchlight, until they reached a wider track rutted with tyre marks and went along side by side to the fence, tilted and rucked like an old bedsheet on the other side of a shallow ditch. The hole was a ripple of shadow in the grey fence mesh.

'Is this it? Garvie?'

He stood looking at the ground around him, a patch of mud pitted and blurred.

'Yeah, that's it. You go. Up the bank on the other side to the road. I just want to check something.'

She emerged alone from brambles by the lock-up,

still packaged in the white canvas rigging of the police cordon, and waited, and a few minutes later Garvie joined her, and they walked down the access road together. Everything around them was silent and still, the dark buildings, the weed-high verges, the unmoving sky, as if they were trespassing on some archaeological remains on a distant star.

'Where are we going?' Zuzana asked at last.

'Tell me when you smell something.'

'Smell something?'

They walked on fifty metres and she stopped, sniffing. 'Ugh.'

'Good,' Garvie said. He lifted his head and shouted once, loud and sudden in the silence. 'Vinnie!'

At once there was a shuffle of shadow at the side of the road, a heavy, surprised-sounding *crump* and the beginning of a hushed retreating noise across coarse grass.

Garvie shouted again. 'Got something for you, Vinnie!'

They found him in the lee of the wall of a former fish wholesaler, ensconced in layers of clothing and cardboard like a modern-day hermit with wild eyes, phlegm-filled beard and a voice of gravel and splinters.

'I didn't fucking do it,' he said as they approached. 'I don't care what the vicar says.'

He spat, partly on the ground but mostly into his beard. 'Swine fubbers,' he grunted. 'Come here all over tits and warts. Got nothing for them. *Fubbers!*'

Garvie nodded politely. 'You know my friend Alex. Used to come down here doing deals.'

Vinnie embarked on a tangled, popeyed bout of swearing.

'Sends his best,' Garvie said. 'Got another friend knows you too, though he's a miserable git. You might remember him. Detective Inspector Dowell.'

At once Vinnie fell silent, chewing his bottom lip furiously, beard wagging wildly in the torch-light.

'He's not really my friend,' Garvie said. 'I mean, he'd like to be, but I'm not ready to move to a relationship. Do you want a drink by the way?'

Vinnie's eyes swivelled onto the can of Special Brew and he instinctively stretched out a long-fingered grey hand, yellow in patches.

'You know it leaves a nasty aftertaste, right?'

Vinnie appeared not to mind. He drank the beer in long, quivering gulps, sharing it with his beard and coat.

'So, anyway, what we wanted,' Garvie said, 'was a chat about the Polish kid you saw that night.'

Enlivened by the drink, Vinnie nodded, laughed out loud, his mouth a sudden dark and glistening wetness opening up in the beard. 'Fuck off,' he said. 'All right.' He made gestures for another beer, and Garvie passed over a can.

'You saw him, didn't you, bundled along by the man, down the road here, to the lock-up that way.'

Vinnie nodded.

'But the cops didn't believe you.'

'Fubbers.'

'Tell us what you saw.'

Vinnie nodded, not to Garvie but as if nudging himself back in time. He threw out an arm and pointed into the empty road. 'Coming yonder out of dark. Got his arm round the bleater tight. Hold him up, see? Or throttle him, I don't know, kill the squealer. Could be. Not making much noise, though. Panting. Huff, huff, huff, huff.' He coughed at length, cross-eyed, hawked with a mighty effort and gobbed with enormous satisfaction onto the ground. He glanced bewildered up at Garvie as if he'd suddenly forgotten what he was doing.

Garvie showed him the pictures from the newspaper.

'This is him, isn't it, the man?'

Vinnie nodded, denouncing him vigorously.

'And this is the kid, right?'

Vinnie nodded again.

'You sure, Vinnie?'

'I see the bleater right between the eyes,' he said indignantly.

'What did the police say when you told them?'

'Fubbing, cod-sucking, fish-titted—'

'They didn't believe you, did they, Vinnie? Why?'

Because they didn't want to pay Vinnie the reward advertised for information leading to apprehension of the culprit. Vinnie righteously anatomized all members of the force in language fit for such a sewer of corruption.

'I see. But how could you be sure it was the Polish kid you saw?'

Vinnie looked astonished at the question. 'I seen him.' He shook the newspaper as if to make it agree with him. 'I heard him,' he added.

'You heard him speaking Polish?'

Vinnie looked triumphant.

'You know Polish, do you?'

'I know it when I hear it. All jabber, see.' He held out a claw for another can, and Garvie gave him one.

Garvie said, 'This is Zuzana. She's Polish, Vinnie. Is this the language you heard spoken?'

Zuzana came closer, but not too close to Vinnie, who regarded her with an unstable expression, and spoke. '*Non mi avvicino,* Vinnie, *se è lo stesso con te – c'è puzza.*'

Vinnie's eyes bulged and he sprayed Special Brew without meaning to. 'The same!' he cried. 'She got it just the same!'

'Sure?'

'Bang on.'

'That was Italian.'

Vinnie looked uncertain. 'So?' he said defiantly. He drank deeply, his glaring eyes fixed on Garvie over the rim of the can.

'Let's try another one,' Garvie said.

Zuzana said in her native tongue, '*Poznajesz cokolwiek,* Vinnie?'

Vinnie looked scornful. 'Nothing like it! Fool me, eh?'

Garvie sighed.

'All right. Never mind about what you heard. What did you see? What was the kid wearing?'

'School uniform,' Vinnie said promptly, as if remembering something he'd heard.

'OK. What sort?'

Vinnie looked at him suspiciously. 'Normal sort. Nothing funny, I'd have twigged.'

'Jacket?'

'Could be.'

'What about trousers?'

'Course.'

'I mean, long or short?'

Vinnie pulled at his beard as if the pain might stimulate his memory.

'Blackish,' he said at last. 'Seen his knees,' he added.

'What colour shirt?'

Vinnie thought for a long time. 'White,' he said at last, sullenly. 'Could be different. I ain't saying.'

Garvie sighed again. 'All right. How many gun-shots did you hear?'

'One,' Vinnie said promptly again. 'Or two,' he added. 'Could be more,' he went on cunningly, 'they don't always know.'

'Before or after you saw them?'

'Before.' His eyes searched Garvie's to gauge the effect of his answer. 'I mean after,' he added.

'OK. Thanks, Vinnie.'

'You bring the money here,' the man demanded. 'It'll be done right.'

Garvie sighed again. 'No money, Vinnie. But you can have another can.'

Vinnie laughed to himself as if unable to believe Garvie's stupidity, and he drank at length with a bitter smile, watching curiously to see what would happen next.

Zuzana said, 'He saw nothing. We should go.'

Garvie didn't reply. For a moment he stood in thought, then showed Vinnie the newspaper again.

'That's him,' Vinnie said automatically. 'Heard him speak the Polish and everything.'

'Forget the kid,' Garvie said. 'Did the police ask you about the man?'

Vinnie shrugged, drank watchfully.

Garvie said to Zuzana, 'I bet they didn't. Not after he failed to identify Pyotor. Not if that moron Dowell was questioning him.'

To Vinnie, he said, 'You said you recognized the man. How?'

'Seen him,' Vinnie said promptly. 'Got the bleater up here, dragging him along. Didn't know whether to gut him or fly him home.'

'Yes, but how can you be sure it was *that* man?'

Vinnie laughed. 'Oh, I know him,' he said. 'Corner boy.'

'What do you mean?'

'Corner boy,' Vinnie repeated loudly, as if Garvie were deaf. 'Up the corner by Bulwarks.'

'You'd seen him before? On Bulwarks Lane?'

'Corner there by the rag-rag shop.'

'By Jamal's?'

'That's the fubber.'

'You sure?'

Vinnie looked astonished to be doubted. 'Corner boy. Hanging round the corner. Seen him with the rag-man, old guy, shouting his tits off.'

'You saw him arguing with Jamal?'

'Stuck it to him proper.'

'That's interesting.'

Zuzana said, 'Did you see him with anyone else there? With Pyotor, Vinnie? With the boy?'

Vinnie turned to her as if he'd only just noticed she was there. His mouth fell open. There was a long pause. 'That's it,' he said in a voice of wonder, as if waking from years of sleep. 'I seen him too. Up there. The two of them. I see him give the kid a slap. Bang. I knew I did. I forgot. The same kid. Bang it went. But I forgot.' He put the can to his mouth and held it there without drinking, and after a while they realized he was weeping.

Garvie put down the last of the cans and a big bottle of juice. 'You'll find it'll take away the after-taste, Vinnie,' he said.

They left him there and walked back down the access road to the hole in the fence. The wind had picked up. The moon held on to a cloud, and let it go, and wrapped itself in another, lightly, like a streaming veil.

'Too late for Abdul,' Garvie said. 'We'll have to walk.'

'I can walk,' she said.

33

They found the track through the scrub and went along it as far as the country road, and walked in silence between fields tarnished silver in the moonlight, past the sewage plant, bland and silent, and on towards Limekilns, the only sound the occasional whine and drone of late cars on the ring road up ahead. They went through the underpass into the streets of Strawberry Hill beyond. Occasionally Garvie glanced at her, but her face was always closed.

At last she spoke. 'Do you remember . . . ?' she began.

Garvie nodded. 'Zbigniew told you Pyotor came back one evening with a slap mark across his face.'

'He thought it was another boy did it. But it was Magee. Pyotor and Magee had met before. Outside Jamal's.'

They walked down Cobham Road, Strawberry Hill's main drag, across Town Road, into Five Mile, and along Pollard Way until they reached the corner of Franks Road which doglegged down to the Bulwarks Lane shops. There was no one about, and they stood there in the silence.

'One thing before you go,' Garvie said. 'What

do you hear about Magee? What do Polish people say?'

'He is a racist. Zbigniew and Bogdana are sure he is the one broke into Stanislaw's shop. They have talked to Polish friends in the city where he lived before who say he has done things.'

'What things?'

'Things that were not reported to the police.'

'Like what?'

'They say he broke into a shop called the *Polskie* Delikatesy. The man who owns it, Janusz, was in hospital for three weeks. And a shop called *Magdalenka*, they say he robbed that too.'

'He was a burglar. That's the sort of stuff he did.'

'Always against Polish shops.'

'Anything else?'

'Something very bad too, I think. A big robbery. Not a corner shop. Someone died.'

'Killed? Someone got shot?'

'I think so. I don't know exactly. Dana said people were scared to talk. He is a frightening person. It is not easy to speak.'

Garvie nodded. 'Listen, Zuza, can you find out more? About the person who got killed.'

'I will talk to Dana again.'

'You'll have to do it quick, though. Time's running out on the whole Magee-in-prison thing.'

'They will release him?'

'Twelve noon tomorrow.'

'All right.'

'Give me a ding soon as.'

'I will do it.' She was looking at him curiously, smiling.

'What?'

'You called me Zuza.'

He hesitated, shrugged.

'Only Alex does that.'

'Yeah, well.' He shoved his hands into his pockets. 'Just quicker. Told you before. Don't like to waste time.'

Though her face was hidden in shadow he thought he saw her smile again. Turning from him, she crossed into Franks Road and disappeared round the corner. For a moment he stood there. Then, instead of going on towards the Driftway, he followed her down Franks Road as far as the corner and stood there fascinated, watching her recede, her figure brightening as she passed under a streetlamp, darkening again beyond, walking so lightly she seemed disconnected from the pavement, as if she existed alone in a sharper, more graceful dimension, diminishing gradually, and as he watched her go he couldn't help thinking of the sound of her voice, still in his ears, that slow Polish sound full of air, and of the air inside her mouth, and of her mouth itself, wide and curving, her lips stretching as she smiled at him. By now she was almost at Bulwarks Lane, only a short distance from her flat behind Jamal's, and he was just turning to go when he saw her reach the road and turn the wrong way.

He frowned. Hesitating a moment, he set off after her.

By the time he reached Bulwarks Lane she'd crossed the road and was walking past the betting shop, and after a moment she turned into John's Street. He jogged down the deserted road after her, and reached the corner of John's just in time to see her cross the road again and go into O'Malley's.

He looked at his watch: half past one. He stood there for a moment, thinking. He went along the street until he was opposite the bar, but all the blinds were down, and he backed off as far as the bus stop and sat down to wait.

It took half an hour. O'Malley's door opened and she came out. Garvie stood behind the shelter but she didn't even look in his direction; she was walking fast, head down, her face strangely expressionless, not guarded but as if she was lost in thought, and she went past him into Bulwarks Lane and turned towards Jamal's.

When she'd gone Garvie stepped out from behind the shelter and stood in the road looking at O'Malley's thoughtfully. And as he looked at it, the door opened again and Blinkie came out. He was on his own. He took two steps into the street and saw Garvie, and stopped. He was wearing a yellow tracksuit and bright blue Zanotti sneakers with gold zips up the sides, and a pink-and-green candy-striped baseball cap branded Nogzilla, and big black shades, and he stood there a moment looking at Garvie, making all his usual twitchy movements, tugging at the groin of his appalling tracksuit, shifting his weight from foot to foot, nodding to himself, his face flickering. He looked down the deserted street, and turned and looked the other way, and grinned. Then he skanked across the road, all the bling hanging off him clicking as he moved. Garvie stayed where he was. Blinkie came all the way up to him and stopped. Garvie kept his eyes on him.

Blinkie peered all round, grinning, and finally put his face into Garvie's. 'You again,' he said. 'I like that. I like fun.'

'Yeah. You said that before. But you don't have your playmates with you.'

Blinkie waggled his head from side to side. He said, 'Know why I like fun?'

Garvie shook his head.

Blinkie's teeth flashed gold. He pushed his face closer.

He said in a whisper, ''Cause they're all scared of me.'

Garvie turned his head to face him.

'All of them?' he said quietly.

They stood close, looking at each other. For a moment Blinkie looked sad. Then he began to laugh. He reeled sideways, laughing. He bent double, and Garvie slowly turned and walked away, leaving him there.

He waited until he was in Old Ditch Road before he made the call.

'Alex,' he said. 'Alex, mate. Give me a ding.'

He glanced back towards Bulwarks Lane. The street was empty, silent, hollow-sounding in the night. He walked on towards Eastwick Gardens.

34

'You seem tired this morning,' Garvie's mother said.

She stood in his doorway watching him get dressed.

After a while Garvie said, 'Yeah.'

'But you went to bed early, you said.'

Garvie went wearily round his room until he found his other shoe.

'Yeah,' he said. Slowly he began to put the shoe on.

'Why so tired then? I'm wondering.'

He finished putting on the shoe and rested.

'Must be all that revision I did,' he said at last.

His mother's face showed the strain of trying to suppress her natural suspicions. 'OK, then. And what you got today?'

'Maths revision class.'

'Sounds good.'

'Got some frees first, but I'm going in early, get some swotting done in the library.'

She seemed to consider this. 'Swotting,' she said at last, with deliberate emphasis. 'Library. Mmm-hmm.' She made a noise like she was tasting something unexpectedly good.

'What?'

'Just, these are words I've never heard you use before all your life.'

Garvie stood and hoisted his bag. He said, 'Well, get used to them, baby. I'm going to prove to you I can pass an exam or two if I put my mind to it.'

He kissed her on the cheek as he drifted past. 'Three,' she called after him. 'Two is no good. You have to pass three.'

'Whatever,' she heard him say. Then the shutting of the door.

Singh stood to attention in the chief constable's empty office, waiting. It was a spacious office on the first floor looking out across the open-plan Administration department through a large plate-glass window. A vast desk occupied one wall, a sleek, expensive slab of highly polished wood inlaid with green leather. On the opposite wall hung a portrait of the chief constable himself, his narrow face colour-less against the rich black fabric of his uniform, the bright splendour of its gold paraphernalia. There was a gleam in his eye no one would mistake for humour. His almost lipless mouth was set to endure in the midst of terrible times.

Singh had received the summons to the chief's office only a few minutes earlier. As the chief's PA had explained, the chief was on his way back from the offices of the city mayor, and had telephoned from his car to say he wanted to see Singh immedi-ately on arrival.

Singh thought about the chief's famed viciousness to officers who had failed in their duty. Singh himself had suffered a duties downgrade, of course, but there were far worse punishments: transfer, suspension, discharge, even prosecution. He thought of the headlines on hoardings he'd seen as he drove into work that morning: *Police Beat My Son! Cop Horror! Injustice!* Photographs of Jamal's ruined shop, the bags of toys found in his lock-up and Khalid's ripely bruised face had been appearing on internet sites since the night before. Dowell had been forced to host an impromptu press conference to explain certain 'unfortunate occurrences' in the police investigation. Singh guessed that the mayor had been asking the chief awkward questions.

He did not move as he thought these things. He remained standing to attention, listening to the silence in Admin beyond, as if, like him, everyone else was waiting for the chief to return, to hear what he would say.

As he stood there in the silence his phone rang. Startled, he looked at it, failed to recognize the number and after a moment's hesitation answered it in a low and wary voice.

'Singh here.'

'Dude! I'm on my way. But, just so you know, I've got to be really quick this time, so no small talk, OK?'

'Garvie?'

'I'll be there in, like, five. Can you meet me

this time, save me having to bust through the lobby?'

Singh was no longer standing to attention. He hunched over his phone, cupping his mouth with his hand, whispering. 'Garvie, listen to me, this is not a convenient time.'

'Don't I know it. If I'm not in my maths revision class in an hour my mother's going to get a buzz from that bitch Perkins.'

Singh peered anxiously through the office window for any sign of the chief. 'Not convenient for me, I mean,' he hissed.

'Yeah. But I've got some information. And I think you're going to like it.'

'Garvie, listen—'

'I've found the link between Magee and Pyotor.'

Now Singh hesitated. 'Are you sure?'

'Nailed on, man. Magee was seen with Pyotor up by Jamal's a few days before Pyotor got shot.'

'By who?' he said at last.

'Vinnie.'

'Vinnie? The wino?'

'And old man Jamal. He saw Magee cuffing the kid. Some sort of argy-bargy. It's the link you've been looking for.'

As he stood listening, Singh caught the curtain-swishy sound of elevator doors opening on the far side of the open-plan.

'I have to go,' he said. 'Do not come here,' he added.

'I might have more by the time I get to you. I've got feelers out with a Polish contact of mine. Like I say, I'll see you in a tick.'

Singh was dimly aware of a long-coated figure approaching across the open-plan.

'Stay away from me,' he hissed into the phone. 'Do not come anywhere near the building.'

He switched off his phone and pushed it into his pocket as the office door opened and the chief walked in. He stood to attention again, feeling a bead of sweat squeeze out of his turban and trickle down his forehead.

The chief glanced at him without expression, almost without recognition, and, taking off his coat, went behind his desk and began to take papers out of his briefcase. Singh noticed that he had left the office door wide open. There was a listening silence from Admin beyond.

After a few minutes, without looking up, the chief said, 'I'm sure you're going to give me the reasons for this fiasco.'

Singh began to speak. In a low voice he described Khalid's suspicious refusal to divulge the contents of his unit at the lock-up; he drew attention to the rumours that Khalid was involved in the drug trade; he explained how he had attempted to calm Khalid down before Khalid had returned to detention, where he had attempted to break out of the building; and he was just beginning to talk about the perhaps over-enthusiastic apprehension of Khalid by the anti-terrorism squad when the chief begin to speak, and he instantly fell silent.

'The problem is not that our security forces are too zealous,' the chief said in his flat, even voice. 'It is that your supposition about the contents of his lock-up was wrong, and that you compounded this mistake by allowing a situation to develop during and after your interview with the suspect. You lost control.'

Singh swallowed and stiffened his posture.

'Sir.'

Slowly the chief stood and came around his desk.

'And that you have created the opportunity for the suspect to bring a lawsuit against the force.'

'Sir.'

'And that you have handed Magee's lawyers all the argument they need to secure his immediate release.'

'Sir.'

'And that you have enabled the media to attack our work.'

'Sir.'

'And that you have made a mistake greater than all these in publically bringing the reputation of the force into disrepute. About which the city mayor has just been questioning me.'

Singh said nothing to that. There was no need, and, besides, he did not feel able to speak.

The chief came across the room until he stood directly in front of him, his face a few centimetres from Singh's.

'I'd be glad to know how you think I should respond to these mistakes of yours.'

For a moment he continued to stare into Singh's face, then at last turned away. And – without knowing how – Singh found himself suddenly speaking.

'Sir?'

'Yes?' There was a faint trace of surprise in the chief's voice.

'Let me interview Magee.'

There was a long pause, and when the chief spoke again his tone was incredulous.

'After your failure with Khalid Baloch, you think you are the appropriate person to interview our chief suspect?'

'Yes, sir.'

'You are aware that he is being released within the hour, that this is our last opportunity to make progress?'

'Yes, sir.'

'And you think you are better suited to this than, for instance, Detective Inspector Dowell?'

Singh swallowed. 'Yes, sir.'

'Why?'

'I have new information. Just come to me.'

'What information?'

'We have a witness who saw Magee with Pyotor in the days before the shooting. It's the link we've been looking for.'

The chief said nothing to this. Singh went on: 'Magee doesn't know we have this information. If

243

I can speak to him I think I can use it to good effect.'

For a long time the chief looked at Singh as if he couldn't decide whether to call for security or tell him to step outside and kill himself.

'Then do it,' he said at last. 'And let us both think of this as your very last chance.'

He sat down at his desk and began to read a report.

Singh thanked him but received no further response, and after a moment he went from the room and quickly through Admin, talking already on his phone.

35

In the monitoring station for 'Interview Room 2', down in the basement of the building, Singh was met by Sergeant Hingley, a young policewoman with a blonde pony-tail and curt features.

'Suspect's in place, sir,' she said. 'We're system-ready.'

Singh nodded.

Hingley said, 'Message from CC. The lawyers are due to arrive any moment. They'll keep them there as long as possible.'

Singh looked at his watch, nodded again. 'When they arrive here,' he said, 'please do your best to delay them further. Every minute counts.'

'Sir.'

Sergeant Hingley sat at the monitoring board, put on headphones and began to tap instructions on a laptop keypad. Adjusting his uniform, checking the alignment of his turban, Singh walked rapidly to the door at the end with the red light above it. The light changed to green, he opened it and went through and the door swung shut behind him.

On the nine screens set into the monitoring-station wall multiple images appeared of another room in which a man sat alone at a square grey table, seen from different angles. He was a tall, well-built man, trim and handsome, with wet-looking black hair combed back from his face, wearing a tight white T-shirt and blue jeans with a broad leather belt. There was a tattoo on his right forearm: a red dragon coiled into a spiral. As the door in the back of the room opened and Detective Inspector Singh appeared, he turned his head with a look of surprise and watched as Singh crossed the room and took a seat on the other side of the table.

The man sneered, his full lips curling. When he spoke his voice was harsh, made harsher still by the poor transmission of sound by the monitoring-room speakers.

'Last time I looked, you weren't my lawyer.'

'Detective Inspector Singh.'

'I remember you, Sikh.'

Settled in his chair, Singh put in an earpiece and spoke impassively into a microphone on the table. 'With interviewee Martin Magee. Eleven fifteen. No other personnel present.'

From an envelope he took three photographs of Pyotor Gimpel and slid them one by one across the desk. And finally he looked at Magee, who sneered again.

Location: high-security interview room, Cornwallis Police Centre, East Wing: large, nearly empty.
Interviewer: Detective Inspector Singh: tense, quiet.
Interviewee: Martin Magee: handsome, sneery.

DI SINGH: You know who this is. How many times had you met him before the night of the eighth?

MARTIN MAGEE: You obviously haven't been on the planet long. Do you want to confer with your colleagues and have another go?

[*Silence*]

MARTIN MAGEE: You're out of your depth so I'll give you a free one. I'd never met the kid. And I've told you all before, and you all know it. End of. Now, when's my lawyer get here?

DI SINGH [*into the microphone*]: Concluding the interview with Martin Magee. Eleven seventeen.

MARTIN MAGEE [*laughs in bewildered fashion*]: Remarkable.

DI SINGH [*retrieving photographs and putting them back into their envelope*]

MARTIN MAGEE: Last time I'll see you I expect, so I'll say goodbye.

DI SINGH [*into the microphone*]: Confirmation for Legal. Case ongoing on the basis of new witness statements. Bail denied.

MARTIN MAGEE [*pause*]: You're full of shit.

DI SINGH: As you say, Martin, this might be the last time I see you, at least outside court, so goodbye. We have new witness statements confirming that you met Pyotor Gimpel several times before the night of the eighth. You've offered no explanation so new charges will now be put in place and we'll proceed to trial.

Our legal department will inform your lawyer. Wait here. I'll get someone to escort you back to your cell.

MARTIN MAGEE: Witness! That crackerjack on the estate's off the scale.

DI SINGH: Yes, he is. But he's not our witness. Our witness is Jamal Baloch, who has the store in Bulwarks Lane. I'll leave you now.

MARTIN MAGEE: What are you talking about? Jamal Baloch?

DI SINGH: He remembers you well. Also remembers you talking to Pyotor Gimpel a few days prior to the twenty-second. And striking him. His testimony will feature in the trial. You'll have time before then to decide how to respond in court.

MARTIN MAGEE: This is . . . Wait. You don't go anywhere till you've explained what you're on about.

DI SINGH: You want me to stay? [*returning to the interview table*] Detective Inspector Singh, resuming the interview with Martin Magee. Eleven twenty-one.

MARTIN MAGEE: You're telling me that kid outside Jamal's, the kid I slapped, was the same one as in the lock-up? The Gimpel boy?

DI SINGH: Yes. The boy you said you'd never seen before.

MARTIN MAGEE: Yeah, well. [*Pause*] It's news to me, right?

DI SINGH: So, you don't deny it?

MARTIN MAGEE: No, but—

DI SINGH: Previously you testified under oath that you had never even seen Pyotor. Now you say you met him just a few days before he was shot. This is extraordinary, is it not? I think a jury will find it extraordinary.

MARTIN MAGEE: You're not listening. I had no idea it was the same kid.

DI SINGH: Really?

MARTIN MAGEE: Well, why the hell would I?

DI SINGH: According to Jamal, you acted as if you knew him.

MARTIN MAGEE: It's a lie. Maybe I'd seen him hanging round Jamal's, I don't know. Maybe I'd seen him, like, once or twice. That's all. There's nothing else in it.

DI SINGH: So why did you strike him?

MARTIN MAGEE: Don't get yourself worked up, Sikh.

DI SINGH: Answer the question. Why?

MARTIN MAGEE: I'm trying to remember what happened, all right? [*Silence*] All right. It's coming back to me. This kid, this kid I slapped, I saw him a few times up there, bothering people. Acting weird, right? That one time he comes out of the shop, comes up to me, says something like 'Don't want you here, don't like you.' Some shit like that. Unbelievable. I just give him a slap and he went away again. Screw loose, that's what I thought.

DI SINGH: 'Don't want you here?' Why did he say that to you?

MARTIN MAGEE [*shrugging*]: Screw loose, like I say.

DI SINGH: It sounds like the sort of thing you would say to him.

MARTIN MAGEE: I told you, I didn't know who the kid was. He just came up to me.

DI SINGH: You heard him speak. So you knew he was foreign.

MARTIN MAGEE: I knew he was a weirdo.

DI SINGH: You knew he was foreign and it enraged you because you are a racist.

MARTIN MAGEE: Not that again. I'm no racist.

DI SINGH: You hold racist views.

MARTIN MAGEE: My views are my own.

DI SINGH: 'Don't like you.' Why did he say that? He knew who you were. He must have seen you before, at Jamal's.

MARTIN MAGEE: I've never been in Jamal's in my life. I go to Bulwarks Lane all the time, to the newsagent's there, pick up stuff. I live here! I use the pavements. I breathe the air. You going to charge me with that?

[*Silence*]

MARTIN MAGEE: Listen, you've got this all wrong. I'm starting to get the picture now. Yeah. You got nothing. Like all this racist shit. Just lies from people who don't know any better. So I'd seen the kid before? Yeah, if this Jamal wants to say so. I didn't make the connection, but

250

OK. I must have seen him once or twice in the street. So what? Means nothing. Truth is, I didn't recognize him at the lock-up lying there covered in blood. Why would I? It was a shock to see anyone there, let alone a kid in his school uniform. I've told you all this before. I went in, I saw the kid, I heard you coming, and I cleared off. I didn't hang about going, *Oh, I wonder who this is, he seems a bit familiar, do I recognize him from somewhere?* If that's what you think you must be mental. No jury'll take notice of that shit. You got nothing at all.

DI SINGH [*pause*]: I put it to you that you were enraged by Pyotor's behaviour outside Jamal's and decided to teach him a lesson.

MARTIN MAGEE: I taught him a lesson by giving him a slap. He wasn't worth no more.

DI SINGH: I put it to you that you were shocked and humiliated to be spoken to like that by someone you assumed was an immigrant.

MARTIN MAGEE: Didn't surprise me at all.

DI SINGH: That you made a plan to punish the boy.

MARTIN MAGEE: What plan?

DI SINGH: That you lured him to the estate on the night of the eighth.

MARTIN MAGEE: What? How?

DI SINGH: And that you lost your temper and killed him.

MARTIN MAGEE [*laughing*]: With what? All this is unravelling now, isn't it? You're just pissing in the wind.

[*Silence*]

MARTIN MAGEE: Listen, if this is all you've got, you got a problem and you know it. Soon as my lawyer gets here he's going to take care of it.

DI SINGH: This conversation isn't over. [*Suddenly silent; hand up to his earpiece, listening*]

MARTIN MAGEE: I think it is. You've run out of time and ideas. You got nothing left at all. I'll see you on the streets, Sikh.

Sergeant Hingley's voice continued to come through Singh's earpiece. 'Sir,' she was saying, 'you wanted me to let you know when the lawyer arrived. He reached the centre fifteen minutes ago, and CC has just called to say they can't hold him any longer. Security's escorting him over. He'll be here any moment. In fact, I think this is them coming in now.'

Magee leaned back in his chair, his feet up on the desk, watching Singh. He began to laugh.

'Thing is,' he said, 'I'm innocent. That's what you don't get.'

Ignoring him, Singh picked up his envelope of photographs and spoke in a brief murmur into his microphone: 'Detective Inspector Singh, concluding the interview with Martin Magee. Eleven forty-nine.'

Magee's face shone.

'Think I'm a racist? Just lies. Think I'd kill a kid? I love kids. Another thing—' he stopped smiling, leaned towards Singh and lowered his voice – 'I ever meet you again on the street and it's fair and proper, the outcome'll be different. You listening?'

'No,' Singh said.

He got up and Magee laughed again. 'I better get ready to meet my lawyer then.'

As if on cue, the door to the interrogation room swung open and Magee turned, chuckling. His face fell.

'Who the fuck's this?' he said.

'It's not Anton Schnopper, is it?' Garvie said, standing in the doorway. ''Cause Toni's dead.'

Sergeant Hingley appeared behind Garvie, flustered. 'Sorry, sir,' she said. 'I thought it was the lawyer and I buzzed him in, and—'

'Love kids, do you?' Garvie said. 'You left Toni dead at the furrier's. March seventeenth, five years ago. He was fifteen. Also Polish.'

Magee's face was suddenly purple. His voice was a growl. 'What the—'

'Two witnesses, but both refused to sign their statements. It never came to trial. Thing is, Mart, they're talking now.'

Magee was on his feet. 'Who the—'

'What did they see scared them so much? Toni fell out of a window, you said. He also fell through it. At high speed. Do you want to hear more?'

There was a crash as the table overturned, and Magee had nearly reached Garvie before Singh caught him in a rugby tackle. There was a cry – 'I'll fucking *kill you*!' – then they went down together in a loud heap, Magee screaming, and Sergeant Hingley leaped forward, shouting for order. There was echoing chaos in the bare room, and to make it worse at that moment three other men ran in suddenly through the doorway, a man in a suit and two police personnel, also bellowing for order, and hurled themselves into the struggle.

The noise grew louder and more chaotic.

And in all this uproar there was only one person who remained calm: Garvie Smith, standing apart and watching it all thoughtfully.

36

In the interrogation room, quiet now with the empty quietness that comes, like embarrassment, after loud noises, Detective Inspector Singh and Garvie Smith sat on opposite sides of the metal table, still lying overturned on the floor. Escorted by the security personnel, Magee had been taken away by his lawyer, who was furiously threatening to bring a case against the City Squad for gross dereliction of their legal obligations to safeguard detainees. Sergeant Hingley remained in the monitoring room. She had told Singh that Detective Inspector Dowell and the chief were on their way over and had asked that he stay in place until they arrived. She had not said anything to Garvie. She had given him a look.

Several minutes passed in silence.

Singh said quietly, 'Why is it that mayhem accompanies you wherever you go?'

'It was important information,' Garvie said. 'I just got it from my Polish contact. Thought you should know.'

'The investigation's compromised. Prosecution risks being invalidated by police incompetence and illegality. Magee has gone free. His rights have been violated. What have you to say?'

'It's a bummer.'

'I will be suspended,' Singh said. 'Or perhaps even expelled from the force.'

'Yeah.'

'It doesn't worry you. Why would it? You don't even think of yourself. Do you understand what you've done? If what you just said is true, Magee's a killer who specializes in hurting children, and you've given him reason to hold a grudge against you.'

Garvie said nothing.

'Well?' Singh said.

Garvie still said nothing.

Singh shouted suddenly: 'I trusted you and you let me down! What have you got to say to that?'

Garvie finally lifted his head. 'I've been stupid.'

Singh rolled his eyes. 'That's a minimal assessment of what you've been.'

'Vinnie as good as told me and I didn't listen.'

Singh stared at him dumbly. 'What?' he said at last. 'What has Vinnie got to do with any of this?'

'What he said was, he saw them going down the access road towards the lock-up.'

'So?'

'They were going down the road all right. But they weren't going towards the lock-up.'

'What do you mean?'

'They were going away from the warehouse. Obvious, isn't it?'

If Singh was going to reply he was prevented by the sound of footsteps in the monitoring station next door. He said nothing, but slowly stood and adjusted his turban. He straightened up until he was standing to attention and stared at the far wall of the bare room, waiting for Dowell and the chief to appear.

37

They went in silence up the stairs, the chief first, Singh next, Dowell last, and across the open-plan area towards the chief's office. All conversations in the Admin pods around them stopped. People put down their phones and stopped typing, and there was complete silence as they watched the three men go through. Before they reached his office, the chief stopped and turned, and Dowell went to stand at his side, and together they faced Singh, standing alone and comically upright in front of them, his back to the Admin staff watching it all in silence.

The chief waited a moment, then said quietly, 'This is as far as you go. It's far enough, don't you think?'

Unconsciously, Singh braced himself.

The chief held out his hand, palm up. 'Give me your badge.'

Singh took the wallet out of his pocket and handed it over, his hand trembling slightly, and the chief took it from him and handed it to Dowell.

'Sir,' Singh began, but the chief put up his hand.

'Take off your jacket,' he said in the same quiet voice.

The colour drained out of Singh's face. With

fumbling fingers he undid the buttons of his tunic. He had to struggle to remove his arms from the jacket, the epaulettes with their two silver pips crumpling, and the sleeves turning inside out, as he tugged himself free, and at last handed it over to the chief, who gave it to Dowell.

Singh stood there in his white shirt, looking more than half undressed. There was a long silence then in which he concentrated on maintaining his upright position, feeling all the time the pressure of the chief's eyes on his, and the eyes of Admin on his back.

'Now your turban,' the chief said, his voice so low it was almost a whisper.

Singh stood immobile. One of his legs began to shake. He couldn't stop it. He was aware of his trouser leg buckling in and out as he stood there.

'It is regulation police issue, and carries the insignia which you are no longer entitled to wear,' the chief said. 'Take it off and give it to me.'

With an almost crippling effort, Singh raised both arms and removed his turban. His hair, bunched into its *joora* knot, secured by its wooden comb, the *kangha*, felt loose and awkward on his head, as if it too felt the shame.

Handing over the turban, his hands shook so much he dropped it and had to bend down to pick it up, an act so suddenly difficult he felt he might faint before completing it. But he did not faint. He picked it up, and handed it to the chief, who at once, almost negligently, passed it to Dowell and, turning, went into his office and closed the door behind him.

Dowell had already turned away, heading for his own office.

Singh continued to stand to attention for a few moments more; then, with steps so jerky it seemed he might actually fall, he staggered away towards the staircase, followed by the silent stares of Admin.

38

A few days passed. The weather continued fine. If anything, it got better. The sun shone carelessly on the fields, the trees, the sewage plant, on East Field Industrial Estate, it shone without a thought on Five Mile, Old Ditch Road kiddies' playground and Bulwarks Lane, where Garvie Smith was walking slowly homeward, wishing he wasn't.

He took out his phone and dialled, and listened, as before, to the message. 'Alex, mate,' he said, 'what's the problem? You got to call me. Do it now.'

Smudge came out of the burger place, chewing.

'Turned out nice,' he said when he could. 'Going down Old Ditch Road later?'

Garvie shook his head.

'Still grounded?'

Garvie just sighed. He left Smudge and went on past Jamal's, open again but still boarded up, and past the entrance to the alley that led to Zuzana's flat, and on, more slowly still, across the road and down the street towards Flat 12 Eastwick Gardens, where Uncle Len would be waiting for him.

Uncle Len had moved into Eastwick Gardens for the duration of exam season. Partly this was the result of discussions between Uncle Len and personnel from the police legal department. Mainly, however, it was because Garvie's mother was more upset than Garvie had ever seen her before. He had done his best to explain things, but in truth it was a tricky gig. Although he hadn't actually missed an exam – a fact he had pointed out several times to both his mother and Uncle Len – it was inconveniently true that, on a regular school day, when he should have been in a maths revision class, he had been apprehended trespassing in a high-security zone at the police centre, where, it was alleged (without much opposition on his part) that he had, almost single-handedly, caused an extraordinary disturbance directly leading to the release of a major suspect in the Gimpel case and a substantial lawsuit being brought against the police service. If he wasn't solely to blame, it was only because he was a minor, and because a former member of the force, Detective Inspector Singh, apparently bore legal responsibility for his behaviour.

So it was not entirely strange that Garvie's mother was upset. But it was shocking. She had said hardly anything directly to Garvie. When she did speak she did not look at him; she turned away and muttered to the wall. Her eyes were wet, her face heavy with distress, and it seemed she no longer knew what to do with her hands, moving them about restlessly, putting them into the pockets of her nurse's uniform and taking them out again, rubbing them together, hugging herself, as if searching continuously for relief. Garvie didn't like remembering it, let alone seeing it. He went down the Driftway slowly, reluctantly reviewing the situation. His mother wasn't the only one upset. Uncle Len was as bad, perhaps worse. It was fortunate for Garvie that his uncle disliked Dowell so much, or he might have followed up the man's complaints of Garvie's 'constant interference in police matters' by really getting the nark on. He was narked enough as it was. Garvie had been forced to admit his persistent interest in the investigation into Pyotor Gimpel's death, and to promise that it would cease immediately.

Garvie let himself into the flats and went slowly up the stairs to the top floor. 'I'm stupid,' he said to the stairwell. 'As stupid as Smudge, or almost. I must have forgotten how to think.'

Standing at the door to number 12, key in hand, he heard voices inside the apartment and paused for a moment. Listening to the murmured conversation beyond the door, he heard a tone he recognized at once, the tone of despair and disapproval that characterized most of the conversations between his mother and Uncle Len in the last few days.

By now he knew the script. His mother would be telling Uncle Len how shameful it was to think that sixteen years of bringing him up had led to this, and Uncle Len would be telling her that it wasn't too late to enforce some purpose and discipline in Garvie's life.

Sighing, he let himself into the flat, and the

conversation stopped and was replaced by awkward silence. This too was familiar, a distressed and accusing hush. He dumped his jacket under the clothes pegs and went into the front room. In one of the armchairs was his mother. In the other was . . . Singh.

Garvie stood and stared.

'Sit down, Garvie,' his mother said.

It was a shock to see Singh out of uniform. The man sat upright and unsmiling in the Smiths' second-best armchair, wearing an ugly brown suit, floral tie and beige turban, looking small and out of place. He said nothing. Garvie didn't say anything either; he sat and waited.

'Garvie,' his mother said, 'the inspector's been kind enough to come and give us some news.'

Singh cleared his throat. 'Yes. As I was saying, I heard this morning that our legal team won't be seeking to prosecute after all.'

'OK.'

'You'll receive a youth caution, and a referral to the youth offending team.'

'OK.'

'They may decide to offer a rehabilitation programme.'

'All right.'

'The caution remains on your record but can only be accessed under certain circumstances.'

Garvie said nothing. He seemed mesmerized by Singh's brown suit. His mother gave him a look. He said, 'OK. Thanks.'

His mother said, 'Yes, thank you, inspector. We've been worried not knowing what would happen. This is a big relief. Garvie, is there anything you want to say?'

'No.' He sat quiet and still, waiting.

She nodded at him, unsmiling. 'It may be, inspector, that this had to happen for Garvie to realize where his priorities lie.'

Singh nodded, cleared his throat. 'Actually, there was something else I wanted to say before I go. Listen to me now, Garvie. It's possible there will be a new case brought against Martin Magee for his involvement in the death of Anton Schnopper. I expect that new witness statements are being prepared. But no arrest will be made until absolutely everything is in place. Until that time Magee's at liberty, on bail, subject to the usual monitoring. It's very important now that you absolutely stop involving yourself in this matter. Is that understood?'

His mother was looking at him.

'Yeah. OK.'

Singh got up and Garvie's mother put out her hand and Singh held it briefly.

'Thank you for everything,' she said.

He nodded.

'And good luck,' she added.

He turned without comment and went out of the flat, a small man in a borrowed-looking brown suit.

After he had gone Garvie and his mother sat together.

'Mum,' he said.

She didn't reply. She didn't look at him either.

'You called him "inspector". Does that mean he's still . . .'

She got up without answering and went out of the living room into her bedroom and closed the door behind her.

When Uncle Len arrived half an hour later Garvie was still sitting there, staring at his shoes. Without looking at Garvie, he went across to the sink and poured himself a glass of water. Then he came into the living room, sat opposite Garvie and unfolded the evening edition of the local paper.

He read out loud. 'Detective Inspector Singh, the officer accused of assaulting detainee Martin Magee, was today formally suspended without pay pending the result of a disciplinary enquiry into his conduct. City Squad is seeking a dishonourable discharge.'

Pausing, Uncle Len looked over the paper at Garvie. 'I'd like to know who put this out,' he said. 'It wasn't formally briefed. I'd like to ask that Dowell if he had anything to do with it.'

He glared at Garvie. 'And there are others,' he said, 'who have something to answer for, even if their names have been kept out of the paper.'

Garvie was silent. He hung his head.

'I never thought I'd see the day,' his uncle said, 'when your mother couldn't force herself to even talk to you.' He folded the paper. 'I hope this is the day you finally see sense,' he said. 'When you realize you have to stop all this nonsense and do the right thing.'

Garvie got to his feet.

'That's what it comes down to, Garvie,' his uncle said fiercely. 'Think about your responsibilities. Forget everything else. Do the right thing. You hear me?'

Garvie sighed, nodded. He turned and went towards his room.

At ten o'clock Uncle Len was watching the television, Garvie's mother had left for her shift, and Garvie was standing at the window in his room, thinking. His reflection stared back, as if silently interrogating him.

Do the right thing, his uncle had said.

A memory came to him, bright and noisy like all his memories, with the exact shapes of things and words in their right order. He was sitting on the fallen trunk of a tree among the bushes at the side of Top Pitch, smoking a Benson & Hedges and waiting for Pyotor, sitting cross-legged on the ground, to finish his vector-notation problems. Sunbeams dappled the leaves and there was a hushed distant noise of traffic and uplifting bursts of birdsong.

It was the fourth or fifth time they'd met there. Each time was the same; Pyotor insisted on it. Garvie set him problems, Pyotor attempted them, Garvie 'marked' his answers. He called him *genialnym matematyk* or *słabe matematyk*, as appropriate.

Pyotor insisted on that too. Garvie wondered what name Pyotor had for him.

He heard himself say, 'Time's up,' and saw Pyotor stop writing at once at once, and he knew even before he looked that Pyotor had got the problems wrong; his workings had been too hasty, too messy.

Glancing at the paper, blowing out smoke, he sighed.

'*Słabe matematyk*,' he said. 'Vectors aren't actually hard, you know. It's just they've got two dimensions instead of one: magnitude and direction. That's all there is to it.'

Pyotor didn't say anything.

'What's this?' He put his finger on the vertical line of the diagram marked $\tilde{a}$. 'It's $\tilde{a}$ sub y. Not $\tilde{a}$ sub x. Sub x is the horizontal component. You know that. It's basic. Childish.'

Pyotor just blinked.

'And how do you find the magnitude of $\tilde{a}$ sub y?'

Again Pyotor made no reply.

'Opposite side to the angle, right? Basic trig. Sin is opposite over the hypotenuse. You know that too.'

Pyotor took off his glasses and slowly cleaned them and put them back on, and stared at Garvie expressionlessly.

'It's not hard,' Garvie repeated. 'You can do it. Why don't you do it? I don't get what's confusing you.'

Pyotor blinked and stared. 'It's different,' he said at last, in his thick, slow growl.

'Yeah. I just said. Two dimensions instead of one. It's different – but it's not hard.'

Pyotor suddenly began to breathe heavily. 'I don't like it, he said loudly. 'It's two things *at the same time.*'

'Yeah. Which makes it easier. 'Cause if it's in two dimensions you can break the problem down into two simpler problems before you put them back together again. Actually there's nothing different about it. It's normal. It's the sort of stuff we all do every day of the week.'

Pyotor sat there completely silent, unmoving. Then he did an extraordinary thing. He smiled.

Garvie was so surprised he forgot to smoke. He had never seen him smile before; he hadn't been aware that Pyotor could smile. It made him look suddenly old and cunning. He wasn't smiling at Garvie. He seemed to have forgotten Garvie was there. He put his paper in his school bag, got to his feet, picked up his violin case and turned to go.

'All right then,' Garvie said after him. 'I'm glad we got that sorted. I guess you'll be off now.'

Pyotor was already going between the bushes along the path that led to Top Pitch.

'See you then,' Garvie had said, but Pyotor hadn't replied.

Now Garvie stood by his window, thinking.

He thought about his responsibilities to others: to Pyotor, who had learned that you can do two simple things to make one complicated one; to Singh in his overlarge brown suit and beige turban; to his mother, who was so upset; to Uncle Len, who had told him to do the right thing.

His uncle was right. But which thing? Briefly his mind went through a series of interrelated problems, he saw the faces of Pyotor, Alex, his mother, Zuzana. Then he moved away from the window, fished his phone out of his bag and lay on his bed. Kept his voice low. It was all a case of breaking it down. It was a risk, he had to admit. But he was in too deep.

'Felix, mate. Yeah. Got a little job for you . . . Nah, said it before, simple for a boy of your abilities.'

39

'Not that way,' Garvie said. 'CCTV at the entrance, remember. Better round the side. There's a hole in the fence.'

Only Garvie had brought a torch. Briefly he thought how much better prepared Zuzana would have been. In darkness they waded through scrub in single file, Garvie leading, Felix next and Smudge at the back engaged in his own private battle with the vegetation growing inconveniently next to the path.

They reached the track and went down it to the fence where the hole was and waited a moment in the clearing for Smudge to pull brambles out of his hair and swear himself back to normal.

Before they went on, Garvie drew Felix's attention to the ground. 'Tyre marks all down the track. What do you reckon?'

'Van, looks like.'

Smudge said in a muttering sort of voice, 'Don't see why we couldn't come in a van. Could have saved me swallowing all these leaves. Don't understand why I'm carrying all the stuff neither.'

He hoicked the rucksack onto his shoulders again and caught up with the others as they went across the little ditch and through the hole in the fence, up the other side and out onto the access road that lay ahead of them pale as foil between shadows of buildings. They walked down it past the lock-up, past the spot where Vinnie liked to sleep, all the way to the warehouse at the far end, and stood for a moment looking up at it. It was the biggest building on the estate. Vast and rank, it loomed above them, twenty-metre-high brick walls smeared with the filth of ages, sprouting with weeds, dark and silent, its three rows of windows black to the black night sky.

'Looks like something in one of them horror jobs,' Smudge said. 'Got nothing in it but zombies probably.'

Garvie turned to Felix.

'You'd be surprised,' Felix said. 'Pays no one to make them look good. But you can still use them. Look.'

The double doors at the front were worn and patched, but the padlock shone with a newish gleam. Above the door was a burglar alarm.

'SECO,' Felix said. 'Said it before: not the best, but better than those SAFEWAYs down there. Doesn't look that old to me.'

Garvie said, 'Likely to go off in a high wind?'

Felix shrugged. 'Can't tell. Let's see what's round the back.'

He led them round the side of the building through deeper shadow and across lumpy banks of feral weeds until they reached the far corner, where a thin-framed fire escape zigzagged down the brick wall like a broken old spring. The tail end of a metal ladder hung down from the end of it, about three metres above the ground.

Garvie bent and fished something out of the weeds and stood there looking at it thoughtfully.

'What've you got there?' Smudge peered over his shoulder. 'Gardening sacks? Amazing what people'll chuck away. It's a new roll too.'

'Come on,' Felix said. 'Don't want to hang about. It's nearly two now.'

Smudge began to complain. 'I hate this bit. Can't someone else do it for a change?'

'No one else has your big bones, champ.'

Smudge plodded over and sank to his knees like a small, weary elephant and Felix straddled his shoulders. With Garvie's assistance, making a series of bass grunts, he rose wobbling under the fire escape.

'Keep still, Smudge.'

'I am still. It's my legs won't stop moving.'

At last Felix grabbed the lowest rung and with a quick squirming movement hoisted himself up and round onto the fire-escape base. He let down the ladder behind him and they went slowly up, Smudge commenting in a steady grumble on the height, age, width and mobility of the fire escape, until they reached the access door at the top and huddled there together on the narrow metal platform perched just below the roof.

'Are we going in, or what?'

'It's locked, you noddy. Pass me the rope.'

Smudge got it out of the bag and Felix weighed it in his hand for a second, the grapple hanging heavily on the end, and flipped it suddenly onto the flat roof above them. At the fourth go it snagged on the brick lip and he tested it.

'See you then,' he said, and ran lightly up the wall and pulled himself out of sight.

'Sometimes I think he's not really human,' Smudge said. 'No bones at all.'

Garvie went up after him, and then Smudge, hauled upwards, groaning and panting, spilled huffing at last onto the flat roof like a beached tuna. Garvie gave the torch to Felix and they went cautiously across the concrete, stopping every few paces to peer at one of the small skylights set in double rows along its length until they were almost at the other end.

'Here,' Felix said. 'See?'

They saw. The frame of the skylight was split in two round all four edges.

'It's been cut and put back. Neat job. Somebody knew what he was doing. Give us a hand.'

They lifted the frame, swung it to one side and put the glass down gently on the concrete of the roof. Garvie handed over the torch and Felix ducked through the gap and flashed the light around. He sat back up with an astonished look on his face.

'Well?' Smudge said. 'What's down there?'

Felix looked at him. 'You'll never guess.'

'Tell me it's not zombies.'

'Want to guess, Garv?'

'Fur coats,' Garvie said quietly.

Felix continued to look astonished. 'Jackpot, Sherlock. Must be a hundred grand's worth. Your long-fur fox, your rex rabbit, your blue mink – all sorts, looks like. Clever. Pick a spot no one'd think of. Make it secure. Ship them in and out when no one's looking. I like it. I like it even more now I know about it.' He looked at Garvie. 'But how the hell did you know about it?'

'Magee's a thief. He knows furs. He did a furrier's a few years back.'

Smudge frowned. 'All right. You think he was up here that night trying to knock off a few more. What's this got to do with the Gimp?'

'Magee likes working with kids. Done it before.'

Smudge's look of astonishment was so big he might have been miming it. 'You're telling us the Gimp was in on it?'

Garvie said nothing. Felix gave a low whistle. 'I get it. Look at the size of the skylight, Smudge. You think Magee could get through that himself?'

Smudge considered the skylight with narrowed eyes. 'The Gimp might have been small enough, but it don't look easy.'

Felix said, 'What was that you told us, Garv? He'd started going to gym class, right? His grandparents couldn't understand it.'

Smudge said, 'I don't understand it either. I mean, did the Gimp even know Magee, Garv?'

'Jamal says he saw them together outside his shop. Arguing. Maybe arguing about this.'

'They were working together?' Smudge gave a low whistle. 'Now that is a turn up. But why would the Gimp do it, though?'

'For a cut, of course,' Felix said.

Smudge considered this. He said, 'You're right. Personal gain every time. A boy like that, likes his games. You've got your new edition GTA coming out September, you've got your—'

'Wasn't that,' Garvie said.

'What was it then?'

There was a silence. Felix said, 'Wait. I remember now.' He clicked his fingers impatiently. 'What was that you said about his baby brother? Needs some sort of expensive operation done abroad.'

Garvie nodded.

'He was obsessive about it,' Felix said. 'He wanted that money to make the operation happen.'

Smudge whistled. 'The little scamp. The cheeky bugger. Now he's Robinson Hood all of a sudden.' He sat back amazed at himself. 'But,' he said after a moment, 'the Gimp! Was he really that sort of kid?'

Garvie said sharply, 'What sort of kid do you want him to be? He was a kid who stole a gun off Khalid.'

'Well, well,' Smudge said at last. 'Told you he was a weirdo. I got an instinct for these things.'

'Another thing about Magee,' Garvie said. 'He

liked working with kids 'cause he could treat them how he wanted. The last kid died too.'

They all thought about that.

'So what happened here?' Smudge asked. 'I mean, in the end nothing got nicked, did it? The coats are still down there.'

Garvie passed the torch to Felix. 'Lean down far as you can and tell us what you see, Felix.'

Felix poured himself into the hole, clung upside down to the skylight's rim on two feet and three fingers and swept the light round with his free hand.

'No bones at all,' Smudge commented. 'And funny little claws too, instead of fingers.'

'What am I looking for?' Felix called up.

'The girder under the roof. See anything?'

'Now I can. Marlow-Gecko, looks like.'

'What, a lizard?' Smudge said. 'A lizard up here? I thought they didn't like heights.'

'It's a type of rope,' Garvie said. 'Magee must have left it here. What else, Felix? What about the girder below? In the dust.'

There was a pause, then Felix's voice came up again. 'Oh yeah. Footprints. Going along. All the way along. And then . . .'

There was a silence. 'Then what?' Smudge called down.

Felix flipped himself lightly out of the skylight and sat down next to them. He squinted at Garvie sideways. 'Then they stop,' he said. 'There's just shuffle marks after that. And then the edge.'

They all considered this.

'Yeah, but,' Smudge said, 'what's it all *mean*?'

For a moment Garvie looked at him, thinking how fast Zuzana would have worked it out. He said, 'You know what they were up to, don't you, Felix? Talk us through it.'

Felix scratched his long nose; nodded. 'Straightforward enough. Get in through the sky-light. Grab the furs. Get out through the fire escape.'

'Hang on,' Smudge said. 'What do you mean, "Get out through the fire escape"? It's locked. We tried it.'

'It's a fire escape, Smudge. Key's on the inside, in a little red box next to the door. Once you're in you can get out. You're *meant* to get out.'

'All right. But what do you mean, "Grab the furs"? Slippy things like that slipping all over the place. Bulky, too. How many furs do you think you could carry down that old fire escape, Mr Boneless?'

'Obviously they had something to carry them in.'

'Like gardening sacks,' Garvie said. 'Magee runs a garden-clearance business on the side.'

Felix nodded. 'No one's carrying anything down the fire escape, Smudge. They'd bag them up here and lob them down. Collect them at the bottom.'

'All right. That's like . . . a plan. But what happened really?'

They both looked at Garvie. He said, 'Something

went wrong. You saw that, didn't you, Felix? What do you think happened?'

Felix puffed out his cheeks, blew. 'I reckon he let the kid through the skylight down onto the girder, and the kid goes along, nearly to the end, and then . . . I reckon he must of slipped.'

He looked at Garvie. Garvie nodded. 'And?'

Felix thought. 'The alarm. Either it was going off already, or he set it off when he fell.'

'And?'

Felix thought again. 'He panicked,' he said at last. 'Otherwise he could have carried on. It was two o'clock, wasn't it, just as the police change shifts. Classic manoeuvre.'

Garvie thought again how much faster Zuzana would have been working it out.

'And then?' he said, helpfully.

'They lost too much time with the kid scrabbling about at the end of the rope. The police were on their way. They had to pull out in a rush. They got the skylight back in place, but they must of been all over the shop. Magee left his rope behind, dropped the sacks at the bottom of the fire escape. Then they went down the access road to the lock-up. Where that vagrant saw them.'

'So Vinnie was telling the truth after all,' Smudge said. 'But why did they go in the lock-up?'

'Magee has a unit there,' Garvie said.

Felix said, 'Makes sense. They'd have opened it up on their way here so they could get the stuff in

279

quick before the police arrived. Very neat. They must have gone back to lock it up.' He looked at Garvie. 'And then . . . something else went wrong. For the Gimp anyway. Just before Plod turned up. Some sort of bother.'

Smudge said, 'You mean Magee went nuts with him 'cause of what happened up here.'

Garvie said, 'The last kid died too.'

'Talk about evil scumbag,' Felix said. 'And now they've let him out. He'll be doing a runner any day, I bet.'

Smudge nodded. 'Find some other kid to work his evil on.'

Garvie looked at his watch. 'Got to get back. Don't want to be missed. I only made it tonight 'cause Uncle Len got called out. Felix, give me a hand with the skylight.'

Ten minutes later they were walking back down the access road. The rain had held off, but the sky was creased with cloud like an old blanket. Garvie seemed lost in thought.

Smudge said conversationally, 'Had Alex on the blower today.'

Garvie gave a him a look.

'Banging on about Zuza. Bit one-track that boy, to be honest.'

Garvie hesitated. 'What did he say?'

'She's been acting funny.'

'Funny?'

'Yeah. Going off seeing other guys. He's been following her, see where she goes on her own. You know what he's like.'

Garvie said nothing to that. They went through the hole in the fence and across the ditch and entered the scrub on the far side, and began to push their way along the narrow path.

'Kept going on about Blinkie,' Smudge called. He spat something. 'I hate plants, don't you? Alex seems to think Zuza's got a thing for him.'

'A thing for Blinkie?' Garvie said sharply. 'Nonsense.'

'Don't misunderestimate the female psychology, Garv.'

He shouted back, 'I'm telling you, Smudge. It's not happening. All right?'

'Bit baffled myself, mate. But I don't know. I was chatting with her the other day. Though it was more like she was chatting with me, to be honest. I mean, she came up to me. Or at any rate I'd only just called her over, and—'

In the darkness Garvie stopped and turned, and Felix bumped into him, and Smudge bumped into Felix.

'Listen to me,' Garvie said angrily. 'It's *Alex* and Blinkie we ought to be worried about. Unless you want to see him dealing again. All that about her liking Blinkie is a-hundred-per-cent nonsense.'

'But Zuza said—'

'And stop calling her Zuza! She's not into Blinkie,

all right? What do you take her for? Listen. I know. All right? I know exactly what's going on. And what isn't going on.'

After he stopped shouting there was a shuffling in the bushes, then silence. Garvie stood there a moment, then turned and went on rapidly until he reached the old road on the other side, and headed down it, Smudge and Felix following a little way behind, exchanging looks as they went.

At the underpass they caught him up.

With the air of someone deliberately changing the subject, Felix said, 'I've been thinking, Garv. About the Gimp.'

'What about him?'

'How funny it is, him turning out to be a thief. I mean, it's not for everyone.'

'No, Felix. Only a chosen few.'

Felix relaxed and the three of them walked on a little way side by side. 'I'm not sure he was thinking of turning pro, though,' Garvie added.

Felix nodded. 'You're right. Probably would have been just a one-off. I mean, obviously it didn't work out that well. And besides—'

Garvie came to a sudden standstill.

'Garv?'

Garvie stared at him fiercely. 'What did you just say?'

Felix looked nervous. 'Nothing. Just that it didn't work out so well for the Gimp.'

'No, the other bit.'

'Nothing, Garv. I just said it was probably a one-off.'

Garvie said nothing. Stared at him in disgust.

'Smudge,' Felix said out of the corner of his mouth, 'this is your fault; you put him in a bad mood with that stuff about Zuza.'

'Not my fault I can't shake her off,' Smudge grumbled.

'It's nothing to do with Smudge. Or Zuza. Nothing to do with you, Felix. It's me.'

'What about you?'

Garvie shook his head in despair. He groaned. 'I've been so stupid. It's as if I've forgotten how to think.'

And without saying more he left, and they watched him striding down Bulwarks Lane. As he went he took out his phone, and they heard him say, 'Alex? Alex, mate? Call me soon as you get this. *Please.*' And then he was gone.

40

It continued fine, wide blue skies and golden light. With its warmth it bathed Five Mile, the estate, the dusty claustrophobic buildings of Marsh, it soaked into the thick margin of foliage that bordered Top Pitch, chestnut and elm trees, elder and brambles growing in tangled green profusion, a bushy warren of wild flowers, sun spots, purple shadows and smokers' dens.

'Why do we meet here?' Zuzana asked, looking round. 'Hidden away like this?'

Leaning against an elm tree, Garvie shrugged; blew smoke upwards. 'No reason. I was just taking time off after ICT.'

'You have managed to sit an exam?'

'I like to do it once in a while.'

She nodded. 'What is it you want to ask me?'

He hesitated, stubbing out his cigarette.

'I have your message about the warehouse,' she said. 'So now we know the bad thing that Pyotor was going to confess. But still there are questions.'

'There are always questions. But that's not what I want to ask you about.'

'No? What then?'

She sat on a fallen trunk looking at him, legs

crossed, as if posing for a photoshoot, natural but extraordinary in black jeans and white T-shirt, with spangles of sunlight in her loosely tousled hair. When she shifted weight everything moved slightly inside her clothes from her hips to her shoulders. He looked away before he spoke.

'I've been calling Alex.'

She just looked at him.

'I've called him like twenty times. No reply. Nothing. What's going on?'

There was a long silence.

'Why do we talk about Alex?'

'We need to, that's why.'

When he turned back to her, she was watching him carefully, her face tense, her eyes unnaturally bright.

'Give me a cigarette,' she said at last.

For a while she sat sipping it, puffing smoke into the shadows.

'Alex is strange,' she said. 'You must not tell him I told you so. He is jealous.'

Garvie nodded.

'Sometimes he is even following me, finding out where I go, who I see. Although,' she added, giving Garvie a look, 'he would not find me here.'

Garvie cleared his throat. 'That's not my point. I don't want to know any of that. I want to know what's going down between him and Blinkie.'

She flinched so hard she nearly dropped her cigarette. 'Blinkie? I don't know what you mean.'

'I think you do.'

'There is nothing any more between Alex and Blinkie.'

'It doesn't do any good, protecting him,' Garvie said.

'I do not protect him.'

'Blinkie goes round to see him.'

'He does not.'

'I've seen it myself.'

She was looking at him so intently, so fiercely, as if she saw inside his mind and knew what he was thinking, and he stood there hoping she wouldn't say what he knew she was going to say. Then she said it.

'He does not come to see Alex,' she said.

'No?'

'No. He comes to see *me*.'

Garvie just stared. She sat trembling, looking back at him defiantly.

'I don't believe it,' he murmured half-heartedly.

She said angrily, 'Why should I not see him? I see who I like. If I want to talk to him, I talk to him. I am for myself, I told you before. Yes,' she said, 'I have seen him at my flat. I have seen him—' she gave Garvie a long stare – 'in O'Malley's bar. *Ach!*' She threw her cigarette into the leaves. 'Alex is too jealous. I know how that ends, it has happened to me before.' For a moment she seemed to struggle to speak. 'Yes. You don't care. Last year, where I lived, it happened. I am not someone's possession; I will see who I want to see.' Her eyes shone in the shadows. 'You think that is wrong?'

'No.' He hesitated. 'But, Blinkie . . .'

'What about him? I think he is funny. He is not always so serious, like Alex. It is other people make him into a fool, he is not like that himself. He is different. I do not say I like him a lot or a little. But if he wants to see me I will say yes when I want to. Alex will not stop me.'

'All right then. But you got to remember, Alex is my friend.'

She stood up. 'Is that why you told me to come here? To tell me these things, to say what I can and cannot do?'

He took a breath. 'Not just that.'

'What else then?'

'I want you to talk to someone for me.'

She hesitated. 'Who?'

'Stanislaw, the guy whose shop was raided.'

She thought a moment. 'All right.' She sat down again, calmer. 'What do you want me to ask? Do you have another list of questions to give me?' She attempted a smile, which Garvie ignored.

'No need. It's very simple. Ask him if the burglar gave him any change.'

'*What?*'

'Doesn't matter. Just ask him.'

'Is that it?'

'Not quite. Got a pen?'

Frowning, she handed one over, and he wrote a number on a scrap of paper and gave it to her.

'What is this?'

'Just in case Blinkie turns out to be less funny than you think. Not sure the police are the brightest, but this guy's not too bad. Bit uptight. You could call him if you needed to.'

As she stood there holding the paper her whole body seemed to stiffen and when she spoke her voice was cold.

'You think you can tell me what to do?'

'Maybe someone needs to.'

Her whole face tightened. She nodded. 'Now I will tell you something,' she said. She was breathing hard.

Garvie said nervously, 'Yeah, well, it'll have to be quick, I've got somebody to see before I get back.'

'It is quick, do not worry. This. People said that Pyotor was difficult. That he did not understand people or care about them. That he was antisocial and selfish. It was not true about Pyotor. But,' she said, 'it is true about you.'

He said nothing to that. He watched her smash her way through purple shadows under the trees and vanish into the sunlight of the playing field beyond. For some time he didn't move, he stood immobile with an unlit cigarette between his fingers and a look of disgust on his face.

It was several minutes before he stirred. 'I'm an idiot,' he murmured.

Glancing at his watch, he hurried through the trees towards Top Pitch.

41

North of Five Mile, a short bus ride away, on a shallow rise above the eastern bypass, Dandelion Hill lay quietly under a film of dust in the early evening sun, a maze-like plot of semi-detached houses arranged in crescents, groves and cul-de-sacs repeating themselves across ten acres like a series of identical false starts. Number five Cross Close was typical. With its flaking pebble-dash and stained plastic window frames, it had the tired air of a house that had been trying for too long to keep up appearances. Garvie went up the path to the front door, rang the bell and waited.

It took several minutes for the door to open. When it did Garvie took a step backwards. Singh stood there dressed in white pyjamas, his head wrapped in a towel, his feet bare, looking like a foreigner. He looked angrily beyond Garvie and up and down the street and back again before he spoke.

'What are you doing here?'

'Well, I was just passing, and I thought . . . What are you wearing, man?'

'How did you know where I lived?'

'My uncle leaves his address book lying around.'

'What do you want?'

289

'I can come back later if you like. I didn't realize it was hair-wash night.'

Singh glared at him.

'I just wanted to see how you're doing,' Garvie said. 'Check you're OK.'

For a long moment Singh said nothing, for a moment he seemed on the point of having a fit, or at least of closing the door in Garvie's face, but at last he controlled himself and stepped aside, and Garvie went past him into his house.

The hallway was white and bare, the living room the same, plain and empty with non-committal carpet and blank walls: there was no furniture in it but a wooden chair, a small table with a couple of manilla envelopes on it and a tiny white bookcase standing in a corner with a temporary look, like last things waiting for the removals men to come back.

'Not that keen on clutter, are you?' Garvie said. He went over to the bookcase. Five shelves were empty; on the sixth there were four objects: a small framed picture of some writing in a foreign language, a wooden comb, an ornamental steel dagger and something wrapped in what looked like a yellow duster. He turned and found Singh watching him warily.

'What is it?'

'My *gurdwara*.'

'Nice.'

'A Sikh altar.'

'What's in the duster?'

'A *gutka*. Scripture. It is not a duster.'

'Do you read it?'

'Of course I read it. It is my guide.'

'And what about the thing in the frame?'

'A *shabad*. A hymn. "From woman, man is born," it begins. "Through woman, the future generations come."' He hesitated. 'It was my mother's favourite text. Garvie – why are you here?'

Garvie glanced round at the room with its bare walls and one chair and no sign whatsoever of anything remotely related to any woman.

'Got something to tell you.'

Singh sighed. 'Wait a moment. I will get another chair.'

While he was out of the room, Garvie took a quick look at the envelopes on the little table. Neither was marked, but in the first was a report headed *Martin Patrick Magee*. He slipped it back in the envelope as Singh returned and they sat facing each other, saying nothing. In his Indian pyjamas Singh seemed no less uptight than usual but more unpredictable. The huge towel piled on his head gave his face a naked look; his nose seemed bigger. The toes of his feet were long and dark and hairless.

'My mother says hi by the way,' Garvie said, trying not to look at the feet.

Singh nodded minimally. 'She has been kind.'

They continued to look at each other.

'So, how's it going with your disciplinary thing?'

'There have been no developments.'

'My experience is they usually blow over.'

Singh made no reply to that. 'What is it you want to tell me?' he said.

'Oh yeah, I was forgetting. About the break-in at the warehouse. Thought you might like to know.'

'Not really.'

'Magee and the kid were up on the roof that night. It wasn't a false alarm you went out to. They set it off.'

Singh said nothing.

'The thing about Magee isn't that he's a racist. It's that he's a thief. And a maniac. It's not about whether the shopkeepers he robbed were Polish or not. It's not about Anton Schnopper or Pyotor being Polish. He used kids and didn't care if they got killed. That's what it's about.'

Singh stood up. 'I'm not interested.'

'Course you are. It's key to the whole thing. Opens it all up. What you'd call a breakthrough.'

Singh said, 'You don't understand. I no longer concern myself with Martin Magee or Pyotor Gimpel. I am no longer working on the case. No longer an active member of the squad.'

'All right. Even better.'

'What do you mean?'

'Go rogue, man.'

Singh remained standing. When he spoke his voice was even and cold. 'You should present whatever information you have direct to Detective Inspector Dowell. That's all I can say to you.'

'Has all that hair-washing softened your brain? Dowell wouldn't recognize a breakthrough if he found it in his mouth.'

'I am currently under investigation and legally prohibited from any involvement in police affairs.'

'Yeah, yeah, I know all that, you just told me. Don't you get it? They've let you down. They've pissed in your pocket. You don't owe them anything. This is your chance to do your own thing, get at the truth your own way, without any rules or regulations or stupid people telling you what to do. Did you hear what they were saying on the radio this morning? Dowell's got hold of the fuzzy end of the Schnopper thing and decided there's a racism angle after all. He's about half a mile behind the facts and he's not catching them up. You don't want to work for that clot.'

Singh said, 'If the witnesses to Anton Schnopper's death give their statements like you said, then there will be a case to answer and perhaps Magee will be brought to justice.'

'I doubt that.'

'Why?'

'I was lying. There were witnesses all right, but there's no chance of them making statements. I just said it to get Magee going.'

Singh's face looked more and more naked. He said, 'You think I'm like you, don't you, Garvie? I'm not. I believe in rules and regulations; I believe in order and discipline and cooperation. When I joined the police service I made a commitment. Commitments are not to be broken just because things go wrong. Without them there is only confusion, and people like you.'

'They're going to ruin you,' Garvie said.

'It's very likely. But I shall not be ruined here.' He curtly slapped his chest.

Garvie got up too and they faced each other. A muscle in Singh's cheek twitched. 'All right then,' Garvie said. 'I'll just have to plug away on my own.'

'I do not recommend that.'

'Yeah, well, there's not much you can do about it.'

'I can inform the police that you have information for them.'

'You'd do that?'

'It is my duty to do that.'

'They're not going to thank you, you know. They'll treat you same as always. Junior Plod. Open your eyes. They don't like you.'

Singh said nothing. He looked incapable of any more speech, his lips clamped together, his face straining. Very slightly he began to tremble.

'Come on, man,' Garvie said. 'This is good stuff; it changes everything. Vinnie was telling the truth. Magee was lying, he wasn't out for a night walk, he was on the estate to break into the warehouse.'

Singh's voice came out in a hiss, angry and sarcastic. 'And now he's free on bail, a dangerous man with things to hide, and you propose to "plug away" at him in your usual interfering, infuriating way?'

Garvie nodded. 'Sounds good when you put it like that.'

Singh shouted suddenly, 'Why are you like this? Haven't you caused enough trouble?' He was trembling so violently now that the towel on his head came loose and a long lock of black hair fell down his neck. 'Don't you ever think about anyone except yourself?'

He lost control of himself. He began to make jerky movements with his arms.

'*Why?*' he shouted. 'Why are you so difficult? Why do you behave as if everything is a game? Why don't you treat people the way they deserve to be treated?'

He was panting now.

'Don't you see what you're doing to your *mother*? Don't you understand what you've done to . . .' He bit his lip, groaning, and turned away to his *gurdwara*. He put his hand out and placed it on the yellow-covered *gutka*, and stood there, head bowed, shoulders shaking, making huge efforts to control himself. His towel finally unwrapped itself and slipped off his shoulders and his hair fell down in wet black clumps to his waist.

Now that he had stopped shouting there was silence in the room; it fizzed in Garvie's ears.

'All right, all right,' Garvie said. 'I was only trying to help. I know you're under pressure.'

Singh said nothing. He breathed deeply in the silence.

'Your hair's all out,' Garvie said after a while.

Turning, Singh was calm again. 'I know you were trying to help.' He moved back into the middle of the room. 'It is only your way, because you have not learned any different yet. I have said too much. I regret it. It is time for you to go.'

At the door Singh said, 'Just one thing more. Look inside yourself, Garvie. Ask yourself what you see there.'

They exchanged glances. Then Garvie went down the path with his usual slouching walk, not looking back, and Singh stood in the doorway, framed by his black hair, as solid and unruly as a thing apart.

When the boy had disappeared from view he went slowly back into the living room and stood there a moment, frowning. Glancing at the manilla envelopes lying on the table, he began to walk in aimless fashion round the room, occasionally murmuring to himself. Nearly twenty minutes passed. At last he came to a standstill by the table. He hesitated for a moment longer, then picked up one of the envelopes and took out a sheaf of papers.

The first page was headed AUTHORISED ACCESS ONLY, and that made Singh hesitate again. It was one thing to fail to return police property, another to access confidential information – a deliberate violation of the police code. But Singh overcame his reluctance, turned the page and began to read.

He went quickly through the facts of Magee's

upbringing and education, more slowly through the accounts of his first offences, and gave closest attention to the last few years. Magee had lived all his life in Heeley, a small city two hundred miles to the south, a restless, vaguely dissatisfied young man resentful of his lack of personal opportunities. By the age of twenty-five he had already served time for armed robbery and had been questioned about a number of other crimes, including the large-scale attempted robbery of a furrier's in which the Polish boy Anton Schnopper had died. After that Magee had registered as a self-employed gardener and moved to a district of Heeley called Hofftown, where he lived alone in a bedsit above a betting shop. In eight months he attracted three police reports of antisocial behaviour: an altercation with a Pakistani shopkeeper; an attempt to disrupt a march through Hofftown of a local gay-pride group; and a bottle fight in a club called Sam Chan's. On 24 June 2010, at ten o'clock in the evening, he had entered a convenience store armed with a shotgun and, aided by an associate called Kim Li, had taken a little over four thousand cash from the post office at the back of the store. Easily identified by CCTV, he was apprehended the following day, brought to trial within the month, convicted on a charge of aggravated burglary and transferred to Firetown Security Facility, where he served eighteen months of a three-year sentence. Released in the middle of January 2012, he returned to his bedsit only to collect basic belongings before making the journey north and settling in Limekilns.

Singh sat upright on his chair, quietly reading.

A man who has made a false start in one place might easily decide to move elsewhere, especially a restless man on the lookout for fresh opportunities, who is already known to local police. But why come to this city, why Limekilns?

Singh sat thinking, as still and lonely in his bare room as the tiny white *gurdwara* standing against the opposite wall. At last he took out his phone.

'Robert? Singh here. Raminder Singh . . . Yes . . . No, I'm still waiting for a date. . . Thank you. Robert, I wonder if you can do me a favour. Just an introduction. I'd like to get in touch with the liaison officer at a security facility near Heeley called Firetown.'

Meanwhile Garvie Smith was lying on his bed in the flat in Eastwick Gardens staring at the ceiling. He had looked inside himself and found there the thought that he was difficult, that he did not understand people or care about them, that he was antisocial and selfish. Singh had directed him to these thoughts, but they had been put there by a Polish girl with an unnervingly direct manner.

As he lay on his bed he frowned.

He had to do the right thing. He knew that already. He just wasn't sure any more what that was.

42

Three days passed. On Friday he stayed all day at school and in the evening revised chemistry. On Saturday he revised Special Maths. On Sunday he found his physics course book, missing all year, and read for the first time about energy, waves and the origins of the universe, none of which turned out to be that interesting. It rained on Sunday night but by eight o'clock in the morning on Monday it was already bright again. Five Mile shone in the sun; the kitchen at 12 Eastwick Gardens was prickly with warm, dusty light. Garvie sat at one side of the breakfast table sucking the end of a pen and reading *Explaining Physics*, and his uncle sat on the other side, drinking tea from a mug and watching him.

'What time does it start exactly?' Uncle Len asked again.

'Eleven. I told you.'

'And where does it—'

'The gym.'

'And how long does—'

'Couple of hours.' Garvie looked at his uncle. 'Relax. You wouldn't want to make me nervous.'

His uncle grunted. 'I couldn't make you nervous if

I tried. Your problem isn't nerves. Your problem is *turning up.*'

'I'll turn up.'

'You'll turn up this time, because this time I'm driving you there.'

Garvie went back to his textbook. He turned a page. Yawned.

His phone rang and his uncle looked at him suspiciously as he answered it.

'Yeah?'

Singh's voice said, 'Garvie?'

Garvie looked back at his uncle, his face adopting a deadpan expression.

'Yeah.'

'Is your mother there?'

'No.' Garvie kept his eyes on his uncle's.

'Your uncle?'

'No.'

'I need to speak to one of them.' Singh hesitated. 'I have some urgent information.'

Garvie mouthed, 'Sorry,' at Uncle Len, and mimed someone talking with his hand.

Singh hesitated again. 'This morning Magee skipped bail. It's imperative that you don't—'

'Interesting,' Garvie said.

There was a pause. 'It's not "interesting", it's—'

'Interesting you're still trying to work it out, I mean. Thought you'd given up.'

Singh said crossly, 'This is nothing to do with what you said to me last night.'

Still staring at Garvie, Uncle Len cocked his head on one side, as if trying to hear the conversation, and Garvie said into the phone, 'That's great then. But you're going about it the wrong way.'

'What?'

'Hertz is a measurement of frequency.'

'What are you talking about?'

'Sound waves. You know. Some people hear more than others. Just like they see more. Top note on a violin, for instance.'

'You're not making sense.'

'Hints, threats, messages left on a phone. Can't get out of the way if you can't hear the train coming.'

'*What?*'

'I'm just saying. Take your example. If the note is 440 hertz there are 440 sound waves per second, and if they travel at a speed of 340 metres per second, obviously the wavelength is 0.773 metres. See you later.'

He rang off, and Uncle Len opened his mouth, and Garvie said, 'Smudge. Got bogged down in waves and radiation. That boy worries too much.'

Before Uncle Len could comment on Smudge's level of anxiety, Garvie's phone rang again, and he frowned as Garvie answered it.

'Yeah?'

Zuzana's voice said, 'Garvie?'

Garvie kept his eyes on his uncle's.

'Yeah.'

'It's Alex,' Zuzana said. 'He has gone. We had an

argument. The same as the other arguments but worse. He said he knew who to blame. Then he went.'

Garvie considered this. 'Why are you telling me?' he said.

'I know what you think. Because of what we talked about. But this is not normal behaviour of Alex. You do not know. Alex is your friend, but I hope you think a little of me too. Do you?'

He thought about this for a moment. 'That's a hard one,' he said at last. 'Let me think.' He watched Uncle Len making angry gestures at the clock and *Explaining Physics*. 'It's like this,' he said. 'Strong forces of attraction between particles in solids. They don't move around much. With gases it's the other way round: weak attraction, random behaviour.'

'*What?* Why do you tell me this?'

'The way to remember it is that it's the opposite of people. With people it's strong attraction, random behaviour.'

'Why are you talking in riddles?'

'Exactly,' Garvie said. 'Oh, and good luck.' He rang off. 'Felix,' he said to his uncle. 'Stuck on solids and gases.'

'You get a lot of calls about revision,' Uncle Len said with a sceptical look. 'I didn't know your friends were so studious.'

'We're all just trying to do our best,' Garvie said.

'What I don't understand is why they call *you*.'

Garvie's phone rang a third time and Uncle Len

302

shook his head in bewilderment. 'Good lord,' he said. 'They really must be desperate.'

Garvie frowned at the phone before answering. 'Yeah?'

His whole body seemed to frown as he listened.

'Yeah,' he said again. And then, 'Do you?'

If Uncle Len hadn't gone over to the window he would perhaps have noticed something odd in the way Garvie held his phone, the way he turned slowly away so his impassive face was hidden.

'Why would I do that?' he heard Garvie say.

There was a long silence.

'Why me?' Garvie said. 'No,' he said. Then: 'Yeah. Fair enough.' Finally: 'All right then.'

There was another long pause after that in which Garvie quietly rang off, counted to three and shouted suddenly into the phone,

'*Nine?* What do you mean, nine? It's eleven, isn't it? All right, all right. I'm on my way.'

At once his uncle was standing electrified at the kitchen table. 'What?' he said. 'What's the matter?'

Garvie was stuffing things into his school bag. 'Got the time wrong. The exam starts in, like, ten minutes.'

'*What?*'

'I know. This is an emergency.' Garvie glanced up at him. 'Thank God you're here to drive me. I only hope,' he added, 'it means you can use the siren.'

43

Magnetic bubble light and siren doing their frantic thing on top of Uncle Len's unmarked car, they sped out of Eastwick Gardens and into Pilkington Driftway. They swerved into Bulwarks Lane, slewed onto Pollard Way, burned down Town Road, whipped up Wyedale Road and drew up with a final electronic *whop* in the driveway at Bottom Gate. It was two minutes to nine.

Garvie pressed his uncle's arm and got out.

'Thanks, man. I enjoyed that.'

'One thing before you go,' Uncle Len called after him. 'Remember to use all the available time. You might think you can't answer a question, but if you just give it—'

But Garvie had already set off up the driveway towards C Block and the gym beyond.

'Good luck then!' Uncle Len called out of the car window at Garvie's retreating back. He reversed onto the street, shaking his head.

Head down and frowning, Garvie walked rapidly past C Block and past the hall, pausing only to sling his bag into a corner of the yard, past the gym and along the driveway to Top Gate, and out onto the street again. Then he began to run. He disliked running. He ran in pain down Claremont Street back to Bulwarks Lane, and past the shops until he came to the taxi rank, where he at last allowed himself to smile. For once he was in luck.

Abdul saw him coming and pulled himself off his cab and greeted Garvie with his usual daft grace, kissing him on both cheeks, smiling sweetly and touching his fingertips to his breast.

'My Garvie man! How is, how is?'

'Is in pain, Abdul. I had to run here. And I've got to get to a place in Brickhouse sharpish.'

'Brickhouse? Is no nice place.'

'I know. Can't be helped.'

'Is *plaisir*, then, my Garvie man. Come. We go quick quick.'

Garvie gave him the address and they drove down Bulwarks Lane onto the ring road and south past the sewage plant. Abdul smiled at Garvie in the rear-view mirror. His smile was rich, deep, white and almost alarmingly big. He was fond of the boy, and even fonder of his mother, who had sorted out his visa for him when he'd arrived from Morocco.

'My Garvie man,' he said. 'You go see friend in Brickhouse?'

Garvie considered that. 'Could be a friend, Abdul,' he said. 'You never know. Or maybe he's just going to kill me.'

Abdul nodded vaguely and continued to smile. Privately he considered the boy a dunce. But there are places for dunces in the world, after all.

'We go quick quick,' he said, 'so you meet your *ami nouveau*.'

They came off the ring road by the big furniture showrooms and drove up the hill, past the crematorium, into the ramshackle slum-like maze of Brickhouse, one of the oldest districts in the city, now dilapidated and shabby.

Garvie sat back in his seat, watching brick strips of houses go by, thinking about the phone call earlier. He'd half expected Magee to get in touch with him, but not so soon. Something must have frightened the man. Thoughtfully, he went over the conversation again in his head.

The first thing Magee had told him was that he hadn't killed the Polish kid. 'I've an idea who did, though,' he'd said. 'You're going to be interested, schoolboy.'

He told Garvie to meet him, to come straightway to an address in Brickhouse, and to come alone. 'Why would I do that?' Garvie had said.

'Think I'm going to slit you? You'll just have to trust me. This is the only chance you get.'

'Why me?'

''Cause you know the rag-head. You can tell him what I tell you. He follows it up, this goes away. You don't think I'm coming in, do you?'

'No.'

'There's too much other stuff. I know how it works with those guys. I'm not going to let them twist me up. I know how to stay out of trouble. Think you're so smart, don't you?'

'Yeah.'

'You can take the pain then.'

'Fair enough.'

'Listen to me, schoolboy. You don't come, or you don't come alone, it's going to get bad. Not for you. For someone you know. I'm leaving in an hour and not coming back, so you better get here now. Understand? Now means now.'

'All right then.'

He sat back in the taxi staring out of the window. The streets pulled by in bits and pieces up and down the hills, houses crammed together at the sides of the roads, buckled and dark with old dirt, pavements littered with the broken ends of things.

Abdul looked at Garvie in the mirror. 'This place sad place, Garvie man.'

Garvie shrugged as they drew up alongside a row of disused garages and got out. There was no traffic, no one about at all, everything was quiet, tired, as if even the houses and trees were exhausted. Abdul pointed down the road, and Garvie nodded.

'Garvie—'

'It's OK, man. Thanks for the lift. I'll give you a ding if I have to.'

He watched as the cab pulled away, then, glancing at his watch, turned and walked rapidly past the garages up a deserted street of boarded-up brick terraces of use now only to stray dogs and graffiti artists, to the end of the row and stood there a moment, looking at the last house. It was bigger than the rest, the only house in the street not boarded up, but it didn't look lived in. Although it was mid morning all the curtains were drawn. Upstairs, an edge of sheet dirty as an old handkerchief hung out of a broken pane.

He asked himself what he was doing here. The right thing? Briefly, he thought of his mother and, more strangely, of Singh, and quickly put them out of his mind.

'It's going to get bad,' Magee had said to him. 'Not for you. For someone you know.'

It was Garvie's last chance to call someone. Singh, perhaps. Or Zuzana. He took out his phone and considered for a moment before punching in a number, and waited, listening. When the message had ended he spoke briefly. 'Alex, mate. Give it up. Call me now.' Then he kicked his way forward through litter and weeds and tried the front door. Just as Magee had said, it wasn't locked, and he pushed it open and went inside.

He knew straightaway that something was wrong. The house felt like a fake. The smell of damp ash, the leaves and litter on the bare floorboards, the wallpaper peeling in tongues from the walls – they all seemed to be hiding something. The silence wasn't silence but the hush of the house holding its breath. He held his breath too but the house didn't drop its guard. Ignoring it, he padded down the hall, peering through doorways into big, broken-down rooms filled with the remains of furniture – chairs with missing backs, a table with a stoved-in top, cupboards without doors – and at the end of the hall he found the door to the cellar under the stairs, as Magee had told him, and opened it onto darkness below. A different smell came up to him, earth and rottenness. After a brief search he found a light switch and the stairwell flickered weakly into view, a narrow flight of bare-board steps down to a miniature wooden door. Holding his breath, he listened again, but the house gave nothing away; there was no sound except for his own pulse thumping in his head. So he went down the steps to the door at the bottom, pushed it open and stood there hunched, peering through.

'Mart?' he called, and his voice sank at once into darkness like a stone into water. There was no light switch he could find; the basement in front of him was a dim shadow, windowless, with a concrete floor and things in corners barely visible. Against one wall he could make out a rack of metal shelving, against another a mattress surrounded with the litter of packets and food. In the wall at the far side was a smaller doorway, open, low and narrow, almost hidden in darkness. In that darkness there was something lying on the ground.

'Mart?' he called again.

Looking about him, he went quietly across the dark room towards the doorway, and when he was halfway there the light in the stairwell behind him was switched off and everything went black.

He said nothing, made no sound.

In utter darkness he stood still, listening. He heard three things, all at the same time. From behind him a noise like breathing, but looser and angrier, with a rattle to it like a plastic bag in a breeze. A sudden crash upstairs: a door kicked in or window blown out, and footsteps pounding in the hall above. And, in the immediate darkness, a slow blurred swirl of almost-silent and invisible movement coming towards him. For a half-second he had the impression, for no rational reason, of someone smiling at him in the dark. Then one of the basement walls seemed to swing loose and slam into him, a tonne of brick and masonry, and he was on the ground, his bones shaken loose, the breath crushed out of him, in his ears jumbled bits of shouting and his own blood stamping like footsteps, and before he could move the wall fell on him again with an annihilating thump and squashed him small as grit.

He wasn't Garvie any more, he was a broken bit of the room, he shared its pain – the pain of the dusty concrete floor, the pain of a corner of mattress, of a fallen metal shelf, all flicking in and out of the darkness like pokes in the eye. Then the pain of electric light brought him back to his body curled in agony on its side, exposed to the world like a fish on a slab.

He mewled.

'Don't move,' a voice said.

He tried to move and his stomach tore itself open and he retched sideways into the dust, his head buzzing with the effort.

He felt invisible, urgent fingers on his head, face, shoulders, and heard the voice again: 'Don't, I said.'

Slowly the dizziness faded; the room put itself back together, left Garvie behind, lying there with his cheek pressed against the floor. Focusing, he saw a man's black rubber boot and with a groan rolled onto his back and looked up at Singh.

'Don't speak,' the Sikh said.

'What are you doing here?' Garvie said in a choking whisper.

Singh made an exasperated face. He was wearing his white pyjamas and a silk black headscarf knotted at the top, and he crouched by Garvie and felt the boy's pulse and peered into his eyes.

'The question,' he said as he worked, 'is not what I am doing here. It is what *you* are doing here.'

Garvie managed a gritty smile. 'You've gone rogue,' he said in a dusty croak. 'Knew you had.'

Singh said nothing to that. He examined Garvie's shoulder.

'Can you move your arm? How do you feel?' He was running his fingers over Garvie's ankles. 'Can you stand?'

Garvie stood and quickly sat down again. Singh continued to check him over. After a while Garvie realized he could talk again.

311

'How did you know where to come?' he asked.

Singh hesitated. 'I have a friend in the centre's databank. I don't think he fully realizes the nature of my suspension.'

'Handy. And I thought you didn't do friends. But I don't suppose he had this address on file.'

'Of course not. With the information he gave me I took a trip to a security facility near Heeley called Firetown. Sit still, please.' He continued to examine Garvie as he spoke. 'You see, I couldn't understand why Magee had come here after his release. Why here, not somewhere else? At Firetown I met one of the men he had shared a cell with, a man named de Clerk. He and Magee used to talk about what they'd do after they got out.'

Garvie said, 'And he's from here?'

'Yes.'

'And this is his place?'

'His brother-in-law's. He remembered telling Magee about it, how his brother-in-law died and his will was challenged, and the house was just rotting away, empty while the lawyer's fees ate it up. Magee would have remembered it as a useful bolthole.'

Garvie nodded. 'Smart of you,' he said. 'I love how methodical you are. But you can stop patting me now.'

Singh stopped. 'You've been very lucky. Nothing broken.' He looked at Garvie. 'And now, you tell me what you're doing here.'

'Me? I just came to meet Magee.'

'You came to do *what*?'

'Have a chat.' He gingerly felt the back of his head.

'A chat? On your own? My God! About what?'

'He gave me a bell. Had something to tell me, he said. Like who killed Pyotor.'

'It wasn't him?'

Garvie shook his head, realized it was a mistake and stopped shaking it. He gave a groan. 'No.'

'How do you know?'

Garvie thought. 'I knew I could trust him,' he said at last.

'Trust him! Look at you.'

'Believe me, he didn't do it. But something must have gone wrong here.' Garvie felt his face, groaned. 'He changed his mind, maybe. Maybe he just loves being on the run.'

Singh looked at him for several seconds. Shook his head. 'He's not on the run,' he said quietly.

Garvie followed his eyes to the doorway in the far wall. Through it he could see a man's legs sprawled on the floor.

'Is that . . . ?'

Singh gave a nod.

'Is he . . . ?'

Singh nodded again.

'Well, don't look at me, man,' Garvie said. 'I didn't do it. I'd only just got here. I came down the stairs and the light went out, and then . . .'

'Then somebody hit you,' Singh said.

'Yeah. I realize that bit.'

'With that thing probably,' Singh said, pointing to a two-by-four lying on the ground nearby.

Garvie looked at the plank with distaste.

'Magee's killer,' Singh said. 'You must have disturbed him.'

'Whoever he is.'

'Yes, whoever he . . .' Singh interrupted himself and fixed Garvie with a suspicious stare. 'Do you know who he is, Garvie?'

'Course not. Don't you think I'd tell you if I knew?'

'No.'

Garvie shrugged. 'Whoever he is, how did he get away?'

'There's an exit through the other basement room. A scramble hole up to the garden.'

'He must have heard you arrive. You weren't exactly quiet.'

'The point was to be quick, not quiet. In any case, it was lucky for you I made a noise.'

They glared at each other.

'Thanks and all that,' Garvie said, 'if that's what you're fishing for.'

Singh almost smiled. Not quite. 'Listen to me now. We haven't got much time. We have to leave as soon as we can. Stay there. Don't touch anything.' He got up and went into the other room where Magee's body lay and began to examine the area with a small metal instrument he took from his tunic.

'What's it look like in there?' Garvie said.

'I'd rather not say.' Singh continued to work round the body, moving out of sight. 'The person who did this must have been very desperate.'

'That's what you said about the person who ripped apart Pyotor's room trying to find his violin.'

Singh's face reappeared in the doorway and looked at Garvie thoughtfully and disappeared again.

Garvie sat thinking. Magee hadn't known exactly who killed Pyotor but he'd said he had a good idea. Garvie remembered his words: 'It's going to get bad. Not for you. For someone you know.' In the end that's why he, Garvie, had come here. But it had got bad for Magee instead.

Garvie sat perfectly still, alone with his headache among the debris of the room, things spilled across the floor around him from the fallen shelving: tools, nails and screws, spare light bulbs in their cardboard boxes, fuses, coils of electric cable; and the rubbish scattered round the mattress where Magee had been sleeping: tin cans, plastic bottles, cellophane wrapping. Ignoring it all, he retired into the privacy of his mind. Someone he knew, Magee had said. Someone desperate, someone violent. Someone out of control. His eyes glazed over.

When he focused again his attention was caught by something lying on the floor by his foot, a small thing, something ordinary and odd among the debris of Magee's food, something that shouldn't have been there. It was so small and ordinary he'd stared at it for several seconds before he realized what he was gazing at.

Wiping his hands, Singh came back briskly into the room, and Garvie casually stretched out a leg and put his foot over it.

'Tell me about the corner shops,' he said.

'What about them?'

'Stanislaw's.'

'The shop at Strawberry Hill is an anomaly. It doesn't fit the pattern.'

'What pattern?'

'Fourteen shops in the city targeted over a period of six months with increasing violence. This is not random. It is not a pattern of burglary at all.'

'What is it?'

'It is the classic pattern of extortion. A protection racket. Organized, widespread. Increasing violence to intimidate.'

'And the shopkeepers receive demands?'

'They pay to protect themselves against further violence. They are too frightened to report it to the police. The perpetrators are very aggressive. Also clever. They work with intermediaries. They too are frightened.'

'When did it start?'

'January.'

'When Magee arrived.'

Singh nodded. 'I had made the same connection.'

'It's the wrong connection,' Garvie said. 'I was just mentioning it.'

Singh shook his head, exasperated. 'It is time to go.'

'OK.'

Singh went round the room rearranging things he had moved, putting them back where they had been. He wiped the handle of the door.

Garvie looked at him curiously. 'You going to call it in?'

'I will contact the appropriate authorities.' Singh hesitated. 'From a payphone.'

Garvie grinned. 'You really have gone rogue, haven't you?'

He shook his head. 'There is no question of "going rogue", as you put it. It is a question of commitment. As usual.' He hesitated again. 'But it's best if we leave things exactly as they were.'

'I won't tell anyone we were here, if you won't. Do we need to swear an oath in blood or something?'

Singh scowled. 'You need to see a doctor about the injuries to your shoulder. You'll have to explain what happened.' He looked at him and Garvie shrugged. 'In the meantime you should contact your mother and uncle to let them know you're safe.'

Garvie shrugged again. 'They won't have missed me. They think I'm in an exam.'

'You have an exam?'

'Not till eleven.' He looked at his watch. 'But I'd better get going. Seeing as it's eleven now.'

Singh rolled his eyes.

They parted in the street without speaking again,

Singh going down the hill towards Brickhouse shops, Garvie putting through a call to Abdul. He waited outside the empty garages. There was still no one about. After a while he took something out of his pocket and looked at it. It was a yellow-and-green sweet wrapper. He had to admit he'd been surprised to find it in the basement. For a moment it had disorientated him, given him the eerie feeling that Pyotor had been there before him. But Pyotor wasn't the only one who bought those sweets, he remembered. There was someone else – someone else who had gone to visit Magee in his hideaway, someone else who knew that Magee hadn't killed Pyotor.

Abdul's cab came climbing up the hill towards him, and he put the wrapper back in his pocket and got in.

'My Garvie man! Is good? Your *ami nouveau* is please to see you?'

'Unfortunately he wasn't there. Not any more.'

'Ah.' Abdul's expressive face crumpled in disappointment.

'Doesn't matter,' Garvie said. 'I've got an exam to get to. And I'm a bit late already.'

'Is OK, Garvie man. We go quick quick.'

And the cab swung round in the road and headed briskly down the hill.

44

In the kitchen at Eastwick Gardens they sat eating salt fish and macaroni. The last of the afternoon sun came in through the window and slicked their faces.

'I know you made it in the end,' Uncle Len said. 'It just seems strange that I drive you to school at nine o'clock for an exam that turns out to be at eleven after all, for which you're still half an hour late.'

'I told you,' Garvie said. 'I got held up in the nurse's office. After I hit my head.'

'That doesn't make it any less strange.'

Garvie's mother said, 'At least you took the exam. For that I must be grateful.'

'I wasn't going to let you down. Even though I'd more or less knocked myself out on those playground steps.' He looked at Uncle Len. 'Don't suppose we could claim compensation, could we?'

Uncle Len ignored him. 'And how did the exam go, when you finally got there?'

'Pretty well. Very well, actually. Really, really well.'

'You think you passed?'

'I'm not sure I'd go that far. But I've still got two to go.'

His mother was looking at his shoulder and the

side of his face. 'What were you doing on those steps anyway?' she asked. 'To fall like that.'

'I don't really remember how it happened, to be honest. It all went dark.'

Garvie's mother and Uncle Len exchanged glances.

'OK,' Uncle Len said. 'Two exams to go. It's almost certain you have to pass them both.'

'Doesn't sound too bad.'

'Chemistry in a week's time. Have you done any revision for that at all?

'Got a week to do it in.'

'And tomorrow: Special Maths.'

'I can do maths. Maths is the thing I do.'

Garvie's mother said, 'It's not the ordinary exam, Garvie. And I wish now we'd never agreed to let Miss Perkins enter you for it. She was only thinking of the prestige of the school. No doubt,' she added, 'she's regretting it now.'

'Sounds like the sort of thing I could probably wing, to be honest.'

Garvie's mother looked at Uncle Len, who said, 'Listen to me, Garvie. I know you're clever. That's not the point. Do you have a plan?'

'I have a plan. Bit of revision. Turn up on time.'

'OK. Do you care?'

'I care. I really care.'

'OK. Listen to me. You really care. You've got a plan. You're really clever. It's not enough.'

Garvie looked at him.

'Even clever people can do stupid things,' Uncle

320

Len said. 'Sometimes,' he said, 'even clever people can't see what's right in front of their noses.'

Garvie seemed about to make one of his usual slippery comments – and then he didn't. Instead, he seemed utterly dumbfounded, as if, all at once, he had woken up to a reality he had never suspected.

'Garvie?'

'That's it!' Garvie whispered, as if to himself. 'I've been so stupid.'

Uncle Len exchanged puzzled looks with Garvie's mother.

'Well,' he said awkwardly. 'Let this be a lesson to you.'

'What have I been thinking of all this time?' Garvie said with bitterness.

'It's all right, Garvie. There's no need to get upset. It's enough that you've taken it on board now.'

Garvie said nothing else. He seemed scarcely aware of the others. He got up from the table in a daze and made his way to his room and closed the door behind him.

'Do you know,' Uncle Len said after a moment. 'I think I finally got through to him.'

Garvie's mother looked at him sceptically.

In his room, lying on his bed, Garvie was on the phone, listening to the ringing tone. 'Come on, come on,' he said under his breath. 'Pick up.'

He didn't. Frowning, Garvie listened to the same old message. 'Alex,' he said when it had finished, 'whatever you're doing, whatever it is you've done, you got to call me now.'

He sat there thinking for a moment. He thought of a sweet wrapper dropped in a house where a murder was committed. He thought of someone trying to break his head open in the dark.

Then he dialled another number.

She picked up straightaway as if waiting for a call.

'Zuza,' he said in a whisper, 'it's me. Sorry I couldn't talk earlier. Has Alex come back?'

'No,' she said after a pause.

Garvie hesitated. 'OK. Soon as he does, will you give me a call?'

'If he does.'

'Listen, that other thing – did you get chance to go up to Stanislaw's?'

'Yes. It was very strange.'

'What happened?'

'I don't know how you knew this, but the man who robbed the shop, he did just what you said. He gave Stanislaw some of the money back.'

Garvie permitted himself a grin. 'Tell me what he did exactly.'

'He came into the shop very late, after Stanislaw had closed. Stanislaw still does not know how he got in. He appeared disguised with a hood and a mask, and he pointed his gun at Stanislaw and told him to hand over all the money in the till. It was a big amount because Stanislaw had just got a lottery licence. But when the man had the money he did not go. He stood there counting it. And when he had finished counting he gave some of it back to Stanislaw. It's crazy. Why would he do this?'

''Cause it would have been wrong to take more than he needed.'

'I don't understand.'

'He needed a specific amount.'

There was a silence. Zuzana said slowly, 'Wait. What are you saying?'

'That clever people can't see what's right in front of their noses.'

From the living room came the sound of footsteps, and Garvie said quickly, 'Listen, got to go. But there's something I've got to talk to you about. I need your help tonight. I'll give you a ding.'

When his mother appeared in the doorway he was busy scribbling calculations in an exercise book.

He looked up and she held his gaze. 'I see you're trying,' she said. 'I see that. But I don't see everything.'

'What do you mean?'

'You might fool your uncle,' she said, 'but you don't fool me. The lesson you need to learn, and quickly, is that it's not about fooling me.' She didn't smile, and Garvie didn't smile either; they looked at each other inscrutably for several seconds before she withdrew.

For some time Garvie considered the equation he'd just written, as if thinking through the problem. Then he reached for his phone again.

45

At two o'clock in the morning East Field industrial estate was still and quiet and dark. It was a warm night, the sky quilted with cloud, the moon a muffled bedside glow. In the shut-up buildings, in the deserted cross roads, in the waste margins of grass and weeds, there was silence.

The only noise, faint and erratic, came from a patch of darkness in the lee of a former fish warehouse: a flimsy muttering, half singing, half cursing, a shuffling of irrelevant words, isolated expressions of quiet indignation and surprise. They came from Vinnie. He lay beadily in layers of cardboard, huffing to himself, tilting his face alertly east and west along the access road in front of him as though following the shifting progress of night breezes with his red-rimmed gaze. From time to time he picked something out of his beard and nibbled at it and muttered something. Occasionally a word could be made out. 'Fubbers' was one. Others sounded like 'cow-fluck', 'fish-arse', 'shipper-tit' – not so much words as incantations against sanity.

Abruptly he fell silent, his head cocked manically to the west, his gaze enlarged as he peered through the darkness. From the warehouse at the end of the road, out of the silence, came a noise of footsteps. Vinnie slid further under his cardboard and pressed his mouth deeper into his beard to guard against involuntary utterances.

As he watched, a movement grew out of the shadows, a puzzling shape, halting and contradictory, struggling against itself, coming slowly nearer and clearer, turning eventually into two figures grappling together in a strangely stumbling walk. Vinnie stifled a gurgle. One of the figures was a man wearing a black hooded top, the other a boy wearing navy shorts and white T-shirt, and they lurched down the road together, the man heaving the boy upright with his arms, the boy limping along painfully, holding his neck, moaning aloud in a language Vinnie had heard once before. It was all exactly, spectacularly as it had been the first time, uncanny, almost eerie. He couldn't help himself. He rose out of his cardboard like an apparition of ancient prophecy and flung his arm towards the pair, who stopped at once, as if he had pulled them out of his dream into reality.

'The same!' he cried. 'I seen it all the same!' He clutched his head and shook his fists in astonishment at them. 'I told you!' he shouted. 'I know that jabber anywhere. Same words, all of them. Try fool me, eh, cod-sucker? Bring the money. Think I don't know Polish when I see it?' And he laughed till he was sick on the ground.

'That's excellent, Vinnie,' Garvie said. 'We

thought it would jog your memory. You got it exactly right. Except for one thing.'

'Eh?'

'It wasn't Polish.'

Silence returned to the industrial estate as they walked through darkness back to their bags, which they had left against the warehouse wall.

'I knew it would work,' Zuzana said.

'You were right.'

'He needed to *see* it again. It would not have worked just to have talked to him.'

'It was a good idea.'

'You were good as Magee,' she said with a glance at him. 'You are stronger than you look. Quite like a man.'

'You were all right as the kid. The dramatic limp. The pathetic little voice.'

She gave his arm a playful slap.

'No, really. And the hand at your neck, masterly.'

'You told me to do that.'

'Of course. Good at details.'

He allowed himself to glance at her as they walked. In T-shirt and shorts she seemed shockingly underdressed, more than halfway to being naked. He hadn't realized how petite she was, but how solid, how small-scale but strong. Her skin shone pale, almost translucent. The T-shirt they had found for her was on the small side; it strained across her breasts and rode up at her waist. The shorts were short, high on her slender legs quivering slightly as she walked, so soft and firm and fluid he thought he could watch them for ever and never understand how they worked or even how they existed in the world. He remembered how she had felt to his touch as they came down the access road together, when his arm was round her waist, his hand under her armpit, the whole length of her tight, solid body pressing against his.

'Don't you?' she said.

'What?'

'I said, you know it all, don't you?'

'Not all. Most.'

'Modest.'

'Part of my charm.'

'I was joking. You are not modest. Or very charming.'

They reached their bags and stood there, talking quietly in the shadows.

She said, 'Tell me. How did you know it was not Pyotor up on the roof with Magee?'

'I was pretty sure once Vinnie said he heard the shots *before* he saw Magee and the kid coming down the road. Sounded like the truth to me. He blurted it out to the police, and then again to us, before he could stop himself. It was the one thing he was consistent about – even though he thought it was the wrong answer. And it was completely obvious once you found out it was Pyotor who robbed Stanislaw.

Pyotor didn't have to help Magee rob the warehouse; he had the money he needed already, the exact amount. Anyway,' Garvie went on, 'he didn't like Magee. And Magee didn't like the look of him. Magee worked with kids he could dominate. No one could dominate Pyotor.'

She considered this.

'Remember *World of Warcraft* too,' he said.

'The computer game?'

'He was a paladin. A tank. Gives protection to his team-mates. Goes into danger, takes the flak. Pyotor was good at it. Perhaps he thought he'd be good at it in real life. I don't know.'

'He *was* good at it.'

'Except for giving change in the corner shop. I'm sure Felix would advise against. Eats into your profit margin.'

'But he knew how much was needed for his baby brother's operation, and it would have been wrong to take more. That's the other thing. His confession. He was going to tell everyone exactly what he'd done afterwards.'

Garvie was silent for a moment. Then he said, 'So much truth sploshing about in the world. Half the time you're up to your knees in it before you realize. Like Vinnie. He told the truth, in his own way. Pyotor always told the truth. Except when he needed not to. I like that. Very practical.'

She began to pull on her jeans over her shorts, and she put out a hand and Garvie steadied her. Her hand was warm and small pressing against his stomach. Her scent disoriented him, a shock of the unfamiliar, as if he suddenly found himself in a place he'd never been before. When she spoke again her voice was quieter.

'Here,' she said. 'Help me with this.' She was pale in the darkness, her dark eyes shining as she looked at him. He held her pullover as she smoothed down her T-shirt.

'So,' she went on, 'he did not come here with Magee.'

He shook his head.

She looked at him accusingly. 'But you do not tell me why he did come. You keep that to yourself. Why would he come here, still with the money from Stanislaw's, instead of going home? To meet someone else?'

He said nothing.

She lifted her arms above her head, almost as if she were about to put them round his neck, and he leaned in to her and pulled the sweater over them, so close to her body he could feel it, like a margin of tickling warmth down his front. 'You won't tell me who killed him either. Why?' She raised her eyebrows. 'Don't you trust me still?'

'It wasn't Magee, I'll tell you that much. Magee just happened to find him there. Exactly as he said, to be fair.'

'But you know who did it. Don't you?'

He shrugged and looked away. 'Well, I still don't know for sure who was driving the van.'

'Van?'

He sighed. 'Course, it all would have been so much easier if only I'd found the violin.'

She frowned, began again. 'All right, I think for myself. I think it is really about Sajid. Am I right?'

'Yeah. But don't forget Khalid.'

He said no more and she frowned again and moved closer and looked up into his face. 'You won't tell me anything else?'

Garvie avoided looking at her.

'Tell me this then. Why did you want me here tonight?'

'You've got a lot of questions,' he said. He shrugged. 'You're good at languages.'

'You could have learned what you needed. Easy, with your famous memory.'

'I needed another person with me.'

'You could have asked Felix. He is just as small.' She hesitated. 'Why me?'

Still Garvie said nothing. She could hear him breathing.

'You say it is about Khalid too,' she said after a while.

'Yeah.'

'Pyotor stole his gun. He brought it here. And the money too. We know this.'

'Yeah.'

'But what about Khalid's phone?'

Garvie said nothing to that.

'The phone is also important, isn't it?' she said. 'I have been thinking. I know I'm right. I can see by your face. The phone is more important than just a phone.' She was smiling conspiratorially.

Still Garvie said nothing.

'I have been wondering,' she said, 'what Pyotor wanted it *for*. To find out who Khalid had been talking to? You can at least tell me this.'

There was a longish silence while Garvie continued to look at her.

'Who told you about Khalid's phone?' he said at last.

Surprised, she hesitated. 'You did.'

He shook his head.

'You mentioned that he—'

'I didn't say anything to you about the phone.'

There was another long silence in which they stared at each other, and when he spoke again his voice was low.

'Enough of this, Zuza,' he said.

'What do you mean?'

'These lies.'

She dropped her eyes and lifted them again, defiantly. 'What lies?'

'You told me you knew Pyotor from Juwenalia meetings.'

She said nothing.

'He didn't go. You told me Pyotor had been obsessed with his baby brother's illness "for months", but his grandfather said they'd only found out about the illness a few days before. I don't think you knew Pyotor at all, did you?'

She stared back silently, her eyes big and vague.

'You told Alex you only came to the city in January,' Garvie went on, 'but you've attended Juwenalia parades for the last ten years. I saw the lists. You've lived here all your life, haven't you? Where? Limekilns? Out at Tick Hill?'

Still she said nothing.

He shook his head, frowned. 'Who *are* you?' he said. And then: 'What do you want from me?'

For a moment she seemed confused, frightened even. Then she smiled. When she spoke her voice was very quiet but somehow very clear. 'You do not like it when there are no answers, do you? When the facts run out.'

He said nothing to that.

'Are you still thinking about Alex? Or about Blinkie? You haven't understood anything, have you?'

He just looked at her.

She said, softly, 'You see, you think I don't know you. But I know.' She smiled. 'Perhaps I cannot solve a mystery. But I can read your mind.'

His reply seemed to stick in the back of his throat. 'What do you mean?'

For some reason they were both whispering now. For some other reason, or perhaps the same one, Garvie began to tremble.

'You want people to think you are so cold, so tough, like you have no heart.'

He felt her hand again on his stomach but couldn't take his eyes from hers. His voice drained away into his chest and set solid.

'It's not true,' she whispered. 'You do all this because you care. Don't look at me as if you can't trust me. You can trust me, I told you before. But now,' she whispered, 'I do not know if I can trust myself. *Jesteś dziwny*,' she murmured, '*ale piękny i myślę, że cię kocham.*'

The words were soft as silk, unintelligible and obvious. Her own voice had disappeared almost to nothing, which was strange because her mouth was so close, next to Garvie's in fact, and he was lost in her scent, in the warmth of her face, in the glow of her eyes, in the touch of her fingers on his stomach – and there was a sudden noise in the access road behind them, a sob or cry or hawking scream, and they staggered apart, both spinning round, and found Alex standing there looking at them in fury and anguish. For a second they were all fixed in place, as if hammered into the moment, then Alex turned and ran in moonlight up the access road towards the gates.

When Garvie turned back to Zuzana she was already moving away. 'I am sorry,' she said, and her voice was oddly formal, loud, as if she was talking to someone else entirely. Then she was running after Alex, and Garvie stood alone watching her go.

46

In the conference room on the second floor of the police centre Singh stood upright as the chief went out at the end of the final morning session, the two lawyers who had presented the police case to the tribunal leaving with him, murmuring together as they passed through the door and into the corridor. Singh's own lawyer and the human-resources manager had gone ahead, and now Singh was alone in the room with Dowell, who sat in full uniform behind a small pile of folders – key evidence against the defendant – watching him curiously, as if still not knowing what to make of the brown suit and beige turban, or indeed of the ritual of standing to attention.

The room, like all such rooms, was impersonal, a place of official processes, as functional as its chrome and leather furniture, in which a civilian like Singh was irrelevant.

After a moment Dowell stood, resting his weight on the folders, and shook his head.

'You know, I hate to see this. I really do.'

Singh made no reply. Still standing upright, he glanced at Dowell, at the folders, before returning his gaze imperturbably to the door, as if determined to remain in his post for as long as possible.

Dowell shifted irritably. 'I'm sorry the tribunal's not minded to reconsider. But you don't do yourself any favours, do you?'

Again, Singh made no reply.

'Granted you made mistakes, especially with the kid. Kids like that need to be taught a lesson, not encouraged. But there was no need to take the position you did. Full responsibility? What's that about? And why didn't you submit a formal statement? I can't believe your lawyer thought that was a good idea.'

Singh didn't even look in his direction.

Dowell looked disgusted. Shrugging, he opened his briefcase and began to put his folders in it, and at the same time, as if suddenly winded, Singh gasped out loud and sat down heavily.

Dowell stared at him in surprise.

As he watched, Singh put his face in his hands and let out a long, quiet groan.

Dowell had seen men crack up before, collapsing without warning after long years of self-discipline, and he watched Singh warily.

'Come on now. Don't take it that way, man.'

A noise like a sob escaped from between Singh's hands, and he began to cough, his shoulders trembling.

Dowell fidgeted. He said, unnecessarily, 'Wait here,' and went out of the conference room towards the café area where the water coolers were – and at once Singh got up, impassive as ever, and went across to the folders Dowell had left behind. When Dowell returned a few minutes later with a paper beaker of water, he found Singh sitting as normal, busily writing in a small black notebook.

'OK,' he said. 'Good. You'll get through this, I know you will. As I was—'

But Singh had tucked the notebook away in his jacket pocket and was walking out of the conference room, leaving Dowell holding the paper cup, his mouth innocently open in outrage.

47

Sajid was finishing his lunch at the table in the back room. With Khalid upstairs resting and Jamal in the shop, he had another twenty minutes on his own before returning to school for afternoon lessons, so he pushed aside the rest of his dhal, quietly fetched the laptop from the cupboard, and loaded *World of Warcraft*. He wasn't going to play; he just wanted to look at it. These days it made him feel confused and frightened, but he couldn't stop himself, in fact he felt an urge to be miserable, so he sat there gazing at the screen, occasionally blinking big, slow blinks. Upstairs Khalid was turning restlessly on his bed. Since he'd been discharged from hospital he was more anxious and irritable than ever. The day before, he'd disappeared for a couple of hours in the morning, and since then he'd hardly come out of his room. In the shop at the front Jamal was talking to a customer.

When he heard footsteps in the passage Sajid hurriedly pulled the plate of dhal towards him again. The door opened and Garvie came in.

Sajid opened his mouth, and Garvie said, 'You know, you should really keep your back door locked. Anyone could waltz right in.'

Sajid looked alarmed enough that it was Garvie. 'You know I'll get into trouble if I—'

'Think about how much trouble you're already in. What I want out of you is the truth for once. And it has to be snappy 'cause I've got an exam, and because it turns out I'm not actually a waster after all I want to get there in reasonable time, so you've got five minutes to tell me what happened that night, starting with . . . this.' He reached out a hand and pulled down the boy's collar to show the yellow bruises round his neck, fading now but still visible. 'And if you want help with questions, I can do that too. Let's go.'

Location: back room in Jamal's convenience store; dim, smelling of dhal and cat.
Interviewer: DI Garvie Smith: brisk, intolerant.
Interviewee: Sajid: anxious, guilty.

DI GARVIE SMITH: You slipped, right?

SAJID BALOCH [*after a hesitation*]: It was the shots made me lose my balance. They sounded really near. Magee hadn't done up the rope right, it got tangled round my neck. I was screaming, and he was screaming at me, and I was scrabbling on tiptoe on that girder thing. I couldn't breathe. I thought he was going to leave me there.

DI GARVIE SMITH: How many shots?

SAJID BALOCH: Three, four, I don't know. Suddenly they stopped. That was almost the worst thing.

I didn't know what had happened.

DI GARVIE SMITH: What next?

SAJID BALOCH: I got free of the rope. He pulled me up and out the window, and we went fast as we could down the ladder.

DI GARVIE SMITH: Then what?

SAJID BALOCH: He kept telling me to hurry. I couldn't walk properly – I'd twisted my ankle – and he sort of dragged me along.

DI GARVIE SMITH: Shouting. In Urdu.

SAJID BALOCH: It hurt. I couldn't help it.

DI GARVIE SMITH: What happened when you got to the lock-up?

SAJID BALOCH: We got a shock. When we'd opened it up before, we'd turned the lights off. Someone had turned them on again. He didn't know what to do. He was swearing and stuff. He said he was going in, to check it out, and he told me to go on to the van.

DI GARVIE SMITH: And?

SAJID BALOCH [hesitates]: And . . . when I got there the van had gone. I was scared, in those bushes, in the dark, on my own, and when I heard the police siren I just started running. I went down the track until I got out of the woods, and I walked home all the way, hiding every time a car went past.

DI GARVIE SMITH: OK. Sounds about right. Now, tell me, who was in the van?

[Silence]

DI GARVIE SMITH: Come on, Sajid. Who was the driver?

SAJID BALOCH [*whispers*]: Khalid.

DI GARVIE SMITH: Khalid, yeah. He fixed it up with Magee, didn't he? And he got you involved too. His little boy band of robbers.

SAJID BALOCH: I didn't want to do it. I didn't like Magee. I'd had enough of getting into trouble. Pete had got me off all that.

DI GARVIE SMITH: But Khalid persuaded you. He needed you, someone small and nimble. He must have thought all that basketball training was going to be put to good use. Besides, he was desperate for his cut. How much did he need?

SAJID BALOCH: I don't know.

DI GARVIE SMITH: Maybe you don't. I can tell you it was exactly a grand. Perhaps he even thought it was easy money. In and out the warehouse, stick the furs in the lock-up, be long gone by the time Plod changes shifts and gets his act together. But then Khalid always was the stupid party. Funny, it makes people think he's not really that evil. He didn't fool Pyotor though, did he? Pyotor saw what was going down.

SAJID BALOCH: Pete kept telling me not to do it.

DI GARVIE SMITH: He did more than that, didn't he? He tried to warn off Magee when he came round to talk to Khalid. Got a slap for his trouble. And he had a go at Khalid too.

SAJID BALOCH: He said he'd go to the police. But Khalid said if he did he'd never play WoW with me ever again. Made him cry. I'd never seen him cry. He didn't look like someone who would ever cry, not all his life. [*Sniffing*] I didn't like it, Garv. I didn't . . .

DI GARVIE SMITH: All right, Sajid. Take it easy.

SAJID BALOCH [*high-pitched, blurting*]: Pete said he didn't want anything to happen to me. Now he's dead! [*Sobbing*] It's my fault. He must have gone out there to try and stop me. You know what he was like; he wouldn't listen, he wouldn't give up, he kept saying he was going to . . . he was . . . he was the . . .

DI GARVIE SMITH: All right, Sajid. Here.

SAJID BALOCH [*blows nose, recovers*]: What now?

DI GARVIE SMITH: Now we're finally going to chat about the most important thing.

SAJID BALOCH: What's that?

DI GARVIE SMITH: His violin, of course. Remember what you told me? He always had it with him.

SAJID BALOCH: Yeah.

DI GARVIE SMITH: That night, when you saw Pyotor for the last time, did he have it?

SAJID BALOCH: Yeah.

DI GARVIE SMITH: Did he take it with him when he left?

SAJID BALOCH: Yeah. Course.

DI GARVIE SMITH: You sure? What did he do *before* he left?

SAJID BALOCH: He didn't do anything. We were in the back room. Khalid had gone upstairs. Pete was crying. Then he just he went.

DI GARVIE SMITH: He said goodbye to Jamal? He fetched his coat from somewhere? He collected his bag?

SAJID BALOCH: No. He just went to the toilet and left.

DI GARVIE SMITH: Where's the toilet?

SAJID BALOCH: Out there at the end of the passage next to the junk room.

DI GARVIE SMITH: What junk room?

SAJID BALOCH: Where we put the out-of-date stuff we can't sell.

DI GARVIE SMITH: Who goes in there?

SAJID BALOCH: Nobody. Khalid keeps it locked up.

DI GARVIE SMITH: Where's the key?

SAJID BALOCH: By the back door. On a peg.

DI GARVIE SMITH: Let's get it. We need to hurry. I haven't got much time.

They went down the passage quietly. Jamal was in the shop serving. Khalid was still upstairs; they could hear him moving about occasionally, quietly creaking.

'I don't understand,' Sajid whispered.

Garvie said, 'Pyotor was a watcher, right? He saw things. He saw Khalid getting worked up about money. He saw that you were going to get into trouble. And he saw where the peg was with the junk-room key on it.'

Sajid still didn't understand.

'When Pyotor left here that night carrying his violin case, his violin wasn't inside it. He'd already hidden it.'

'Where?'

They came to the end of the passage and Garvie unlocked the door and they went into one of the untidiest rooms he'd ever seen. There was junk everywhere, stuffed into shelves, heaped in landslips, piled in towers, strewn in cascades, scattered in bag bursts. Pallets of videocassettes, boxes of disposable cameras, cartons of CDs, stacks of Pokémon cards. Out-of-date catalogues and directories. Forgotten-cartoon-character juice boxes, cans of unsellable vanilla Coke and Crystal Pepsi, caterers' packs of Tongue Splasher bubble gum, spangled ketchup.

'I hope this isn't going to take long,' Garvie said.

It didn't. Perhaps it had been hidden once. Not any more. It lay in bits at the side of a pallet.

'His violin,' Sajid said in a wondering voice. 'What's happened to it?'

It had been destroyed, smashed to pieces in a frenzy. Garvie said nothing. He began to examine the remains, turning them over rapidly in his hands, like an archaeologist. A bone-like shaft of stock. Sharp fragments of the cracked-open body. Black shiny chin-rest. Pegs still trailing strings. Scraps of label ('Gusta', 'Kle', '00', 'ebo') and a shell-like splinter of highly polished rib showing the small, dark brand of two letters. For several minutes he stood there staring at it all intently.

'How clever,' he murmured at last. He began to laugh.

'What's going on?' Sajid said.

'He hid it. The thing he loved most, that he never let out of his sight, he left it behind.'

'Why?'

''Cause he thought someone might come looking for it.'

'Why?'

''Cause he'd put something inside it.'

'What?'

'Evidence. Pyotor saw what went on, he heard what was said, he knew what was going down. He had a plan. And he hoped it wouldn't go wrong.' He stared at the violin mess. 'But it did go wrong,' he said. 'And someone did come looking for the violin, and they found it, and they smashed it up. Look at the way it's been pulverized. It must have been done by someone who really, really hated violins. Don't you think?'

He turned to Sajid. 'Your brother's a pretty desperate guy, isn't he? Shop like this ought to do OK, but he needed a grand, and he needed it badly. Why?'

Sajid shook his head. 'I don't know.'

'You should. Pyotor knew.'

'I don't understand.'

Garvie looked at him thoughtfully. 'What did he call you, Sajid?'

'What do you mean?'

'Pyotor liked to give people names. Didn't he call you something?'

Sajid bit his lip; nodded. When he spoke his voice wobbled. 'It sounded odd, but sometimes he called me *Pyotor's friend*.'

Garvie nodded. 'Good,' he said quietly. 'Remember that. Because now you're going to tell me something else.'

'What? I've told you everything.'

'But here's the weird thing. You haven't asked me who smashed the violin.'

Sajid looked at the bits of violin and gave a quick half-glance at the door.

Garvie said thoughtfully, 'Isn't there something else you want to tell me about Khalid?'

'No,' Sajid said quickly.

'What about that night? You were up on the warehouse roof, you heard the shots, you came down; Pyotor was dead and Khalid was gone.'

'He didn't do it. I know he didn't. He was waiting in the van and when he heard the shots he panicked and drove off. He told me. He didn't go near the lock-up. He never even saw Pyotor. He didn't know Pyotor was *there*.'

'What about yesterday morning?'

Sajid hesitated. 'He was in the shop.'

'He was out at Brickhouse meeting Magee.'

'How do you know?'

Garvie held up a sweet wrapper. 'Though, to be fair, Magee wasn't around to confirm it. He was already dead.'

Sajid stood with his mouth open.

'Khalid's desperate, we've already established that. Desperate and angry. Desperate and angry . . . and frightened. Frightened for himself – and frightened for you. Frightened people do the worst things.'

Sajid said nothing.

Garvie said sharply, 'Who smashed the violin, Sajid? Who's Khalid frightened of?'

For a second they faced each other, motionless, then Sajid made a break for the door, but Garvie was too quick for him, and after a scuffle he got him in a headlock.

'Who is it?' he said.

Sajid panted and thrashed. 'No one. I don't know.'

'I think you've got a good idea.'

Sajid struggled silently.

'Last chance, Sajid. Or I'll haul you upstairs and get Khalid and we can all go see Plod together.'

Sajid went limp and Garvie released him. 'Think you're so smart,' the boy said in a tear-blurty voice.

'Just tell me who it is.'

'Your mate!' Sajid shouted. 'Alex Robinson!'

Then he ran from the room into the passage, leaving Garvie grim-faced and alone in the junk room of lost things.

48

He went down Bulwarks Lane in a daze. It was a warm afternoon, the air fuzzy with sunshine. Newspaper hoardings outside the newsagent's relayed the latest – *Murder Suspect Found Dead*: *Police Baffled* – but he didn't pay them any attention. There were people strolling on the pavement, from time to time he sensed them round him, but he didn't see them; to him they were no more than shadows. His gaze was fixed elsewhere: in a junk room, in a basement hideaway, in a lock-up. After a while he found himself sitting on the bench outside the burger place smoking a Benson & Hedges. Sucking in smoke in long therapeutic drags, spooling it out into the air, he tried to get his thoughts in order. They did not want to be ordered. Like the plumes of his smoke, they loosened and came apart, showed him separate, disconnected things. An image of Alex standing in the access road, his face twisting through degrees of shock, like a man who begins to realize his shoes are on fire. Alex in the darkness outside Zuzana's flat whispering sullenly with Blinkie. A green-and-yellow sweet wrapper on the floor next to a dead man. Pyotor's smashed room, his smashed violin. A man with a temper. A man out of control.

Alex? He'd trust Alex with his life.

At the moment his thoughts were disorganized, arbitrary as an unbroken code. But just out of his mind's reach there was a cipher that would show the hidden pattern and make sense of them all. He knew it.

And after a while he realized what it was. Sajid had just given it to him.

'Oh, Alex,' he murmured. 'Alex, Alex, Alex.'

He blew smoke, lifted his face to the sun, failed to feel soothed and began to bite a fingernail. He took out his phone and wondered who to call. Alex? A tricky manoeuvre, possibly nuclear. Singh? Could he trust the policeman not to jump to conclusions? The person he most wanted to call was the person he couldn't talk to at all without complicating things even further; just thinking about her confused him.

As he sat there looking at his phone thinking these things, a text came through.

We need to sort this east field 3pm. A.

He sat looking at it for a long time, frowning. Shadow people walked past, their shadow voices insubstantial as the smoke drifting above him, shadow traffic shimmering in the road, as he gazed at the words on his phone's screen. At first he thought it changed everything. Then he saw that it made no difference at all.

He replied at last. *ok*. Sat back, braced himself for the trip out to East Field.

Then he remembered his exam. Looking at his watch, he saw with horror that time had got away from him.

He ran. He reflected, with some indignation, that he'd been doing a lot of running lately, and that, despite the claims of so-called experts, in his experience it didn't get any easier or more likeable. He ran grimly down Bulwarks Lane with stitch like a Chinese burn in the tender parts of his lungs. Without stopping or – to his surprise – vomiting, he ran past the end of Badger Lane, past the roadworks depot and across the strip of waste ground by Town Road to Bottom Gate and up the drive past C Block.

As he reached the gym he got a call, and he stopped to look at his phone. It was Zuzana. He stood there a moment, frowning, letting it ring. Then he cut it and went into the building.

It was empty except for a single table and chair set out under a basketball hoop, and at first he thought it was deserted. He hoped it was. Then there was a movement by the door of the stock room at the far end, and with a clicking of heels Miss Perkins emerged from darkness into the light. She seemed to gather intensity as she made her way across the sprung floor towards the entrance where he hunched panting over his knees, trying to look casual and not that late.

'Bit delayed, miss,' he said, when he could. 'Sorry.'
She remained silent until she had come to a

complete standstill in front of him, fixing him with her strange eyes. He remembered seeing a wildlife programme in which weasels did something similar to rabbits.

She spoke. 'Higher mathematics special paper began at 1 p.m. You will see from the clock above you that the time is now nearly a quarter to two. Is there a reason, Smith, why you are three-quarters of an hour late?'

'I expect so,' Garvie said. 'Though,' he added after a long pause, 'to be honest it escapes me. I've just done a lot of running, miss; it must have affected my memory.'

She said nothing to this.

'Look,' he said, 'if it's easier, we can just forget the whole thing. Doesn't look like it's going to inconvenience anyone. And, as it happens, I really ought to be somewhere else very soon.'

'You are the only candidate for this special examination at Marsh Academy,' Miss Perkins said, 'and one of only a dozen candidates throughout the city. For that reason it will very much inconvenience *me*.'

'Oh.'

'I am satisfied that you have received no prior assistance, so you will be allotted the full hour and a half, finishing at three fifteen.'

'Oh. Really?' He glanced at his watch.

'I shall invigilate you myself.'

'Are you sure? I wouldn't want to put you out.'

'You will begin immediately, Smith. Go to your desk.'

For a moment he entertained the thought of bolting. But it was only a moment. After his run, he didn't feel strong enough. Besides, Miss Perkins looked quick enough to catch him. In resignation, he walked before her to the desk at the far end of the hall and sat down. Miss Perkins positioned herself obtrusively about three metres away, her eyes fixed on him as if without her continuous attention he might disappear, and with a sigh he turned over the paper and began.

Forty-five minutes passed.

'Yes, Smith, what is it?'

'Finished, miss.'

She ignored him.

'Miss?'

'What is it now?'

'Like I just said, I've finished.'

'The exam takes an hour and a half, Smith. You have taken forty-five minutes. Therefore you have not finished.'

'Yeah, but, what I mean is, I've done all the questions.'

'Nonsense.'

'But I have.'

She took two steps towards him and lowered her head. 'I don't care,' she said quietly. 'You will stay precisely where you are for another three-quarters of an hour.'

Garvie looked at his watch.

'Thing is, it's half past two, miss.'

She looked at him, surprised. 'This is relevant in what way?'

'It's when the exam's scheduled to end. Officially, it's over now. Those other eleven kids have finished. I can leave and there's no risk of me helping them.'

She continued to look at him. 'I hope you're not going to do something very stupid,' she said.

'It's just that there's somewhere I've really got to be now. Sorry.'

He stood up, making the standard universal facial gestures of apology, knowing that these were unlikely to register in whatever domain Miss Perkins existed.

'If you leave now I will be entitled to cancel your paper,' Miss Perkins said at last.

'Yeah. But wouldn't that inconvenience you?'

'If you fail this paper, Smith, I believe I'm right in saying that you will fail to attain the minimum standard required to stay on at school.'

He thought about that; nodded. 'Maybe I've passed, though,' he said.

'You're free to let yourself down,' she replied. 'Are you free to also let down your mother? Are you going to be free all your life to let down those who try to help you?'

He had nothing to say to that, so he turned and walked slowly away.

At the entrance he looked back and Miss Perkins hadn't moved; she was still standing next to the desk, as if fixed, terrifyingly, in a continuing moment of fury and judgement, and his self-control broke, and he ran out of the gym and up the drive to Top Gate, the stitch in his side kicking in almost immediately.

49

In another part of the city Singh ran too, bleeding from the head, out of the apartment to the top of the stairs, where he paused only a moment to listen to the crash of the footsteps below, before vaulting over the banister into darkness. Landing on cardboard boxes piled at the side of the stairwell, he rolled sideways and was on his feet to see the man called Yazhov vanish through the doorway into the alley beyond. For a moment he stood perfectly still, expressionless, removing a splinter of glass from a wound above his left eye, then he leaped lightly through the door and continued the chase, back straight, elbows pumping, eyes fixed on the man ahead who clattered down the alley, skidding on the greasy cobbles, and disappeared into a side street.

The streets in this part of Brickhouse were dark and narrow. At one end of the district was The Wickerwith its long line of bars, bowling alleys and casinos; at the other end the crematorium. In between, below the crowded ribbons of tiny terraced houses up the hill where Magee had been killed, were sunless old lanes between tenements and boarded-up workshops, damp brick alleys used only as rat runs by drivers beating the daily jams between town and the ring road.

Singh put on speed. He rounded the corner and accelerated after Yazhov along an alley buckled with cracked flagstones and crowded with overflowing industrial bins. He cursed himself. It was bad enough to have been taken by surprise when Yazhov smashed the glass tumbler in his face, but worse not to have secured the exit as soon as he entered the apartment. He'd arrived at the place less than an hour after getting the gun dealer's address out of Dowell's folder, stopping en route only to change out of his brown suit into his white *kurta* and topknot, and was fortunate enough to find Yazhov at home after he had been released on bail. But something had made the Russian nervous and after answering the first few questions distractedly he'd panicked, flinging the glass into Singh's face and bolting out of the door.

Singh rounded a second corner into an even narrower alley overshadowed by dirty brick walls. He could hear traffic from The Wicker nearby. Yazhov was only fifty metres ahead now, running raggedly, looking back over his shoulder, dragging over bins as he passed, and Singh put on speed, hurdling the garbage, keeping his head up, arms pumping. Too late he caught a glimpse of a low-slung van as it pulled abruptly across him out of an entrance. In a screech of brakes it caught him as he leaped and tipped him into the air, and he rolled over the bonnet and onto the tarmac, and sprang to his feet, running faster, ignoring the shouts behind him, emptying his mind of everything but the need to catch Yazhov. He went at speed through a gateway and found the man waiting for him with a half-brick. The brick missed; they fell together. Up on his feet, Yazhov caught him a couple of punches in the face, but he rolled with the third and as Yazhov staggered forward Singh stepped round and took hold of him, pushed down on his shoulder and pulled back his arm.

Yazhov froze. He opened his mouth and gagged, fell to his knees and crouched there motionless, white-faced, as Singh kept up the pressure on his arm, both of them fighting for breath.

'All I want is an answer to my question,' Singh said at last. 'You did a deal with Khalid Baloch.'

'I have already told the police! I told them everything!'

'No, you didn't.'

'What didn't I tell them?'

'You didn't tell them how *many* guns you sold him.'

50

Garvie had not stopped running. He ran down Bulwarks Lane clutching his side as far as the taxi rank. Pausing only to ascertain that Abdul's cab wasn't there, he ran on erratically, occasionally looking at his watch, and down Pollard Way. He ran through the Strawberry Hill subway onto Cobham Road, past small shops selling Hoover parts and buttons and fishing tackle, past a long row of maisonettes, to the ring road and through the underpass to the other side. He ran down the country lane, checking his watch every few minutes, going at a steady, grim pace between empty paddocks, all mud and stones and tyre tracks, as far as the sewage plant propped up against the sky like a vast and simplistic piece of technology as outdated as a fax machine, and when he got there his phone rang and with relief he slowed to a walk to answer it.

'Garvie?'

'Yeah.'

Singh hesitated. 'Where are you? It sounds as if you're outside.'

'Could be.'

'You're out of breath.'

'Just finished an exam. Went for a little run to celebrate. What do you want?'

'Something you ought to know. I've just talked to the dealer who sold Khalid the gun.'

'Yeah?'

'It was two guns he sold him, not one. Pyotor might have taken one of them, but Khalid still had the other.'

'Well, well. Everyone's been misunderestimating Khalid, as Smudge would say.'

'What do you mean?'

Garvie looked at his watch. 'Haven't got long, but here's a couple of things right back at you. Khalid got to Magee before we did yesterday.'

'He went to see Magee? Why?'

'It was their first chance to talk through what the hell went wrong on the fur-coat job.'

'Khalid was in on it?'

'And he roped in Sajid as well. Literally. Through the skylight.'

'So they were all there that night. With Pyotor. And Khalid probably armed.' He paused. 'It all comes back to Khalid, doesn't it? Khalid with the murder weapon at the lock-up. Khalid going out of control. He must have been the one smashed up Pyotor's room looking for the violin. And then Magee. You're right. We read him wrong.'

'Yeah well. Turns out everyone's been misunderestimating Pyotor too. He's always been one step ahead.'

'What do you mean?'

'Two simple things make one complicated thing.'

'What?'

'Basic vector notation. If you can't get from A to C, go from A to B first, then B to C's easy.' Garvie looked again at his watch. 'I'm running out of time, man. Did you have a chance to check out Pyotor's photograph collection before you got busted?'

'Yes. I looked at the dates, as you suggested.'

'And there were some missing?'

'That's right. He took pictures all the time, every day. He'd been doing it for years. But there were three days, quite recently, when he hadn't taken any.'

'He'd taken them, don't worry. He just hadn't put them in his collection. He put them somewhere else, for safekeeping. They were different.'

'Pictures of what?'

'He thought Sajid was going to get hurt.'

'You mean he saw Khalid plotting with Magee. He knew the robbery was happening.'

Garvie said, 'He knew *why* the robbery was happening.'

Singh paused. 'What do you mean?'

'Why Khalid needed the money. Two simple things. He got the evidence together, put it in a safe place. That was the first thing. The second was to hold up Stanislaw's shop with Khalid's gun—'

'He did that? I knew there was something strange about that robbery.'

'Then he went to the industrial estate.'

'To stop the robbery?'

Garvie looked at his watch. Sighed. 'I'm not sure he even knew the robbery was taking place that night.'

'What? You've lost me. What was he doing there then?'

'Think of it this way. The gun wasn't the most important thing Pyotor stole from Khalid. The phone was.'

'The phone?'

'Yeah. It was only then he could set up the meeting at East Field.'

'Meeting with who?'

'With the person who could stop it all.'

There was a silence. Singh said, 'I don't understand.'

Garvie looked at his watch. 'Well, that's a shame because I haven't got time to explain.' He sighed. 'Time to start running again.'

'Wait, Garvie!'

'You want to do something useful, you could go to Jamal's. You'll find a smashed violin in Khalid's junk room. Unfortunately there was nothing in it.'

'Garvie! Tell me where you are. Tell me where you're going.'

'I'm going to meet someone.'

'Who?'

'Can't be done, man.'

'Why?'

Garvie thought about that for a moment. 'You

know why,' he said sadly. 'You can't trust me. No one can, I know that now. Not even,' he said, 'my best friend.'

And he set off, quickening his pace down the lane to East Field industrial estate.

51

It was as deserted by day as it was at night, the cross roads empty, the buildings shut; no traffic, no one about. It sat in stillness and silence under the perfect blue sky, almost picturesque, a ruin. Garvie trotted in through the main gate and down the road to the junction, and looked up and down. The smart operational hoardings surrounding the lock-up had been dismantled by the police and the building stood as before, beaten up, ugly, two storeys of semi-wrecked blackened brickwork enlivened only by a banner, now old and faded, above the entrance advertising discount storage.

This is what Pyotor saw that night, Garvie thought. *This was one of his last memories.*

Before he could go on his phone rang and he looked at it. It was Zuzana again. With it ringing in the palm of his hand, he hesitated. The phone rang on and on, and he stood there helpless until at last he couldn't stand it any more.

'Garvie?' he heard her say. 'Garvie?'

'Don't bother,' he said quietly after a moment. 'I know it all now. I know what Khalid's been doing. I know what Alex has been doing. And I know what you've been doing.'

'Garvie! Where are you? I need to talk. I can explain!'

But that was all he heard, because a goods train went by with a scrapyard din of squealing metal, a long chuntering hell-wail of wheels and chains, and he shook his head – it seemed somehow appropriate – and without saying any more hung up. Taking a breath, he walked down the access road to the lock-up. As he'd expected, the door was ajar. For a moment he hesitated, looking up and down the deserted row, then he pushed it open and went inside into dimness and silence.

He thought again to himself: *This is what Pyotor saw. This lobby. These doors.* Like Pyotor, he had come alone to his meeting, with no one to trust and no one to trust him. And he felt he knew what the boy felt that night, and that he was doing exactly what he did, walking across the lobby into the room behind, where Pyotor had ended up, and down the passage between the lock-up units to the metal staircase at the end, and up the stairs to the desolate storey above.

He stood at the top of the staircase, smelling the staleness, as musty and mineral as rabbit feed, listening to the silence, deeper and damper than the quietness below. It was darker than he'd expected. The windows were small and screened with grime, the skylights crusted over with filth. Gradually his eyes adjusted; he scanned the wide space, the heaps of builders' materials so old they'd fused in place, the breeze-block partitions between bays now collapsed, the rust-mangy girders, pools of black water, grey vegetation sprouting in the walls. When he walked across the floor his footsteps seemed to make no sound, as if he too were now a part of its deadness.

In the centre, where he could be seen, he stopped and waited, looking round.

After a moment there was a noise at the far end. A scrabbling. A soft panting, clicking of claws on concrete.

He braced himself.

Out of the shadows a dog emerged, straining against its chain. It wasn't Genghis. It was bigger than Genghis.

'Hello, Blinkie,' Garvie said, and the man followed the dog into the light. He was wearing a maroon tracksuit with a wet sheen to it and a Nike SnapBack, and he skanked behind his dog on thick-lipped, gold-dipped Nike dunks as if he was wading through molten bling, and stood grinning his gold grin and blinking, while his dog locked eyes with Garvie.

'Sur-*prise!*' Blinkie said after a while.

'Not actually,' Garvie said. 'Alex never signs his texts.'

Blinkie's dog began to tremble, its lips unfurling from its jaws, and Garvie tried to plant his feet more firmly on the concrete floor, and Blinkie looked at him thoughtfully. 'Don't like dogs, little boy, do you? Clocked that.'

Garvie kept his eyes off the dog. He heard it, sla-vering and panting, as he made himself as nonchalant as possible. 'What's it called, by the way?'

'Mother.'

'Nice.'

'She was a nice mother. But she's got some bad habits.'

Blinkie sneered, and Mother seemed to sneer with him, rising up against its chain, mouth dropping open like an oven door, and Garvie felt much less nonchalant. Blinkie reached round and fondled Mother's chops, staring at Garvie with those idiotic eyes, his head bobbing on the stalk of his neck. 'Know who I am?' he asked softly. 'I'm the king of dogs.'

Garvie felt sick. He said, 'You killed Pyotor. A sixteen-year-old kid with his hair brushed flat and his shirt tucked in and his tie done up properly, and you met him here and shot his spine out. Don't worry, I know exactly who you are. Blinkie.'

Blinkie gazed at him; blinked twice, waggled his head.

'Pyotor knew too,' Garvie went on. 'He clocked you at Jamal's putting the screws on Khalid when he wouldn't pay you protection.'

Blinkie carried on fondling Mother.

'You told Khalid to pay up or you'd hurt Sajid, didn't you, Blinkie? Pyotor didn't like that.'

Blinkie cocked his head on one side as if he was listening, though it wasn't clear if he was listening to

Garvie or tuning in to noises from another planet.

Garvie went on. 'Must have been a surprise for you when he turned up here instead of Khalid. He'd been checking Khalid's phone when your text came through telling him to meet you here with the money that night. He told you all this himself, I bet, when he came here. Didn't he, Blinkie? He always told the truth, when it suited him.'

Blinkie nodded thoughtfully. 'He was a lucky boy. But he's a bit dead.'

Garvie said, 'A thorough boy. He'd got you your grand. He'd written a cease-and-desist contract for you to sign. And, in case you didn't like that, he'd got evidence of what you'd been up to safely stowed away. It was easy enough, Blinkie. Which bit of it didn't you understand?'

Blinkie frowned. 'You want to stop calling me Blinkie?'

Garvie said, 'How about I call you whatever Pyotor called you? I bet he had a name for you.'

Still frowning, Blinkie took a little plastic bag out of his tracksuit pocket and shook it about so it made a teasing, shushy noise, and Mother began to dance on the end of her chain.

Blinkie's face twisted. In a few seconds it was a mass of tics and grimaces. He said in a whisper, 'That kid. You know what he called me?' His mouth writhed silently as if he had forgotten how to work it. 'Do you?' he said eventually. 'Do you *know* what he called me?'

'If I wait long enough I suppose you're going to tell me.'

Blinkie took a step towards Garvie, Mother rearing and straining in front of him, and Garvie couldn't help taking a step backwards.

'Kid like that. Kid like that comes here. Kid like that comes here and . . .' Blinkie blinked so hard his eyes went out for several seconds and when they reappeared they seemed bigger than his glasses. His voice went rusty, it crackled when he shouted.

'*Do you know what he called me?!*'

'Someone who can't express himself?'

Blinkie drew breath. He whispered. '*Stupid man! That's what.*'

'*Stupid man.*' Garvie nodded. 'Yeah, sounds right to me.'

'A retard like that. That's what he called me. *Me!* I'm saying. A retard like . . . I mean,' Blinkie said, 'who the fuck did he think he was?'

'Sajid's friend,' Garvie said. 'That's who.'

Blinkie did a double take. He shook his head, astonished. He went loose.

He held up the bag. He took his wet fingers out of Mother's mouth and put them in the bag, and took them out crusted and white, waggled them about and looked at them for a moment.

'I don't use,' he said softly. 'But Mother does.' He grinned. 'Fun time!' he said. 'At last!'

He reached forward, pulled back his dog's lips and rubbed the powder into its purple gums, and the dog reared up madly, its eyes sunken into its head, and began to chomp the air, spraying drool around, and Garvie fought hard to stop himself trembling.

Then there were footsteps on the metal staircase and they turned to look. Alex appeared. He stopped at the top of the stairs and looked at them as if unable to recognize them or work out what they were doing there; then he walked slowly over through the rubbish and puddles, past Garvie without looking at him, and took his place next to Blinkie.

'Your guy gave me the message,' he said. 'What's going on?'

'You can give him back his phone now,' Garvie said to Blinkie, and Blinkie took a phone from his tracksuit pocket and tossed it to Alex, who stared at it, puzzled.

'You idiot,' Garvie said to him. 'You really messed up this time.'

Alex stared back at him sullenly.

'I suppose he told you all you had to do was lean on Khalid a bit, pass on the message "Blinkie wants his money".'

Alex said nothing. He breathed, staring at Garvie, sunk in his fury.

'It was you told him I was looking for the violin, wasn't it? Didn't mean anything to you, but he was onto it straightaway.'

Still Alex said nothing.

Garvie shook his head. 'I trusted you, man.'

'Trust!' Alex said in a furious voice. 'Don't talk to

368

me about trust. How long was it going on between you and Zuza?'

'Wise up, Alex. She was only ever looking out for you. You thought she was interested in this muppet? She's got eyes. She played him. All she was interested in was finding out how stupid you'd been. She was trying to protect you, man.'

Blinkie scowled; he smacked his lips and spat on the floor.

'Meeting him in O'Malleys. That's all it was about. It was from him she found out that Pyotor had got hold of Khalid's phone.'

Alex didn't seem to be listening. 'What about you and her, Garv?'

He hesitated. 'She played me too, if you want to know. Same thing. Trying to find out what I knew. All the time she had your back.'

'She lied to me. About not living here.'

'She wanted a fresh start. She'd walked away from a bad situation and she wanted it to be different with you. Don't you get it? She was trying to make it work.'

Blinkie was trembling again, eye-rolling. He gave Mother another wet rub of powder and the dog went crazy on the end of its chain, while Blinkie strained to keep it under control, laughing.

Garvie couldn't help looking at it. He felt his legs begin to shake. He said, 'Alex! Alex mate. Snap out of it. He told you the truth when he said he was getting out of dealing. He forgot to tell you he was getting into extortion.' He got no response. They stared at each other like it was a competition.

Blinkie was struggling to restrain Mother. He said to Alex, 'You're not listening to this spank boy, right? I told you, be smart. He got into her big time.' He said sideways to Alex, 'I can trust you on this, right?'

For a moment Alex said nothing. Then he said, 'Yeah.' He stared at Garvie for another three seconds and began to bite his lip.

'Let's do it then,' Blinkie said, and Alex swung sideways and chopped him in the throat.

Blinkie went down like a kite, crashing onto the floor, all arms and maroon sleeves flapping, and the dog leaped into the air, plunging and skidding. It sprang free from Blinkie's grasp and turned to the boys. Flattening itself against the ground, massive and ugly, it stalked them as they backed together onto a shallow pile of rubbish in the middle of the wide, empty warehouse space, where they stopped and faced it.

'We didn't do anything,' Garvie said sideways, eyes on Mother.

Alex's eyes were on the dog too. 'No?'

'I feel bad all the same.'

'It's over with Zuza.'

'Of course it is, you idiot.'

'I've been stupid.'

'Me too. Let's be smart now.'

They said no more. The dog came to a halt a few

metres in front of them, rolling its lips back from its teeth until its wet jaws stood up, as interlocking and well-oiled as the parts of a machine. It gnashed them together twice, as if to show how well they worked.

Garvie said, 'I don't know if you remember this, but . . .'

'You're scared of dogs. I know. Since you were a little kid.'

Garvie felt the sweat break out on his forehead. He willed his legs to stop trembling. He made himself crouch down and slowly put his hand out.

Alex said, 'What the fuck, Garv? It doesn't want to play.'

'I know that.'

'Get out if you can,' Alex said, and stepped forward.

The dog coiled into itself like a spring and leaped at him, crashing through the air like a flying bullock, and Garvie put his hand into the split bag of cement at his feet and flung powder into its face, and it went through the powder like a plane through cloud and took Alex with it, chomping at his shoulders. Entwined, they rolled and twisted on the concrete, the dog making pneumatic gnashing noises with its jaws, its great body heaving, straining with muscle, rank with animal stink. It reared up whining and snarling, blindly shaking its head from side to side, trying to clear its eyes, and Alex punched it in the side of its head. It turned to Garvie, who froze, half-brick in hand, mesmerized by its face so close to his, a mashed mask of fury as it lunged forward and took a bite out of his forearm, and he gritted his teeth and clubbed it twice, and the dog reeled sideways, spilling blood from its lips.

'Here's something for Pyotor,' he said. And as he lifted the brick again something slammed into the side of his head and he fell face down onto the ground.

Everything vibrated. His eyes felt loose. Vision blurred, he squirmed round and Blinkie kicked him in the knee and he felt a snap and a flash of pain as he rolled away. When he looked up the man was struggling dementedly with something in his track-suit pocket, jerking about as if electrocuted, until finally he yanked out a gun, grinned at last, and was swept aside by Alex falling on him suddenly from behind.

The gun skittered away across the concrete, and Blinkie and Alex struggled together among builders' rubbish. Garvie yelled as Mother reappeared, crushing Alex to the ground, squatting over him, big shoulders high, gnashing, and Alex got both hands round the dog's collar and butted it suddenly in the snout with a crunch, and it staggered sideways and fell on its face. 'Alex!' Garvie shouted again, and the boy looked up, too late, as Blinkie swung down and blatted him flat with a roof tile.

There was a moment of stillness, an exhausted tableau of panting and retching, dust swirling slug-gishly in stirred-up patches of sunlight.

Slowly Garvie began to drag himself towards the place where the gun lay on the floor, but Blinkie went ahead of him, staggering and swearing.

Before he could reach it there was a rapid patter of footsteps on the metal staircase behind them, and Blinkie glanced back, magnified eyes swivelling in cartoonish astonishment, frozen to the spot. Then he turned and ran, and at the same time someone came past Garvie at high speed, running on light feet, vaulting rubbish, a blur of white, and reached Blinkie as Blinkie reached the gun. They clashed, struggling together, and when they came apart Blinkie had the gun.

Singh stood very still in front of him.

Blinkie pointed the gun at Singh.

Singh moved. He danced closer as Blinkie fired, gliding past him, kicking as he turned, and the gun flew out wide across the floor. Blinkie slashed out with a knife and Singh rocked back on his heels, and Blinkie shoved forward, twisting, baggy maroon sleeves swinging round him, slashing wildly, the metal sweeping through empty glinting arcs on either side of Singh, who swayed left and right in front of him until, as if coming to the end of a practised routine, he slipped suddenly behind him, lifting his arms in a swift almost delicate scissoring gesture, and the man crumpled at once and lay with his deflated trackie around him like a collapsed parachute.

There was silence.

The Sikh stood there motionless, head bowed as if praying, his mind elsewhere, a slight figure in white pyjamas, calm and quiet in the still-surging shadows.

Garvie yelled, 'Singh!'

And Blinkie's dog crashed into the policeman from behind, lifting him off the ground, hurling him through the air and thrashing him head first against a girder, where he fell and lay still.

Now there was only Garvie and Mother.

The dog swung its heavy head towards the boy. Slowly it began to move towards him.

Garvie tried to lift himself off the ground but fell back, and lay there helplessly as the dog stalked across the floor towards him, head lowered, shoulders raised, moving stiffly on bunched muscles, its jutting face covered with blood and mouth-foam, open jaws spilling drool.

Garvie went white. The saliva dried in his mouth, his pulse pounded in his head. He backed away crabwise as far as a pile of gravel, and threw a handful of it in the dog's direction, and its snarl widened until its whole head seemed made of teeth, and it came on, creeping slowly, as if wading through heavy sand, its muscles straining and trembling under its sweat-glistening hide.

Gradually it quickened its pace. Lifting its head, it pushed forward with long, regular strides. Its momentum built, carried it quicker. Garvie just had time to see its ears go back, tail curl under, eyes fix themselves on him, black and wet, before it charged. From five metres away it launched itself, low and huge, all jaws and thickened muscle, a blur suddenly exploding sideways with a scream, crashing past him into a girder, and Garvie lay there drenched and dazed.

His face and front were wet with blood. He thought at first they were all dead now, lumps of rubbish in the rubbish-strewn warehouse. But there was a noise, and his eyes focused and shifted, and he saw Zuzana standing nearby with Blinkie's gun still in her hand, her face white in shadow.

She dropped the gun.

They stared at each other for a long moment, and she stood there as if uncertain what to do, and he turned his face towards Alex, and after a moment's hesitation she turned and ran to where the boy lay on the ground, just beginning to stir.

The last thing Garvie heard was Alex's voice. 'Is Garvie OK?' After that, nothing.

52

Some things don't change. Other things change around them. A boy is murdered, an arrest is made, a big dog is put down. Headlines are written, policemen tell the media that justice has been done in the end. But the weather stays the same, all steady sunlight and soft air and summer breezes. Three boys loiter in a corridor as they've done many times before. One has an arm in a sling and walks with a crutch, one is fiddling inside the lock of the classroom door, one is keeping lookout, glancing down the corridor with an expression of utterly unnatural ordinariness on his face. The school music room is the same too, with its corner piano, stacks of orange plastic chairs and astringent smell of wax, and the stock room, where the old-fashioned musical instruments are kept, has been unchanged since the beginning of time.

Smudge said from the doorway, 'Still only seven, Garv. You got some sort of problem with counting?'

'Get them out, will you, Smudge? Let's have a look.'

Grumbling, Smudge disappeared into the stock room; they heard him mumbling to himself. 'First it's violins, then it's furs, then it's violins again . . .'

Felix said, 'So it wasn't Magee.'

'He was up on the roof with Sajid.'

'And it wasn't Khalid.'

'He was in the van outside the fence, waiting.' Garvie looked at the violin that Smudge brought him, and shook his head. 'Next,' he said, and Smudge went back, grumbling some more, into the stock room.

'And it wasn't Alex.'

Garvie said, 'No, Alex was too busy being stupid.'

'I don't get Alex.'

'No,' Garvie said to Smudge. 'Next.' He sighed. 'You told me Alex owed Blinkie. You were right. Alex got into some serious trouble on someone else's turf six months back and Blinkie gave him protection. But Blinkie never does anything for free. No,' he said to Smudge.

'So he called in the favour?'

'That's it. After he shot Pyotor, Blinkie couldn't be seen at Jamal's. He got Alex to go round and lean on Khalid for his grand. I thought Alex was dealing again. No, Smudge,' he said. 'Bring two next time, will you, speed things up; someone'll come in a minute.'

'What about Magee?'

'Bad luck all along. His fur job got scuppered by the shooting. He got nabbed by Singh at the murder scene. Then Khalid led Blinkie to his hideaway.'

'And Blinkie killed him.'

'He was worried Magee would work out what had happened that night once he'd quizzed Khalid. He *had* worked it out, he told me.'

'And what about Zuzana?'

Garvie said quietly, 'Nothing to say about Zuzana.' He took the two violins and looked at them. 'No, Smudge,' he said. 'Not those either. Typical. It's always the last one. Go on, bring it out.'

Smudge brought over the last violin. 'End of a totally pointless exercise. Hope you've enjoyed it.'

'Very much,' Garvie said. 'I can see you working with old instruments in the future.'

Felix said, 'So it was all about the Gimp.'

'Pyotor and Sajid.'

Felix was frowning. 'What I don't understand,' he said, 'is why he thought his plan would work. I mean, getting Blinkie to sign something? Can the man even write his own name?'

'Even clever people can't always see what's right under their noses. Blinkie doesn't operate by the laws of human nature. Everyone in Five Mile knew that, except Pyotor. Once he told Blinkie he had all the evidence he needed to make sure he went down, he thought Blinkie would go along with it.'

'Evidence which he'd hidden somewhere for safekeeping.'

'That's it.'

'Where?'

The door to the music room opened and the

temperature dropped a couple of degrees. On clicking heels Miss Perkins walked in and stopped and looked at them.

Smudge said automatically, 'We were just . . .' and fell silent.

Glancing quickly at all points of exit, Felix made himself inconspicuous behind his more solidly built friend.

Her gaze swivelled onto Garvie.

'Smith,' she said.

'Yes, miss.'

'As you are aware, the music room is out of bounds.'

'Yes, miss.' He leaned over and took the last violin off Smudge.

'And the instruments, I need hardly remind you, are all county-music-service property,' Miss Perkins said.

'You'd think, wouldn't you?'

She looked at him as she'd looked at him many times before, coldly, mistrustingly, and he felt a familiar resentment, the urge to go his own way.

He dropped the violin on the floor and it failed to bounce. He lifted his foot and stomped on it and smashed it into bits.

There was the sort of silence that accompanies all acts of appalling folly. Smudge battled hard to stop himself bursting into tears.

'I will inform the authorities of what you have just done,' Miss Perkins said, her voice scarily normal. 'There are three witnesses. I expect you to be prosecuted. I shall, of course, inform your mother.'

Garvie lowered himself awkwardly to the floor and with his good hand delved among the remains of the violin.

'Here,' he said.

She stared at him for a moment. 'What is it, Smith?' she said at last.

'Pyotor Gimpel's memory stick, miss. Got important stuff on it. Pictures. Phone recordings. Think I'm right in saying the police offered a reward. You can have it. Keep the money. Or give it to the school.'

'So we can replace the violin you've just broken?'

'Not yours actually. Belonged to Pyotor. You can check it out; it doesn't have the school brand on it. Clever of him. He hid the memory stick in it, then switched his violin for one in the stock room. Easy to do.'

'Yeah,' Smudge said. 'They all the look the bleeding same.' He put his hand over his mouth.

Garvie said, 'You'll find the remains of the school violin in Jamal's stock room. If they haven't tidied it up. And I bet they haven't. I met the guy who smashed it. I don't know his real name, but if you get to meet him I think you should call him Blinkie. He's in prison on a murder charge.'

Miss Perkins listened to this without comment, her rigid face pale.

'So you see,' Garvie explained, 'I haven't really done anything wrong. For once.'

Miss Perkins looked at him. 'You have done something very wrong. You have tried my patience too far.' She put the memory stick into her jacket pocket, walked to the door and turned back.

'Half past two,' she said. 'I note that you were meant to be in your chemistry exam thirty minutes ago, and I shall mark you down as a fail.'

Then she went. None of the boys said anything. The temperature of the room remained chilly.

53

In his bed in the men's ward on the twelfth floor of City Central Hospital former Detective Inspector Singh lay thinking. Sunlight fell in thin woollen folds across the bed, gleamed on a bedside plastic glass, plastic vase filled with freesias. Warm air swarmed in the bright window. Singh paid no attention to any of this, head resting on the pillow, his gaze directed at the ceiling, a plastic tube up his nose, a drip feed in his forearm and a brace around his jaw.

He paid no attention either to the headline of the newspaper lying on his bed: *Mission Accomplished by Suspended Squaddie.* He was daydreaming of Lucknow, its orange dust, its flawless blue sky, of the guru who taught him *viraha yudhan*, a burly man with a bushy beard and tiptoeing step, whose eyes never left Singh's as he showed the boy his moves, swaying round him, catching sunbeams out of the air with his rapid, thick fingers. Singh heard again his guru's dark brown voice. 'How strange to think that all this violence comes from God.'

There was the sound of footsteps in the corridor outside and the door opened. Garvie came in. He was wearing a rucksack and he limped across the room with a noise of clinking bottle glass and sat in the chair next to Singh's bed. Neither greeted the other, and Singh continued to stare at the ceiling.

After a while he said, 'I'm not allowed visitors. The nurses are very strict about it.'

'Yeah. Told them I was related. On your mother's side. Your great-great-grandfather was my—'

Singh waved a hand and Garvie fell silent.

'Whatever you've brought with you I'm not allowed either. Nothing to eat or drink from outside, they said.'

'It's not for you. I'm on my way to Old Ditch Road, see the boys. Picked up some refreshment.'

'I can imagine,' Singh said drily.

For a while they were silent.

Garvie said, conversationally, 'They've admitted Alex in downstairs. I've just been to see him. Skull fracture and haemorrhage, open wounds to shoulder and neck, something called cellulitis. Yeah. He's a bit down in the dumps. Still, he's getting lots of care and attention.'

Alex was in between operations, confined to bed, encased in a sort of protective frame, like an exhibit. Smudge and Felix had been earlier and had left the remains of a bunch of grapes and a couple of packs of Benson & Hedges, which had been removed by the nurse, and a half-bottle of Glen's, which she hadn't yet noticed under his pillow. Garvie had sat with him for an hour or so, not saying much, occasionally giving him sips of water from a beaker with a straw.

'By the way,' he said to Singh, 'I meant to ask,

How'd you know to turn up at East Field when you did? Was it Zuzana?'

'Zuzana Schulz, the Polish girl, yes. She called me on the number you'd given her.'

'I suppose she must have guessed where I was 'cause she heard the goods train going by when she called me.'

'That's what she said. She was concerned for you.' With some effort Singh moved his head and looked at Garvie. 'Haven't you talked to her about it?'

Garvie shrugged; shook his head. He'd seen Zuza only once since the palaver at East Field, in the hospital lobby downstairs. She'd just been to say goodbye to Alex. It had been one of those moments that happen at the wrong time in the wrong place in probably the wrong universe. She was going to catch a train to the airport, on her way to Kraków, to where her parents were relocating. There was nowhere in the lobby to sit, even for a minute; they stood there in the double doorway surrounded by the smoking decrepit in their wheelchairs, old men and women in flimsy bed gowns, hooked up to portable drips and oxygen tanks, gazing at them with fish eyes through drifting currents of smoke.

Neither of them had spoken. Looked.

At last Zuzana had stepped forward and smiled, and it was like the first, original smile, pert and amused, as if she'd just thought of something funny to say, and her eyes were the same too, large and dark and shining. But she said nothing. There was nothing to say. She put her hand to her lips and softly touched his cheek with her fingertips; then she was gone, outside, walking in that rapid, fluent way towards the taxi rank.

Singh had turned his head sideways and was looking at Garvie curiously, and Garvie said, 'Are they strict about smoking in here?' He glanced at the window. 'I could let in some fresh air, get rid of the smell.'

'It doesn't open,' Singh said. 'Perhaps they're worried I might jump out.'

'Feel like jumping?'

'Not all the time.'

Garvie nodded. 'That sounds about right. Life's a bore, isn't it? Though not so boring as it's going to be for Blinkie. He's going down, right?'

'No question. Pyotor's evidence is clear enough. And the gun taken from him at East Field has been confirmed as the murder weapon.'

'All over then.'

'All over.'

Garvie gave him a sidelong look, hesitated as if wondering how to phrase what he was about to say. 'Your . . . dishonourable discharge,' he began at last.

Singh returned his gaze to the ceiling. 'Not yet finalized,' he said quietly. 'I'm given to understand there may be possibility of a reprieve. But I don't know.'

'What will you do if there isn't?'

'Something else.' After a while he said, 'What are *you* going to do? Stay on at school?'

'Small problem with that. Exam-related.'

'So what then?'

He shrugged. 'Something else.'

Singh looked at him sternly. 'What does your mother say?'

'Plenty. She's got reason, I know.'

'Your mother is a lovely lady. She brought me flowers.'

Garvie turned in surprise to the vase of freesias. 'She brought those? For you?'

'She has been several times to talk to me. Of course, she worries about you.'

Garvie said nothing to that and Singh said nothing more either, and they sat there in a silence for several minutes, as if contemplating the future or perhaps avoiding contemplating it.

There was a knock on the door and it opened at once, and Detective Inspector Dowell came in. As usual he was wearing full uniform, including hat, and he carried a black leather briefcase. His walk was brisk and purposeful, but when he saw Garvie he stopped and his expression turned through several degrees of hostility.

'Well,' Garvie said to Singh, 'best be off. The boys get restless without their refreshment.'

He hoisted his rucksack onto his back with a loud chinking of glass and went across the room as far as Detective Inspector Dowell, who stepped across to stop him.

'What are you doing here, son?' he said in a soft and dangerous voice.

'Been trying to tempt the inspector to drink and smoke. But he's oddly incorruptible. You knew that already, of course.'

Slowly Dowell's face changed colour, beginning with his ears. His eyes hardened, his lips shrank. Smiling pleasantly, Garvie moved to go round him, but Dowell blocked him off.

'And where are you off to now?'

'Old Ditch Road. Kiddies' playground.'

Dowell nodded, considering this. 'I know what goes on at that playground.' A sour expression came into his face, a sudden suspicion. 'What's in the bag?'

'Nothing much.'

'Show me.'

Garvie hesitated. 'Just some groceries I picked up for my mum.'

'I said, "Show me."'

Garvie took off his rucksack and opened it and removed the contents. A bottle of orange squash, some cans of beans, packets of cereal, a glass jar of olives.

The silence was broken by a noise from the hospital bed, and both Garvie and Dowell turned in surprise. Singh was laughing. Garvie had never seen him laugh before; and he looked younger and sillier. Garvie had never seen his teeth before either. They were very white and all different sizes. He made a noise like a five-year-old, high-pitched and disorderly.

'Did you want to take any of these down to the

lab so my uncle can test them?' Garvie asked politely.

Dowell lowered his big head, whispered, 'I'm going to be watching you, son.'

Garvie put his hand up to the side of his mouth and whispered back, 'Likewise.'

He stepped past him to the door, and paused. 'Hey, Raminder,' he said. 'remember that Sikh proverb you told me.'

'Proverb? What proverb?'

'Something about Scottish policemen and over-tight trousers.'

Singh was laughing again, and Garvie had gone, and Detective Inspector Dowell stood disregarded at the foot of the bed with his briefcase in his hand, looking like a man beginning to realize he has stepped in something foul.

On the bus Garvie got a call from Smudge.

'Listen, mate. Not being funny, but we've been waiting, like, hours. If I have any more goes on the swings I think I'm going to be sick.'

'Relax, Smudge. I'm on my way.'

'Did you get the drinkable?'

Garvie took the half-bottle of Glen's out of his jacket pocket. 'Yeah.'

'Full?'

'Not exactly. The volume's proportional to the unused capacity by a ratio of about one to four.'

There was silence.

'Not quite empty,' he added.

'Oh. Right. What about the other stuff?' Smudge said.

Garvie patted his other jacket pocket. 'Yeah, got that too.'

'And the sherbet lemons?'

'Ah, no. Forgot those.'

'That's a shame. They're my favourite bit to be honest. By the way, I been meaning to ask you, you know how to speak Polish, right?'

'No.'

'Yeah, but, you did.'

'A few words, Smudge. I've forgotten them now.'

'You don't forget anything.'

'I'm making an exception in this case.'

'It's just I heard Zuza's got a sister, right, and I was wondering maybe I'd learn a bit of the lingo. You know, improve my chances. Hey, maybe we could learn it together.'

'I'm not going to be learning Polish, Smudge.'

'No?'

'No, Smudge. No need.'

'You mean—'

He rang off and put his phone away. The bus swayed into Bulwarks Lane, pulled slowly by the shops, past the burger place and Jamal's and Zuzana's flat, and he sat there staring at it all through the grimy window, a blue-eyed, black-haired boy in old leather jacket and slouch jeans, looking bored.

Acknowledgements

It's a pleasure, as always, to thank my colleagues at DFB, who are both exemplary and unique. Editorial conversations with David Fickling and Bella Pearson, and feedback from other DFBers, and from Pari Thomson, have helped to fundamentally shape the finished book. Thank God for Talya Baker's excellent copy-edit and Julia Bruce's eagle-eyed proof-read, which both tightened the text and caught stubborn errors. Anthony Hinton shepherded the book through the production process with customary efficiency. I am grateful too for help with the maths from Ted Walker and Michael Holyoke, and for guidance on the Polish from Katarzyna Deja, and on the Italian from Sandy Fredman. Will Fickling donated a tiny bit of his extensive knowledge of gaming. For strict instructions on clothing, I am indebted to my daughter Eleri. My agent Anthony Goff has been unfailingly calm and astute in all negotiations involving the sometimes tricky Garvie Smith. But as usual my greatest debt, for everything I can think of, is to Eluned, Gwilym and Eleri.

About the Author

Simon Mason has written novels for adults (*The Great English Nude*, *Death of a Fantasist* and *Lives of the Dog-Stranglers*) and younger readers (the Quigleys series and *Moon Pie*), and a work of non-fiction, *The Rough Guide to Classic Novels*. He lives in Oxford with his wife and two children.